Dangerous Series -Book.1

Amber Alert

*A Christian Contemporary Romance
with Suspense*

Linda K. Rodante

LONE MESA PUBLISHING

LONE MESA PUBLISHING
www.lonemesapublishing.com
ISBN: 978-0692548332

Amber Alert
Copyright Linda K. Rodante

Unless otherwise noted, Scripture quotations are taken
from the HOLY BIBLE, NEW INTERNATIONAL VERSION, Copyright 1973, 1978,
1984, by International Bible Society. Use by permission of Zondervan. All rights reserved.

Dedication and Thank-you

This book is dedicated to the Father and to Lord Jesus Christ without whom there would be no Christmas, no new life, no eternal life. Thank you for forming me, loving me and shaping and guiding me. May the words of my mouth (and computer) and the meditation of my heart be acceptable in your sight, my Lord and my God.

And to my mother, Elaine Knadle, for her constant love for her children, and her enthusiastic love of Christ, for her courage in following Him and being a witness in Jerusalem, in Judea, in Samaria, and to the ends of the earth.

And continuing thank-you to so many others!

The Word Weavers critique group of Tampa, Sheryl Young, Janis Powell, Sharron Cosby and all the rest. You are great critiquers and friends.

Becky Zuch, friend and beta reader, patient listener and constant encourager.

Sue Wayne, my boss at Trinity College for encouragement and always giving me time off for whatever writer's conference was upcoming, and for her encouragement.

Kathy Blackwell, friend, critiquer, and beta reader.

Members of Highest Praise Family Church for reading my first manuscripts and encouraging me.

The Christian Indie Author Facebook group. Too many to list, but you know who you are.

The Friendly Writers Facebook Group. Thank you for encouragement, critiques, and sharing the struggle.

Teri Burns, editor at Lone Mesa Publishing, for doing the impossible and bringing all my ideas and the needs of this manuscript together.

Kathi Macias, multi-published author and encourager.

Debby Tisdale Mayne, multi-published author, friend, and encourager.

Sandie Bricker, multi-published author, encourager, managing editor for Bling Romance.

Varina Denman, friend, encourager, author of *Jaded, Justified, and Jilted.*

Jessica Kirkland, agent with Blythe Daniel Agency, for her patience and encouragement.

ACFW (American Christian Fiction Writers) and all the good people, information and conferences, for those who judged my contest entries and for their critiques.

Cec Murphy's scholarship to Florida Christian Writer's Conference, and to his assistant, Twila Belk, who encouraged me to submit to Cec's anthology, *I Believe in Healing.*

Donnie Whittemore, former Tampa Sheriff's Deputy and Lt. Colonel in the Army for his answers to numerous questions over the years.*

Mark Mynheir, retired officer, Palm Bay Police Department, former SWAT team member, and multi-published author for his encouragement and help with police procedures. *

My husband, Frank, for financial support and encouragement in what proved a longer endeavor than either of us foresaw.

Both my sons, Justin and Matthew Rodante and my daughter-in-law, Melissa, for their encouragement and patience.

My extended family, sisters, brothers, nieces, nephews and all others for encouragement and help.

Wes Knadle (deceased), my dad, for giving me my first typewriter (when such things were the main means of writing) when I was 12, and by so doing, encouraging me to keep on keeping on.

*Any fault with police, court, or paramedic procedures is strictly mine and not others' (between not fully understanding the explanation I was given or taking "poetic" license and stretching what was real to fit the story).

Chapter 1

Sharee Jones stalked over the dark field away from the church. Moonlight yellowed the area in front of her and a breeze tossed her mass of curls.

Calm down, Sharee. The teen didn't push your loyalty buttons by design. Abbey Somers had no idea she'd trampled the character of a woman who supported you after a broken engagement two years ago—while slogging through a tragedy of her own.

Sharee inhaled, catching the scent of jasmine and damp earth. All she needed was a few minutes of peace. No one would miss her for a while. Ahead of her, the inky blackness of the pond reflected the moon's light, and cypress trees stood like sentinels against the sky. Bushes clung to the bank except where the church's maintenance crew of one had cleared them.

She crossed the last few feet to the pond, put a hand against the tree's trunk and stared at the moon's cold presence.

A growl rose from the darkness. Her heart lurched, and she froze.

Grrr...

She strained to see through the darkness, but black foliage obscured her view. She inched her head sideways. A bear? Surely not this close to the city, but... Someone had reported a Panther the other day. Her heart started an erratic beating.

Come on, Sharee, you can't freeze. Move backward. Slowly. A step at a time...

Clouds raced past the moon. The night shadows flitted over the animal. Whatever stood there, it was huge.

The growl came a third time. Her throat constricted.

God, I need help.

She glanced over her shoulder. The church lights glowed fifty yards away. A long fifty yards. She swallowed. *Just stay still. Don't move.*

The creature snarled and shook its head. Recognition hit, slid over her. A dog.

Her throat closed, and the scar under her hair constricted. She gave a quick look at the church. People filled the fellowship hall there. The baby shower proceeded without her. If something happened, no one would miss her. Not for a while.

She prayed again and forced herself to edge backward. The animal's liquid eyes caught the moonlight and followed her. She stopped. Something large was in its mouth. As she tried to focus, the dog dropped its head and released its prey. A rounded form rolled across the dark ground. Her heart jumped.

A baby?

No!

No, it had to be a doll. What if she tried to get it? Crazy. She could throw something. If she threw her shoe, would he chase it?

Sharee leaned forward, narrowed her eyes and tried to see better. A sharp, quick bark jolted her. The tingling beneath her hair increased. *Don't freeze, Sharee. Think!*

"Cooper!" A shout came from her left. "Cooper, come!"

She wrenched her head in that direction, but one dark silhouette melted into another. She couldn't see anyone. The dog turned and trotted off. As he neared the trees, moonlight outlined his massive form, and the night swallowed him.

Thank you, Lord.

Her shoulders dropped, and the tightness in her chest eased. Bending over, she snatched the object from the ground. As her fingers closed around the hard plastic, a wave of thankfulness surged through her. *A baby doll. Nothing more.*

The pale light illuminated its life-size form. She turned it, and the canine's saliva oozed through her fingers. Ugh. She shifted her hand to find a dry spot, and the moonlight fell on the doll's face. Sharee stared.

The eyes were black ovals, and a long, deep gash opened the throat. Her hands tightened. The dog couldn't have done this. Could he? Someone had mutilated it. Some sick person.

Her focus returned to the trees. No dog. Nothing there. Good. She turned and started in the church's direction. Its lights formed the same welcome glow she'd seen on many Christmas cards.

"Sharee?"

Her breath caught. She stopped and spun around. A tall figure closed the space between them. The same dappling shadows that had danced over the dog flickered across him.

He stopped next to her. "Sorry about the dog. He likes to run when I take him off the leash."

The ball in her stomach eased, and relief spread upward as she recognized his voice. John Jergenson, maintenance crew of one. Ah. She had seen the animal before, a year or so ago. But at half the size.

"That's Cooper? He's grown. He's huge, in fact."

"If I'd known someone was outside, I would have kept him close. He didn't scare you, did he?"

"No. I'm fine. I came out for a breather. The baby shower's gone on for a while. I just needed a moment." The dog materialized beside him, and she stepped away. "I never realized Labs got this big."

"He's large for the breed. Especially, if you're shor—" He stopped.

"Especially, if you're short? Petite or vertically challenged?" She tried to contain the spurt of annoyance, but she'd heard the euphemisms too many times.

"Sorry. I didn't mean…"

"And *he*'s huge. *And* running loose. He'd scare anybody."

His pause lasted a second. "Except you."

"What?"

"You said he didn't scare you."

She took a long breath. Why had she snapped at him? The man had always been polite. Distant, but polite. Perhaps the irritation with Abbey still lingered. She tried to catch his expression, but the evening light and his height—six-foot-something to her five-foot-two—prevented a helpful view of his face.

"All right. Sorry. Yes, he scared me."

She heard his chuckle.

"Well, I'm sorry he interrupted your break."

Yeah, a break. Lynn had almost pushed her out the door. "Take five, girlfriend. If you clobber the girl now, it will definitely have an effect on the baby shower. Marci won't miss you for a few minutes."

John shifted, blocking the moonlight. "You and Lynn have been here all afternoon, and you have a crowd tonight. I would have slipped out myself."

Of course he would. Crowds, as everyone knew, were not for him. "So, you've been here today, too? On a Saturday. Extra work this week?"

"Some things I wanted to finish." His voice flattened. He wrapped the empty dog's leash around his hand.

She'd heard the tone before—the one that kept her and every other church member from inquiring into his life. He could say "none of your business" with just the tone of his voice.

He motioned toward the doll. "You brought some of the decorations with you?"

"No. Cooper had this in his mouth. Now that scared me. It looked real."

"It did? Moonlight can do that. Distort things."

"Yes. And look at it." She held it out. "Someone has blackened its eyes and slit its throat."

He took the doll and examined it. "Someone's got a bizarre sense of humor."

"I don't call that humor. It's gruesome. Especially tonight." When he just looked at her, she added, "Because of the baby shower."

He flipped the doll over once more, frowning. "Yes, I see what you mean. You said Cooper had this?"

"Yes."

"I didn't see it when I made rounds."

"When was that?"

"About two hours ago. Not long after your party started."

"Shower."

His brow lifted. "Shower?"

"Baby shower."

"Oh." The moonlight caught the twist of a smile. "Of course."

"I better get back."

"I'll walk you in." He gave a sharp whistle and called the dog.

Her shoulders tightened. The dog appeared, running out of the gloom. When he stretched his nose at her, she edged away. John reached for the Lab's collar and tugged him to his side.

"He won't hurt you."

Memory of the dog's growl brought her head up. "Since you're here, you mean."

He shook his head. "No. He's gentle, despite the size. But I'll walk you in. Don't worry."

"All owners think their dogs are friendly. Not all are."

"True."

"And I don't need an escort."

His mouth twisted again. "I'm going that way myself."

"Oh. I... Okay." She clamped her mouth shut.

They both turned and headed for the church. The moonlight painted a silver line around the pond's edge, and a soft breeze circled filled with the scent of night-blooming jasmine. Crickets chirped. Sharee breathed in the peace.

As they neared the fellowship hall, the back door opened. Light splashed across the walkway, and the pastor of New Life Church appeared. A moment later, the door reopened.

"Pastor Alan." Roseanne Sawyer stepped into view, her hand reaching for him.

The pastor slanted a look over his shoulder and sidestepped the hand. "Yes, Roseanne?"

In the light spilling from the window, the woman's red hair and jeweled purple tunic stood out. Crystal earrings twirled. "I need to talk to you, Pastor."

"Something special?"

"My finances. I've juggled my money and my budget since the divorce, and I just don't know what to do anymore."

The pastor thrust his hands into his pockets. "You'll need someone trained in that field. I'm not a financial counselor, as my wife will confirm. Come by the office tomorrow, and Daneen will give you a referral."

"But you're the one I want. I don't trust others. You…"

"Roseanne, let's you and I and Daneen talk tomorrow. I'm only here to pick her up from the shower."

"But I don't know if I can make it tomorrow—"

Sharee and John stepped forward into the light, and her words trailed off.

"Hello, Roseanne." Sharee forced a smile. She never knew if it would work but trying was necessary.

Roseanne frowned as her gaze shifted from Sharee to John and back. An eyebrow arched. "Where have you two been?"

Sharee glanced up at John. The short beard gave him an easy-going look, but the brown eyes held an unmistakable irritation. He said nothing.

She gave Roseanne another smile. "I just wanted to get away from the shower for a few minutes. So, I walked out to the pond."

"Really?" The gaze flicked back and forth once more. "But aren't you in charge?"

"Lynn and I are. It's under control, don't worry."

"Oh, I'm not worrying. It will be breaking up in a few minutes, anyway." Her eyes dropped to the doll John held, and her mouth opened. "Where did you get that?"

"In the field."

"What's wrong with it?"

"Someone playing a joke, I think." John's tone ended the conversation. He turned to the pastor. "You have a few minutes, Alan?"

"Yes. Walk with me to the office." The pastor looked at Roseanne. "Call in the morning, Roseanne. Daneen can help you." He made an indication with his head, and the two men fell into step beside each other. The dog trotted at their heels.

"Well, what was that? He can talk to John but not to me?" Roseanne's voice hyped.

Sharee bit her lip. "It is late."

"Not for John, obviously."

"No, but Pastor Alan doesn't see women outside office hours or by himself."

"Yeah, well, now I have to come back tomorrow." Roseanne crossed her arms over her chest. "Where did John find that doll?"

"The dog found it. Someone slit its throat and gouged the eyes out. Kind of gruesome."

"In the field?"

"Yes. I don't know why kids do that stuff."

Roseanne said nothing but stared into the darkness where the men had disappeared. With a quick look back at Sharee, she reached for the fellowship hall door, opened it and vanished inside.

The door closed like a slap.

What is it today, Lord? I've tried with Roseanne. I've tried with Abbey. Two new people in the church, and I keep running into walls. She sighed and followed Roseanne inside.

Lights and laughter met her, startling her back into the baby shower as if she'd stepped from a hot, humid day into air conditioning. Her shoulders loosened and her gaze traveled the room. White cloths covered a dozen tables. Cobalt, sapphire, and silver balloons rose from the center of each. Tulle, intertwined with silver ribbon, swirled around a large table at one end. She and Lynn Stapleton had spent hours cooking and decorating. Now, chocolate cake leftovers, soiled dishes, and torn gift wrappings littered it.

She smiled. Good.

Another quick glance showed her that the girl she'd clashed with earlier had disappeared. Abbey Somer's rant against their guest of honor had caused turmoil minutes before the shower, and her smirks during the event had caused Lynn to shove Sharee out the door.

Sharee glanced at Marci Thornton, the mother-to-be. The woman looked exhausted, even as she continued to smile and hug the women surrounding her as they said their goodbyes.

Where's Stephen? He should be here to pack the car and drive her home. Marci's doctor had restricted her driving privileges. No surprise. At eight months along with her seventh child, Marci looked like she could deliver any minute.

Lynn broke from the group and sent her a look that told her what she wanted to know. Everything had gone smoothly. Good. Marci's pregnancy had raised a storm of controversy. Why did people think it their place to criticize how many children a couple had? A stack of used cups flew into a plastic bag she'd grabbed. No, she hadn't just stood and listened when Abbey Somers started criticizing her friend. She'd spoken up and ignited a conflict between herself, the teen, and others.

She should have handled that better. Being ten years older than the teen should mean something. Sighing, she dropped a bunch of plastic ware into the bag, wishing she could drop some marbles of understanding into the agitator's head with as little difficulty.

"Well, Miss Jones," Lynn said, "I'm glad you made it back."

Sharee smiled. Lynn held a plastic bag, too, into which she stuffed used paper cups, plastic ware, and napkins.

"Have I ever left you to clean up by yourself?"

Lynn shifted waist length hair out of her way and grabbed another pile of used plates. "After Abbey said what she did, I thought you might take the rest of the night off."

Sharee's smile widened. "She stretched my new resolution to the breaking point, that's for sure."

"I do think I saw you swallow what you wanted to say one time." Lynn laughed when Sharee wrinkled her nose. "Don't worry. If you hadn't said something, I would have. And it wouldn't have been pretty either."

"That's good to hear."

Lynn grinned. "Everything went well while you were gone, and the nay-sayers didn't sour the shower. Marci has lots of beautiful things for the baby."

"That's what's important."

Sharee eyed her friend's designer outfit. The word "beautiful" described Lynn the way sensuous described JLo. Lynn's five-foot-seven-inch height, long blonde hair, and blue eyes made her runway material. Sharee wrinkled her nose again. Even if she straightened her head full of curls and put on five-inch heels, she'd never make it into the competition.

"What?" Lynn asked.

"You look great. As always."

"And you do, too. You know I envy your curls. My hair refuses even the slightest wave."

Sharee rolled her eyes. "Here we go again. You want my curly hair, and I wish mine were straight."

"And together we cover all the bases."

Sharee closed the trash bag and hoisted a dirty serving dish. "Everyone loved your fancy appetizers."

"They should have. I spent oodles of time on them." Lynn stopped at the next table. "I plan on getting some of the women to bring meals to Marci's place the first week."

"Good. She'll need it. And I'm asking Pastor Alan about the Christmas program."

"You haven't asked yet? You know he needs time to think things through."

"It's only September."

"Late September."

"He'll be fine."

"With all the stuff you want to do? He'll have a cow." Lynn grinned and headed for another table.

Sharee grabbed a serving dish and headed for the kitchen. Maybe she'd talk with Pastor Alan and Daneen this week. She elbowed open the kitchen door.

ॐ

"She doesn't deserve a baby."

Sharee stopped with the door open. The two girls huddled together on the far side of the room.

"Abbey, just quit. I don't want to hear this again." The second teen bent her head and long gold hair slid like a waterfall in front of her face.

"Well, it's true." Abbey's voice rose. "She doesn't deserve another child. Not…not when you lost yours."

Sharee let the door swing shut behind her, the noise adding an accent to her entry. She deposited the dishes on the counter and threw a look in the girls' direction.

"Abbey, we had this discussion earlier." She met the girl's hard stare with one of her own. "You shouldn't have come if you felt this way. And you're badgering Ryann." She walked over and hugged the other girl. "You doing okay?"

Ryann Byrd nodded but didn't say anything.

Compassion squeezed Sharee's heart. "You could have stayed home, Ryann."

"I know, but I wanted to be here for Marci."

"And I know Marci appreciates it. This was hard for you."

"Yeah. It's okay, though."

Abbey grabbed Ryann's arm. "Let's go. Everything's over here."

Sharee focused on the other girl. "Abbey, you didn't leave a note for Marci, did you?"

"No. Why would I?" The teen's voice displayed her hostility.

"I found one on the floor in front of the table with the presents."

"So?"

"So, when I opened it to see if I could find out which present it went with, I found a nasty message inside."

"Well, I didn't write it."

Sharee studied the girl. Was she telling the truth?

"What did it say, Ms. J?" Ryann sniffed.

Sharee frowned, debating the wisdom of telling them. "That having too many children was a sin against God."

Ryann looked shocked. "That's not true!"

"No, it isn't. It was just a way to make Marci feel bad."

Abbey tossed her head. "Well, I didn't write it."

Some others in the congregation had made their feelings known, too. If, as Marci said, she and Stephen had decided to let God number their children, what right did others have to interfere?

"But I don't understand, Ms. J." Ryann's whisper interrupted Sharee's thoughts. "I know Will and I did wrong having sex before marriage, but did God take my baby as punishment?"

Tears pooled in the girl's eyes. Sharee closed her arms around her again. "No, sweetheart. I don't believe that. God is a god of love, but there are causes and effects in life, and Satan is real. We don't always know why things happen, but just know that God loves you. He will get you through this."

"It's not fair." Abbey edged closer to Ryann. "What happened to Ryann wasn't fair."

"Life's not always fair, Abbey."

The girl scowled and pulled on Ryann's t-shirt. "Let's go."

Ryann threw an apologetic look at Sharee, and the girls left arm-in-arm. Sharee sighed. Abbey's Goth look clashed with Ryann's preppy clothes. How did two such different girls become such close friends?

"She's right, you know."

Sharee spun around. Roseanne Sawyer stood holding the door. Her earrings dangled and twirled, and her voice matched Abbey's.

She stepped farther into the room. "It isn't fair. If God is such a good God, why does he allow these things?"

And why do people act as if God is their personal Santa Claus and should deliver whatever they want down the chimney? Sharee opened her mouth to answer but closed it quickly. Any answer she gave would reflect her feelings toward the woman and her irritation with Abbey rather than a respectable discussion of God's goodness and his plans.

She'd said what she needed to say to Ryann. At least for now. But if she replied to Roseanne's question right now, she'd regret it later.

"Well?" Roseanne asked. "You don't know the answer yourself, do you?" Her challenge hung over them both before she turned and barreled back into the fellowship hall.

Chapter 2

"Are you crazy?" A man's high voice leaped at her as she climbed from her CR-V. Sharee lifted her head and looked around.

Across the parking lot, Bruce Tomlin gripped the arms of his wheelchair and glared at Abbey.

"You think I ran into her on purpose?"

Sharee missed Abbey's soft reply, but she shook her head. What was the girl up to now?

"Of course, you did." Bruce pushed backward in the wheelchair. "What else could you have meant by that?"

The wheelchair's movement revealed two people huddled together on the ground. Ryann was attempting to lift Marci Thornton to her feet.

Sharee jumped forward. "Marci! What happened? Are you okay?"

The woman didn't answer, but she grabbed Sharee's outstretched hand. Ryann and Sharee helped her to her feet.

"Are you all right, Mrs. Thornton?" Ryann's voice trembled. "What about the baby?"

"No. I...I'm okay."

"Are you sure?" Sharee's arm slipped around her friend's waist.

Marci caressed her rounded abdomen. "I think so."

"Let me call your doctor."

"No, I—"

Bruce's wheelchair edged closer. "Marci, I can't believe I didn't see you. Are you sure you're all right?"

"Yes. Don't worry. It's my fault. I was reading something, and I stepped from between the cars."

"I'm not letting you take the blame for this. I was going too fast and didn't see you."

"Don't' worry, Bruce. I'm okay."

"You're due soon. You should probably see the doctor." He leaned forward in his wheelchair. "You don't want anything to happen to the little guy."

Ryann's hand went to the woman's stomach. "He's right, Mrs. Thornton. I'll drive you home. You can call the doctor from there."

Sharee squeezed her arm. "That's a great idea. And I'll bring your car later, Marci. Lynn will help me."

"I've ruined our lunch plans, Sharee. And the program—"

"Don't worry about it. I'll talk with Lynn. We'll get back to you. Right now, you and the baby are what's important. Let Ryann take you home."

Marci's protest sounded frail. "I can drive."

"No." Sharee shook her head. "You're not supposed to be driving, anyway. I should never have agreed to meet you here."

Ryann leaned in close. "Let me help."

"I...well...I guess." Marci thrust a paper at Sharee. "Here. Someone left this in my car. Just burn it."

"What?"

"Burn it." Marci's voice echoed the disgust in her eyes.

"My car's right over there." Ryann pointed. "Abbey can sit in the back." She threw a smirk at Abbey, who scrunched her face. Ryann slipped her arm around Marci, and they started for the car.

Sharee watched them go. Ironic that Ryann would come to Marci's rescue, and Abbey would have to help—or, at least, endure it—in some way. She glanced down at Bruce. "Ryann's the sensible one, but I wonder how she's feeling inside."

"You mean because of her miscarriage? That still bothers her?"

"It was traumatic for her. She's a teenager, and she was five months along. The baby is well formed by then. She lost a child. Yes, she's having a hard time."

"I hadn't thought about it like that." He changed his grip on the wheelchair. "I've been out of touch with the youth lately. And to have Abbey accuse me of running into Marci on purpose. That's ridiculous. Marci stepped from behind the car, and I couldn't stop in time." His voice faded. "I was going fast, but usually, I see everything." Bruce slapped the wheelchair's arm. "Well, the truth is I can't see a lot from this height."

Sharee's heart ached for him. Bruce had played basketball with such passion, his laughter echoing across the court, and the youth had loved his leadership. The two years since his accident had seen him struggle to get back to as normal a life as possible. Marci's involvement, as the driver that day, had left her quieter, more serious. Then Ryann's pregnancy and miscarriage. The father of the baby leaving the church. Even her own problems with Dean... So much had happened over the last couple of years. It had all taken a toll on the church, too. Somehow the idea of the church working together on the Christmas project felt right. Maybe God would use it to bring healing.

Sharee touched Bruce's shoulder, and he shifted away.

"I don't need your pity."

"You're not getting it. But you've had a rough two years. Just like Marci. Only yours has been tougher. I admire what you've accomplished."

A short silence followed. "Thank you."

Shoving on the wheels of his chair, he rolled to the van and clicked the remote. The back door rose. The lift came down. Bruce rolled onto the lift; and in another minute, he had maneuvered into the driver's seat. His electric wheelchair sat off to the side, but he hardly ever used it, preferring the old one for building muscle.

"He's come a long way, hasn't he? Doesn't baby himself."

Startled, Sharee lifted her head and looked into John's dark eyes. "What? Oh. Yes, he has."

An engine started, and they both turned. The van backed away from the curb and followed Ryann's car as it exited the parking lot.

"I remember arriving here the weekend of the accident," John said.

"And I took off for Tennessee that same weekend." She sensed his eyes on her again, but she stared at the van as it disappeared. They hadn't mentioned that day since. She wouldn't mention it now. A lot had happened.

"He's come a long way, but I wonder if he's doing as well inside as he's doing outside. He's angry still."

"Don't you think he has a reason?"

She glanced up to see him studying her. "Well, yes, but if he stays that way, he'll be miserable."

"Maybe he should just paste a smile on his face and pretend everything's okay."

She leaned back, surprised at his tone. "I didn't say that."

"No?" A line appeared between his brows. "Tell me something. Does this God of yours demand we take everything he dishes out without complaint?"

Whoa, where did that come from? "I didn't say that either."

"No?"

"No." His words brought back Abbey's and then Roseanne's questions at the baby shower. "You know, God is not the author of all the bad stuff that happens to us. There's an enemy out there, whom everyone chooses to ignore. But he's real and active. And a lot of the stuff that happens to us is our own fault. My heart goes out to Bruce and to Marci and the other woman involved in the accident. It was horrible. But if Bruce had worn his seatbelt that day, would he be walking now? Maybe. Just maybe. So often, we do what we know is not right and then we blame God for the consequences."

"But couldn't this all-powerful God have prevented what happened?"

"He could have. Of course. And sometimes He does, but often we reap what we sow. We make our own choices and experience the consequences of them. Only, most people don't like that—to take responsibility for their actions. We just blame God."

She stared at the field, and silence stretched between them. Sharee lifted her head again, checking the dark eyes looking down at her. Her stomach dropped at what she saw there. *Oh, Lord, why do I always jump in there and blurt out what I'm thinking?*

"Some of us take responsibility very seriously." The words were clipped. He turned and strode back toward the work buildings.

Sharee watched his retreating back. Her heart squeezed. He'd been angry, yes, but the pain... She bit her lip then whispered, "He's not just my God, John. He's yours, too, and He loves you."

Chapter 3

The jangle of her phone the next morning woke her. Sharee reached for the nightstand, slapped her hand over assorted items and felt for the familiar rectangle.

"Hello?" Her voice pushed past a dry throat and remnants of an interrupted dream.

"Sharee?"

She struggled to clear her head. "Lynn?"

"Yes, guess what?" Lynn's wake-up-now voice burst across the airways. "The baby's here!"

"What?"

"Marci's baby. Joshua Michael Thornton. Six pounds, two ounces."

Sharee propped on an elbow. Her alarm clock showed 5:02 A.M. "The baby?" She fought the wave of tiredness that rolled over her. "Marci's baby? Is he okay?"

"Yes. Yes. He's fine, but I had to tell you. He's a little early, but I heard Bruce knocked Marci down with his wheelchair. So, I assume that's why."

"He did." Sharee tried to stop a yawn. "Marci's okay, too?"

"She's fine. But they'll keep the baby a day or two to monitor him."

"How did you find out?"

"Daneen called last night about the food for Marci, and Stephen beeped in—from the hospital. She and Pastor Alan ran over there. I told her to call when the baby came. Guess what?"

Recognizing the tone, Sharee rolled onto her back to get comfortable. Lynn and her gossip. "What?"

"Abbey and Ryann showed up."

"Really? Was Ryann okay?"

"Yes. In fact, she seemed pretty excited about the baby."

"And Abbey?"

"Abbey was Abbey. What can I say?"

"She wasn't rude to Marci, was she?"

"No. In fact, she didn't get to see her, but she and Ryann stood at the window of the preemie unit and saw Joshua."

"I wonder how they found out."

"Matthew Thornton and Ryann are close. He was a great help when she lost the baby, remember? After the boyfriend did his disappearing act. I bet he called her."

"Could be."

Lynn giggled. "I wish I'd been there."

"I bet you do. God is good, isn't he? Both Marci and the baby are okay, and that's what counts."

"You're right on, girl."

"Thanks for calling. I'm going back to sleep. Bye."

Sharee put the phone back on the nightstand. A new baby. She plumped her pillow and snuggled down under the covers. After a few minutes, she rolled to her back and stared at the ceiling. A little while later, she pushed the blanket off, swung her feet to the floor and clicked on the lamp.

The paper Marci had given her lay on the nightstand. She unfolded it and reread the title: "A list of Congenital Diseases and Problems for Babies of Aging Moms." At the top, someone had written, "You're too old to have children. Your baby could be born with one of these." Who had left this in Marci's car? And why?

Sharee sighed, turned off the light, but didn't move. Silence stretched through the apartment. A familiar urging tightened her insides. She bowed her head and began to pray.

స్

Sharee shoved her hands into her jacket and grabbed her purse. She had waited a whole week after Pastor Alan gave his okay for John to give his, and now John wanted to see her—today.

Daneen's voice was warm with amusement when Sharee picked up the phone earlier. "Sharee, I'm sorry I had to call you at work, but John just agreed; and he wants to see you this afternoon. We need the time, he said, since this is such a last-minute request."

"Last minute?" Sharee let her voice rise. "He's the one that took a week to agree. You'd think I was asking them to build the Taj Mahal instead of a few mock-ups for a Christmas project."

"It will take some doing."

"Anything worth anything takes some doing."

Daneen chuckled. "Yes, it does. Your boss doesn't mind if you take off early?"

"No, I talked told her about the project earlier and said I might need some time off. I have a lot of PTO coming."

She whirled out of the parking lot and flipped on the Christian radio station. Downtown Ministries could do without her for the last hour. She had no clients, and eight years of faithful service to the homeless counted for something.

Glancing down at the speedometer, she realized she needed to ease back on the gas and her enthusiasm. Sometimes her excitement turned people off. She didn't understand it herself, but every year the Christmas program filled her with fire—in the same way a potbelly stove heated the room of a log cabin.

She took a breath. John hadn't helped on the other Christmas programs. He kept to maintenance. Of course, the program this year was outside and more extensive. Which was why Pastor Alan had asked for his help. Sharee had known they'd need it. Still, his agreement to assist was unusual.

She parked and darted across the lot to the office. Three heads swiveled her way when she snatched open the door. Pastor Alan, Daneen, and John all sat in the front office.

"You're earlier than expected." Pastor Alan threw her a smile. "Not much traffic?"

"Not much. I think I got here on autopilot."

"You want to sit down and catch your breath?"

"No." She tried to stop the grin and couldn't. "I don't want to keep John long, but I could if I'm not careful."

"I warned him, Sharee. He agreed to do this, but when I told him you wanted to build a city—"

"A city?" Her voice rose. "That's not true. I mean…" She transferred her focus to John. "Of course, there are buildings; but they're mock-ups. Not the whole building. And we'll need to do Herod's court. And the manger scenes. You'll have volunteers to help like always. You know how the congregation pitches in to help with whatever you need—we need, in this case. But you'll have to…" She stopped.

The two men had exchanged glances, and John's mouth twitched.

"Well," Pastor Alan said, the corner of his eyes crinkling. "John will make sure it gets done, but go easy on him. The congregation will have your head and mine if you run him off."

Daneen tapped on her desk. "I don't know why you're giving her a hard time. From what I can tell, there's a month to build the sets and a month for rehearsals. It will be fine, Sharee."

John leaned back in his chair and eyed them both. "If there are no problems."

Sharee wasn't going to let him fluster her. "I'm depending on God to bring it all together."

"That and a whole lot of workers."

She wanted to say that God would bring the workers, and hadn't He already brought John? But she bit her lip. She'd promised that she'd work on her tongue—on not spouting off before she thought.

She sighed. "Can we discuss this in the field? I can explain it better there."

John rose from his chair and pulled a leather jacket from the back of it. "Okay. I need to see what I agreed to. Alan already has me wondering if I've bitten off a plug too thick to chew." He walked toward the door.

Sharee cleared her throat. "Uh. Do you want a legal pad or something? You know, to write on?"

"A legal pad?" He slipped his arms into his jacket and shifted his gaze to Pastor Alan.

The pastor grinned at him. Sharee frowned. What was so funny?

John ran a hand over his stubbly beard. "Sure. Why not? Daneen, you have a legal pad there?"

Daneen opened a desk drawer, drew one out, and handed it to him along with a pencil. John turned and held the door for Sharee. She ducked under his arm. This should prove interesting. John either worked by himself or at the head of a group. How would he do taking instructions from her?

They walked in silence for a minute, while she tried to balance her enthusiasm with the undercurrents in the office.

"So." She hesitated a moment before forging on. "Do you feel like you pulled the short straw or what?"

He tilted his head toward her. "Must have."

The glimmer of light in his eyes stopped her from saying anything else. He and Pastor Alan doubtless had a great discussion before she arrived. At her expense. Well, good. Let him be amused, as long as he didn't hold that debate about Bruce against her.

They stopped just inside the field under one of the large pines. The wind swept cool fingers along the ground. Sharee shifted in that direction, enjoying the feel of it in her hair. After temperatures in the high eighties, the unexpected cool front that moved through last night was a blessing. She zipped her light jacket.

The legal pad under one arm, John slid his hands into his pockets. "Tell me what you have in mind."

Sharee tamped down her eagerness. If she poured everything out, she might find herself working the project like a giant panda. Alone. "I'm wondering where to start."

"Let me ask some questions then."

"Okay."

"Since it's a Christmas program, you'll want a barn and a manger, right?"

"Right, but I'll need two barns and two mangers."

He raised a brow but didn't ask the obvious question. "Okay. We'll talk about that later. Let me get a handle on a few things. What needs to be completed first?"

"The bleachers."

He crossed his arms and raised both brows this time. "Bleachers?"

"Yes. We have to have someplace for people to sit."

Quiet settled over them. She grinned. She couldn't stop herself.

"Hmm. Wait here." Strolling across the parking lot, he disappeared into the garden shed.

Sharee hugged herself against the chill. How could she tell him when she didn't feel like she knew it all herself? She had a vision. Well, no one else would call it a vision, but what else could she call it? Something stirring inside her. Bits and pieces had shifted together when she talked with Pastor Alan, but the whole thing appeared more like a lake brushed with morning fog.

Don't let me mess up, Lord. And don't let it seem ridiculous to John. Help him see it, too.

John returned with two folding chairs. He handed her one and opened the other, sat, and put the legal pad in front of him.

"All right, let me ask another question."

His questions, she realized later, helped her take a brush to the picture inside and, with sure strokes, erase the fog. He challenged her basic theory of dividing the field into seven stages. Why not five or six areas, he wanted to know. Or why not one?

She explained the vision of the drama, how it would play out in seven areas with live animals, a choir, and costumed actors.

His eyebrows came into play again. So, they'd need holding pens for the animals? She had to admit she hadn't thought about that.

Back to the seven areas. He wasn't going to let that pass easily.

She folded her hands in her lap and prayed for patience. "It's a huge six-pointed star on the ground, highlighted by a spotlight. The actors will move from one area to another as they go through the Christmas story, and the spotlight will follow them."

The pencil stopped moving. His head rose once more. "A star on the ground? Why?"

"I don't know. That's the way I see it. Each area will have its own backdrop or building, and the characters will slip from one scene to another in the dark. It will work well if the set-up is a star. Not five-pointed, but six-pointed. The middle of the star is the seventh area and will be the city of Bethlehem."

"A whole city?" His voice remained low.

She wanted to laugh at his tone. "No. No. Really. I told you earlier. Not the whole city. A backdrop. You know?"

"Just so we're on the same page."

She glanced at the notes he'd written. "Good thing I suggested the legal pad. We've got the page right there." His look did nothing to stop her grin. "I'm sorry. I'm excited about this. I think it's going to be wonderful. At the end, I'm going to ask someone to talk about Jesus and give an invitation."

"An invitation?"

"You know, for them to accept Christ."

He nodded but said nothing.

She sobered and sat straighter. "You know, perhaps I wasn't fair when I asked Pastor Alan if he thought you would help us." His quiet watchfulness unsettled her. "I mean, you might not believe in what we're doing. I had no right to ask you to give up your Saturdays between now and Christmas. I wasn't thinking. I—"

"Sharee." His voice stopped her. "I said I would do it. Don't belabor it."

She studied him for a minute. "Okay, but I…"

"You're doing this for the neighborhood, for the community, Alan said."

"Yes, I wouldn't be asking you or the congregation to do this if it was just for us. We could have a nice little celebration inside, sing songs, have food. We've done that before, but I told Pastor Alan I want to send invites to the addresses within a couple of miles around. I'll invite those who come to my work, too. We minister to a lot of people. I think Downtown Ministries would offer to bus them over."

"Are you planning on using the youth?"

"I haven't thought about it."

"Think about it." His eyes focused on the legal pad again. "So we start with the shepherds and angels, then the manger scene, move to the wise men coming, Herod's court, the Inn, then the wise men bringing gifts—where you want another manger scene—and a final scene where everyone will sing and someone give their testimony and an invitation?"

"Wow. You condensed that."

"Why don't you just use the same manger scene for the wise men and their gifts?"

"I want it to look different. Many people think it was actually two years later. That Jesus was no longer a baby, but a child." He said nothing, so she continued. "Anyway, I don't want to do that, but I do want the scene to look different than the first."

He nodded. "Give me a couple minutes." He flipped the page and began sketching.

Sharee rose, moved next to him, and cocked her head to see it better. "You do that well."

A smile appeared and left. "Wait, and I'll show it to you."

His hands moved over the pad with a deft artistry, a line here and there brought the buildings, even some of the animals, into quick relief.

"But you know…" She leaned over and studied the sketch.

He raised his head. "Yes?"

Eyes as warm and dark as coffee searched hers. A touch of amusement showed in their depths. She'd noticed that already, but his look held no animosity, no hardness.

Something clicked inside her. He wasn't giving her a hard time. The questions he asked had meaning and focus—finding out what she wanted and narrowing it down. His workmanship had excellence as an epitaph. Everyone in the congregation had commented on it. And if he was to do what she wanted, he had to know what that was.

She took a step back from the closeness of his eyes, trying to think what she'd just said to him. "I…uh…the star has six different scenes. The space in the middle is the seventh. The last scene."

He dipped his head in acknowledgment. A breeze circled them. She stepped back further, rubbing her arms.

"Are you cold?"

"No, I'm fine." Her concentration switched to his sketch. "Can we make the middle of the star…" She pointed to his drawing. "Can we make that bigger? That will be the backdrop for Bethlehem. It includes everyone in the program. Can we do that and keep the shape of the star?" The layout was in her mind, but was she getting it across to him?

She stuck out her hand for his sketch. His lips quirked, and he handed it to her. She took it and moved away from him, overlaying it with the diagram in her mind. The quick walk generated welcomed heat. In a minute, she returned.

"You know, if we take a fat triangle and put another fat triangle on top of it going the other direction…" She put her hands together, finger splayed and turned them opposite each other. "It will form the six-pointed star, and it will make a fat middle. Yours are too skinny."

"You want fat triangles? We can do fat triangles." He flipped to another page, drew one triangle, flipped the pad around and drew the other on top of the first and raised a brow for confirmation. Sharee bobbed her head. He labeled each section and stood.

Sharee jumped back to get out of his way and knocked her chair over. It clattered to the ground. His smile widened, and warmth filled her face. She bent to pick up the chair.

"Do you have any idea how big this star will be?" he asked.

"Well…"

"I didn't think so. I'll do some measuring tomorrow. Alan wasn't far off, you know."

"What do you mean?"

"You want us to build a city."

"I don't think...I mean...I—"

"Don't stumble all over yourself." He studied the pad for a moment. "Let me digest this, do some measurements, and talk with a couple of the other men."

"Okay."

"You're excited about it."

"What?" She tilted her head back and met his look. "Yeah, I am. I feel that God has given me something to do. It is exciting."

He nodded. "Look, when you come next time, wear something warm, will you?"

Her mouth opened, but nothing came out. She just gawked at him.

He slipped both chairs under his arms. "I couldn't decide if I needed to offer you my jacket or not."

"Oh." Offer his jacket? He'd opened the office door for her, too. Someone had raised him with manners.

He indicated the tablet under his arm. "You've given this some thought. And we honed in on a few things that needed attention. Makes my job easier. We'll talk in a few days." He headed across the parking lot.

She hugged herself and smiled as the wind swept past. Talking with John had been less difficult than expected. Perhaps he'd do the spotlight. The old one the church owned was heavy and would need someone strong. John had the type of wiry strength needed. He'd lifted and carried much heavier things when they had work parties out here.

She grinned again and scanned the field. Anticipation rose like a kindling fire.

༄

John put the chairs down in the shed and glanced out the window. Sharee stood with her arms crossed, a smile lighting her face, her auburn hair shifting in the wind. Like a lion's mane—only curly. He grinned at the thought and caught himself.

Hmm.

He'd smiled more this past hour than he had for...well, for a while. Of course, the pain inside his chest had eased over the last couple of months, the overwhelming emptiness giving way to an ache like a valve tapping. Its constant drumbeat kept him aware that something needed fixing. But no fix would change his life.

When he accepted Alan's job offer two years ago, he'd wanted to get away from the questions, the reminders. And he wanted nothing else now—no reminders, no complications, no relationships. He rubbed his chin.

Not that Sharee would create a problem. Except for that first day when he'd found her sobbing by the pond, they'd stayed apart. He'd made sure of that, made sure she realized that first day was unusual. Not that he had to worry. She'd stayed as far away from him as possible, too.

He turned from the window. No, she wouldn't be a problem. Too skittish for one thing, too serious about her faith for another. He'd agreed to help with the sets, and that's what he'd do. Nothing else.

He reached for the door, stopped and rolled his shoulders. Something didn't feel right, though. He looked out the window again, watched Sharee walk back to her SUV and frowned. He hadn't played chess with God this long not to be aware of the moves.

On Wednesday evening, Sharee pulled into the church parking lot a few minutes before the service began. She climbed from her SUV and leaned back against the door. The sun-smeared sky glowed with color—pinks, melons, salmon. Deep gray clouds stretched across it, pulled like angel hair, their edges alive with fire.

Stunning, Lord. You do good work.

Her gaze dropped to the SUV, and she sighed. The problem with her Honda CR-V might prove to be something else altogether.

Moving to the front, she popped the hood and secured it with a prop rod. At her apartment, the car had sputtered and stopped—had done it twice, in fact—before it caught. What if she had trouble after church? Holding back her long curls with one hand, she reached to loosen a connection with the other. The terminals appeared all right, but maybe they needed cleaning with steel wool. She'd seen her dad do it. She would try that, and if that didn't work, then the battery…

"Anything interesting under there?"

Sharee jumped and jerked her head around. "Oh! John. You startled me."

He rested his hands next to hers on the car. "Are you having trouble?"

She stepped back and reached for the prop rod. "Not really. Just checking the connections." Her voice trailed off as she took in his appearance.

He had on a dinner jacket, dress pants, and a white shirt, open at the collar. Since he'd started doing maintenance around the church, she'd never seen him in anything but jeans and t-shirts.

Something crunched behind him. Without moving, John asked, "Do you think the lady has a problem?"

"That's what I came to see." Pastor Alan appeared next to him.

"I'm fine." Sharee pulled her gaze from John's. "It just had trouble starting earlier, and I thought, well, maybe I needed to clean the terminals."

"Could be." Pastor Alan stepped next to her. "Why don't you climb back in and crank her up?"

Sharee rolled her eyes. Did they think she couldn't take care of this? She'd been on her own for eight years—since college graduation. She could take care of herself. Pushing past John, she climbed into the driver's seat. And when she turned the key, the car acted like the proverbial cat and purred to life. *Of course.*

Through the window, she caught John doing his best to keep a grin off his face. He'd seen her reaction. *Great.* She scowled at him and searched for something to say but could not get past his new look. The long-sleeved white shirt, dark olive pants and matching jacket highlighted his tan face and dark eyes. A now-smooth, not scruffy, chin completed the look.

"Well, don't you look different."

Pastor Alan poked his head around the hood. "It sounds all right to me, Sharee. Catch me if you have any trouble after the service. John, your ride's here. Let me talk with her a moment."

Sharee climbed from the car and watched a black Jaguar slide to a stop. An attractive woman close to her own age rolled down the driver's window. Black lace covered the girl's shoulders. A teardrop diamond necklace and long, straight hair accentuated her attractiveness.

Sharee's hands went to her own unruly hair. She shoved the curls back from her face.

The driver leaned her head out the window. "*Pastor* Alan, so nice to see you." Amusement edged the words. "I can't get over how much you remind me of a kid I once knew. Of course, I'm sure that boy's enjoying hard time these days."

The pastor leaned over and said something that Sharee didn't hear. The girl laughed. Sharee brought her gaze back to John.

"So, how many times have you cleaned battery terminals?" he asked.

"I...well...enough."

"Which means never, I take it."

"That's not what I said."

"This coming from a Christian woman who would never lie."

"I'm not..." She frowned. "Well..." Sharee stumbled to a halt. She was lying.

"Just what I thought. Look, if you—"

"John." The voice came from behind him. "My birthday won't last forever. Are you coming? Or do I have to hijack the Man of God to take me to dinner?"

Pastor Alan leaned against the car door, his mouth forming a wide smile. John turned and strolled toward the passenger side of the Jaguar. He rested his hand on the top and looked across at Sharee.

"If you have trouble with the car, girl, swallow your pride and ask for help." He dropped into the passenger seat, and the car pulled away.

Sharee watched it disappear around the drive. Beside her, Pastor Alan cleared his throat.

Sharee's head swung his way. "Who is that?"

"Someone I've known most of my life." He stared after the car. "But haven't seen for a while. Someone who needs the Lord."

"Oh." She stared down the drive to where the car had disappeared. "John looked different today, and he seemed different the other day. I mean, when we were talking about the program."

"Did he? How?"

"I'm not sure. Not so serious. He seemed lighter. Easier to talk with."

"About your Christmas program?"

"Yes."

"It took him a while to make up his mind. Since he did, he'll do a good job."

"I know. He always does."

"Have you ever told him that?"

"Told him what?"

"That he does a good job. Everybody appreciates a word of appreciation."

"Hmm. Well, when do I get the chance? Unless you two drag us out here for some project you've dreamed up, I hardly see him."

"Every one of those projects, Miss Jones, has benefited the congregation more than us, and you know it."

She grinned. "I do."

His smile matched hers.

"Pastor, wait!" A woman's voice came from behind them. "Wait! I need to talk to you." Roseanne hurried across the parking lot. A crimson dress was accented with light-catching sequins, and a matching comb held back the red hair.

"Hello, Roseanne."

The woman shot a glance at Sharee then turned her attention to the pastor. "I need your assistance, Pastor." Her hands fluttered in emphasis, and the light captured the wink of numerous rings on her fingers.

"What can I help with today, Roseanne? No finances, I hope."

"I want to help Marci with the baby, but she says she has six other children, and they can help. That's ridiculous. She's got to wait on them, and on the baby, and on her husband, too. I know how that works. She needs help, and I have time. It's just pride making her say no."

"Now, Roseanne." Pastor Alan's voice soothed. "If Marci says she doesn't need help, you can't—"

"It's not just that. I'm new here. I need something to keep me busy. Since my move here and the divorce, well, I have to get re-established. What's a church for if not to help people?"

"You're right, but Marci..."

"The rest of your *flock* are all chipper and fine," Roseanne said. Her eyes narrowed as she glanced at Sharee. "No problems there. So, why can't you convince Marci that I can help with the baby?"

"Well." Pastor Alan's gaze touched Sharee's. He'd noticed Roseanne's attitude, of course. "Let's go talk with Daneen. Maybe she has an idea."

They headed toward the church, and Sharee dropped behind. Pride. The word had surfaced twice in a few minutes. She twisted her head and eyed her SUV.

Why had she not wanted to tell them about her car? "Swallow your pride," John had said, and Roseanne's remark about pride left a tinge of guilt, too, even though her reference had been about Marci.

She pulled a soft peppermint from her pocket, unwound the wrapper and popped the candy into her mouth. *You trying to tell me something, Lord? I don't like asking for help. Is that pride?*

Was she still trying to prove something to her parents? Being an only child had its plusses and minuses.

Behind her came the drumbeat of running feet, raised voices, and throaty laughter. She shifted and glanced over her shoulder. Five or six girls from the youth group ran toward her.

A warning leaped through her even before she saw the pistols. She spun toward her car.

"Quick! Get her! Don't let her get away!"

Chapter 4

The warning and resultant blast of adrenaline gained her nothing. Sharee ran for her CR-V, but the group of girls surrounded her before she reached it. Spray from the water guns soaked her back and chest. Laughter rose and encircled her.

"Hey! Stop! Wait!" Sharee put up her hands for protection and recognized Ryann and some of the other youth as they surrounded her. Since she'd taught the girls' Bible class and pulled a number of jokes on them, they had found ways to make sure the weights and balances of "get even" stayed in their favor.

"Girls!"

Zings of water drenched her hair and ran down her clothing. She fumbled for the car door and yanked it open. Someone shoved it closed. Giggling and squeals rose, and one girl up-ended a cup of water over her head. Icy fingers streamed down her neck and slid under her collar.

Sharee screeched. "You're gonna regret this!" She tried to sound firm and tried to keep the laughter out of her voice. Managing to pry open the door, she squeezed her body into the car then had to fight to get it closed. Water shot past her.

"My car!" Sharee protested. "You're soaking my car!"

More giggles surrounded her, and she couldn't help laughing herself. "All right. All right. But you're in *so* much trouble!" She yanked on the door.

"We got you, Ms. J. We got you!"

More water blasted her, sharp bursts that saturated her hair and jacket and the inside of her SUV. She wrestled the door closed and locked it. The girls circled the car and flooded every inch of it before running off.

She huddled there for a while, shivering and wet, and then moved her head to get a good look in the rearview mirror. Her curls were soaked and matted. By the time she went home and changed, church would be over. She left the parking lot shaking her head in amusement and determination.

She'd get them back all right. Wait until she thought of the right plan.

A few miles passed. A picture of Abbey standing behind the others, arms across her chest, flashed across her mind. Sharee turned onto the highway. Abbey hadn't joined in the other girls' prank. Instead, she'd stood apart.

She remembered her own high school years. Even with other Christian students at her school, she'd been a loner, too. Maybe that's why she was one, still. It hadn't changed that much, especially with guys. Except for Marci and Lynn, she had few close friends. Friends at work were just that. Work friends. They rarely spent time together outside of work. Everyone had families and other interests and church. Not that she complained. No. God had somehow inserted Himself into that hole. Particularly over the last two years...

Since Dean.

She stared past her car back to the darkening sky. The warm colors of a few minutes ago had changed. The fire corals had muted to cool apricots mixed with pale gray clouds.

Abbey's face flashed into her mind again. *She's hurting, Lord. I see that. I need more patience with her.* Sharee took a deep breath. *Show me what to do.*

❧

The dry, brisk air heightened every sense before she started across the parking lot for the field. A glorious day. Sharee's anticipation jumped higher as she noticed three rows of chairs already there. John had started working on something already. He'd wanted to talk with her again.

She stopped in front of the chairs. Stakes, rope, and some tools sat on one, a towel and plastic water bottle on another. She glanced toward the two buildings that contained the tools and machines needed for work around the property. If he was anywhere, it was probably there.

As she started that way, he came around the corner of one building. He wore sweatpants, a sweatshirt, and running shoes. Another outfit she'd never seen.

"You jog?" Sharee asked when he was close, trying to keep the surprise from her voice.

Cooper rounded the building, too, trotted up to her, tongue lolling, and pushed against her legs. Her throat closed. She stepped away from him. A moment later, she reached a tentative hand to pat his head.

Be nice to the dog. The owner is helping big time.

"Yeah, you?" He watched her a second then studied the field.

"Yes."

He nodded, wrote something on the tablet then lifted his head. "You jog?" His tone mimicked hers.

Heat rose in her face. "I'm sorry. It's just that...I've never seen you..."

And yet, he had a runner's lean build. Why had she never thought about his life outside of work? Just because he didn't talk about his private life didn't mean he had none. A mental picture of the girl in the Jaguar surfaced. Obviously, he did.

John grabbed a stake and a hammer and headed off across the field. "Bring the rope, will you, and the other stakes?"

She snatched up the others and headed after him.

He hammered the stake into the ground, straightened, and held out his hand. Confused, she shoved both hands at him. He took the rope, looped it through a hole at the top of the stake and tied it in a quick knot.

"I've never seen you jogging either, and I'm trying to work in some barb here about jogging and your height and what short strides you must have, but I just can't put it together. Take it that I owe you one. In the meantime…" He lifted a stake from her hand, began to unroll the rope, and walked off.

She stared after him. *What?*

He played the rope out and flashed a look over his shoulder. "Come on, girl, get with it. Stakes, please. This is your project."

Sharee gaped at him, unsure how to take his attitude. So different from the other day. She forced her legs to move. He looped the rope through a hole in the second stake and strode back across the field and came to a stop.

Sharee marched over and slapped another stake into his outstretched hand. What had her height to do with anything? Just because his stature reached cell tower status didn't mean he could insult her.

"You're speechless." His eyes held amusement.

She contemplated his grin, the clothes, and the cocky attitude and narrowed her eyes. "I've got a handful of sharpened stakes, and you're giving me a hard time."

He laughed aloud, reached over, and took the stakes. "Just in case. Come on. I want you to see this once we mark it off. I've placed the chairs where I think your bleachers should be—to give us an idea." He pounded in the third stake, tied the rope, and returned to the first one. "Your first fat triangle."

In a short time, they finished the second triangle that finished the large six-pointed star on the ground. When they stood next to the chairs, she saw the scope of the area marked off.

"Wow. That's big."

"For what you've planned, that's what we'll need. You're not leading animals from one section to the other without this much room. And you're right about the bleachers. We'll need them for people to see what's happening."

She cocked her head. "I was right on that?"

He chuckled and looked back at the chairs. "Yes, you were right, and is this the right place for the bleachers?"

"I think so, don't you?"

"Looks best to me. You want easy access from the parking lot."

She nodded. "I...uh..."

He lifted a brow when she stopped.

"I...well, I appreciate what you're doing here, that you agreed to help. I...we...couldn't do it without you."

After a moment, a slow smile appeared. "Was that a thank you?"

"Yes."

"Seemed hard for you to say."

She shook her head. "Will you quit that? I'm trying to thank you. Quit baiting me."

"Sorry." But his eyes were back-lit with laughter.

"You know, there is something else."

"What is that?"

"I thought we might need...well, a platform or something from which we can direct everything. Instead of trying to do it from the ground."

"A platform?"

"Yeah." She pointed between the bleachers and the north side of the star. "Something about eight feet off the ground. We'd know how each scene went. We could direct things from it, use the spotlight..."

"A platform?"

"Like a control tower."

"A control tower?"

"Yes."

After a moment of quiet, he said. "You're serious?"

She nodded.

"All right, but I'm not sure on this one. We have to think about time and cost. Did Alan give you a budget?"

"Uh...no."

The dark brows lifted. "Let me talk to him." He turned and called for the dog.

Cooper appeared from around the office and ran forward, circling her. Sharee's heart lurched, and she crossed her hands over her chest.

John slipped his fingers under the dog's collar and pulled him back. "He's a pussycat. Really."

"Yeah."

"Sit, Cooper. Stay." The dog sat back on his haunches, and John turned to Sharee. "Help me with these chairs. It's getting dark."

They folded the chairs and headed back to the shed, carrying some under each arm.

"How's the car?"

She shifted the chairs. "It's running."

John opened the door to the shed, and they stacked them inside. "Clean the terminals?"

"As a matter of fact, I did." She lifted her chin. "Ha!"

His mouth curled on one side. "Did it help?"

"It seemed to." They headed back to the parking lot.

"Look, may I say something?"

She crossed her arms, trying to keep her impatience under control. Didn't anyone think she could take care of herself? She took a long breath. "Okay."

"It's possible you need a battery. If you take it to a station that does auto repair work, you can have them test yours. If you need one, usually they'll sell you one there and install it for you. It's an easy solution. You don't want to be stranded somewhere."

His concern seemed real.

She took a long breath. "All right." If it happened again, she'd do it, just not before payday.

She glanced up as the light from the parking lot's pole lamp switched on. The sun had slipped past the horizon, and the cool stillness of the evening hung over them.

"I've talked with some of the other guys," John said. "George and Sam will help me get a head start on this. We'll get the frame done on the bleachers. You can make an announcement Sunday to start work the following Saturday. You'll need a lot of volunteers."

A white van came around the drive and parked near them. Sharee peered at it—an older model Dodge van. The doors opened, and Roseanne and Marci climbed down.

Sharee chuckled. "Marci's out already with the baby. With Roseanne."

"I'm glad everything went well for her. Especially after the car accident."

"You mean Marci? When Bruce knocked her down the other day?"

"No. The car accident."

Sharee nodded, remembering Marci's stressed call to her a day later. "We were going to that out-of-town youth rally. Stephen took the kids in the van, and I followed with Bruce in the car. A woman just came out of nowhere, ran the red light and crashed into us. Sharee, it was horrible! The woman was screaming. Bruce was bleeding and out cold, the car crushed on his side. I didn't know if they'd get him out. But they did, and then the ambulances took us to different hospitals. Pastor Alan said Bruce might not walk again, and that the other woman's son died. Sharee, how can I live with that?"

"Marci, if the woman ran the red light, it's not your fault."

But the accident had crushed the whole church, in a way. Only now were they coming out of it. Sharee swallowed and watched Marci reach into the back of the van. She turned a moment later with Joshua in her arms. Sharee smiled. Things were looking up. Hopefully, the Christmas program would help, too.

Another car pulled into the lot, its lights raking them as it passed and parked next to the van.

Matthew Thornton climbed from the second car and took the baby from his mother. When he had strapped him into the car seat in the back, Marci climbed into the front. They waved to Roseanne and then to Sharee and John when they drove past. Roseanne took the back exit and disappeared on the road behind the property.

Sharee crossed her arms across her chest. "Marci still feels responsible for the crash, and that's ridiculous. She wasn't the one cited."

"That doesn't always remove the guilt."

His voice had changed, deepened. Sharee looked up, but he moved toward their vehicles. She caught up with him. A cool wind penetrated her shirt, and she rubbed her arms.

"Where's your jacket, girl?"

Girl? He'd called her that before. Sharee huffed. "In my car."

"You trying to catch pneumonia?"

"What? There you go again. You know, it's not freezing out here. I know if I need a jacket. And don't call me girl."

He grinned. "Just wanted to see if I could activate that chip on your shoulder."

"I don't have a chip on my shoulder. I..." Sharee stopped. The man was amusing himself at her expense, and she was adding to his pile of kindling. "I hope you're having a good day today."

"It's ending well."

She slid her eyes his way and shook her head. He chuckled, and she did, too. At some point, he'd let go of the dog. It trotted beside her as they made their way to her car. She did her best to ignore him and looked for a distraction.

"John, what did you do before you came here?"

He stopped short, in mid-stride. She almost stumbled trying to stop beside him. A moment later, though, he reached for her car door and opened it. She slid inside.

"Drive safe." He shut the door and walked across the grass toward the office. The dog followed. Their retreating figures blended into the twilight.

Sharee watched until he opened the office door. A slice of light dissected the darkness and went out.

"Well," she said aloud. "That question had about as much chance as a kite surfer in a hurricane." She shrugged and prayed for the car to start. It did.

∽

Inside the office, Pastor Alan leaned back in his chair and watched his cousin pace back and forth in front of his desk. "Why didn't you tell her?"

John shrugged. "You think I should?" He swung around, striding to the other end of the office. "It's been three years."

"Yes."

John stopped. A muscle bulged in his jaw. "You think I should forgive him."

"You should have forgiven him a long time ago."

Chapter 5

Marci's voice sounded broken, and a baby's cry rose in the background.

Sharee's heart stuttered. Not again. "Marci, what does it say?"

"It's a printout of a Wikipedia site entitled "Child Mortality." Who…whoever sent it highlighted all the reasons that babies under the age of five die."

Sharee drew in her breath and gripped the phone tighter. "This has got to stop. You should call the police."

"I…I haven't told Stephen yet."

"What? Why not?"

"Well, we argued so much during the pregnancy that…I…I didn't want him to say I was hysterical."

"Hysterical? Why would he say that?"

"He thinks I've been hormonal this time. I'm so wound up."

"These ridiculous notes would upset anyone."

"Yeah." Quiet followed.

"Marci? Is there something else?"

"I can't talk now, Sharee. You're at work. I'll start crying again. Besides, I can hear Joshua in the bedroom. I have to go."

Sharee breathed out her frustration. "All right, but call me later."

"I'll try, Sharee. You know how hectic it gets around here."

"I know. I wish I could be there."

"I hear Joshua again. Thanks for letting me cry all over you."

"I only wish I was there so you could. Oops, I hear him, now, too. Okay. Talk to you later."

≈

Marci and Joshua weren't in church, but the rest of the family was, taking up a whole row as usual. Sharee smiled down the row at each one before asking Stephen about Marci.

"She seemed a little down on Friday when we talked. Is she doing okay?"

"She's fine. Just new mother stuff, tired, a little overwhelmed. Neither of us is getting any younger, so it takes more out of us. At least, the older ones help with the younger ones now."

Sharee nodded and moved to her seat. Surely, if Marci told him about the notes, Stephen would understand. New mother stuff, maybe, but when someone harassed you with nasty notes, you had a right to be upset.

She sat and listened as the worship songs started, and then she bowed her head and prayed. Warmth flooded through her. God was in control. He'd use whatever was going on for good.

When church ended, she headed for the parking lot but caught sight of John's truck in the field. A trailer attached to the back held stacks of wood. More wood rested in groups on the ground. He lifted a board from the trailer and placed it with others.

How can I tell him what he's missing, Lord? She walked toward him, praying under her breath.

John glanced her way, grabbed a two-by-four and set it on his shoulder. He looked her way again before setting it down near others of the same length.

Sunlight brightened the large pine nearby and painted its needles with liquid gold. The wind whipped past, and Sharee slid a hand down her thigh, holding her dress in place.

"Hi."

He straightened. "Hi." His gaze dropped then rose. A smile appeared. "Well...don't you look different."

She remembered her comment from the other day and ducked her head. "You don't forget much, do you?"

His smile broadened, but he didn't answer, just waved a hand at the area they had roped off the other day. "I measured the space we'll need for the bleachers, and I think we've got the angle right, but that can be adjusted if needed."

"I didn't expect you to be working on Sunday."

"It's as good a time as any for me."

"John, you know..." Her tone must have warned him, because she saw him stiffen, eyes narrowing. She hesitated but started again, "Do you ever wonder—"

"No."

The one syllable said everything she needed to hear. She sighed. He wasn't interested in talking about God today. She'd have to pray for an opening another time.

"Okay. Have you had lunch? I'd be glad to run pick something up for you." A movement to her side caused her to glance down. She did a quick side-step.

Black liquid eyes stared up at her. Not Cooper's, another dog. A puppy.

The inquisitive brown face seemed to smile at her. A wet, cold nose touched her knee. She retreated once more, but her heart warmed at the small dog's expression.

John leaned down, took hold of the collar and tugged the puppy away from her.

Matthew Thornton's voice came from the parking lot. "Sampson! Come here!"

Sharee watched Matthew run their way. Ryann, Abbey, and another boy followed close behind.

"Thank you, Mr. J." Matthew reached for the dog. "He's gotten away a couple of times. I've chased him all over."

"He's enjoying the weather." John let loose of the collar. "But your uncle's farm would be his place of choice, I'm sure."

"Yeah, I know." Matthew scratched behind the dog's ear and clicked a leash on him. The dog's tail wagged.

"And where is he during church?"

The others laughed, and Matthew sent them a sideways glance. "Well, we take turns walking him during the service."

"A reason to slip out, huh?"

"Yeah." Matthew gave him a conspiratorial wink.

"When did you get him?" Sharee asked.

"Just this past week. Mom finally gave in." He shot a look at John. "Our uncle's dog had a litter of puppies, so we had our choice."

John ran his hand along the puppy's back. "I'm sure this is the pick of the litter then."

Matthew nodded and glanced at Ryann. "Come on, we better cut out if you want to babysit Joshua."

The teens turned and zigzagged their way to the parking lot, the puppy running ahead, his enthusiasm curtailed by the leash.

Sharee watched until they disappeared. "Are Matt and Ryann going out?"

"I think it's more friendship right now."

She rubbed her arms, tilted her head, and studied him. "I heard you were helping with the youth the last couple of months. In fact, I heard some stories about you and some of the pranks the youth pulled lately."

"All lies, I'm sure."

"Are they?" She let her tone indicate what she thought of that. "Then you didn't help them pull those pranks on the College and Career group?"

He smiled but remained silent.

"I happened to be at the end of one of their pranks the other day."

"I heard." Amusement now.

Sharee eyed him suspiciously. "I get even."

He raised a brow but said nothing more.

She stared past him to where the teens disappeared. "I wonder what goes on in Abbey's life. She's so serious and unhappy."

"True, but Ryann's stepped up. Offered her friendship."

"Yeah." Sharee smiled. So like Ryann. Her hand slid down to the skirt of her dress again. The breeze tugged at it.

"Having trouble with the dress?"

Sharee gathered the skirt tighter. "Yes." Warmth rose in her cheeks as she struggled to keep it from flying up.

His mouth opened then closed, and he turned abruptly to the trailer, reaching for another two-by-four.

"I offered to pick up some lunch for you. What would you like?"

He hefted the board. "Feeling guilty that you're not working?"

"No. But I appreciate the fact that you are. On your day off. Thank you." There. She'd done it right this time.

He turned back to her. "You're welcome."

His smile brought a returning one from her. Why had she thought him standoffish? "Something for lunch?"

"No, thanks. I'm fine. I won't be much longer. I need to take Cooper for a run." His gaze dropped to her dress again. "If you brought a change of clothes, you could come with us. I'll hold Cooper back to accommodate your stride."

"You'll hold Cooper back?" Her confusion morphed to irritation and extinguished the warmth she felt. "Are you taking pot shots at my height again?"

The light in his eyes made her scowl.

"That is just...so...Ah! Get your own lunch!" She whirled and marched back toward her car.

His laughter followed her.

༄

Sharee decided to take off early from work after seeing John in the field the day before. If he could spend extra time working on the project, she could, too. Things would get busy at work as soon as cold weather swept in. An exodus of homeless from up north making their way to Florida would keep their office as full and crammed together as a bait ball. Then her extra time would be nil.

She pulled into the back parking lot at church and looked around. No John. So she headed for the work buildings. Sounds of metal and grinding came from behind them. She rounded the corner and saw a number of large metal boxes set on work tables.

John tilted a head at her with a brow raised.

"Thought I'd come to help you work on the Christmas project." She looked at the metal units set on the tables. "Those look like air conditioners to me. Of course, it could be hot in December. I guess we could attach them to the bleachers."

He gave a wry smile, acknowledging her attempt at humor. "Alan is hoping I can keep these antiques running for another year. It's cheaper to run these in each classroom than to redo the whole building with central air. Of course, the classrooms are as old as the air conditioners. One more year before he'll let me do anything about that."

"Oh."

"We'll get your project done. Don't worry."

"I wasn't. I just thought I could be of some help."

"We discussed getting aluminum bleachers, but they're more than Alan wants to pay. I went online and found some plans for wooden, portable bleachers eight seats high. I've ordered two of those." He reached for a rag and began to wipe down some of the tools. "Do you have a guess at the number of people you might expect—for one evening?"

Sharee propped herself on an end of the table. "It's hard to say. Maybe two hundred people each night? That's what we'd like. We're planning on two Saturday nights."

"Two hundred? That will be close." He finished with the tools and pulled a blue tarp over the air conditioners. "Look, I'm almost through here. I'm planning on going for a run. Want to come?"

"With you? After that remark yesterday?"

One side of his mouth hitched. "If I promise not to—what was it you said—bait you?"

She crossed her arms and studied him. Run with him? She glanced around. And the dog?

"You're already dressed. Your jeans and Nikes are fine."

She frowned. "I don't think so. I'm not a long-distance runner."

"We won't go far." He straightened. "Unless you lied about that, too."

"About what?'

"Running."

She made a face at him. "No, I didn't lie."

"How far do you run?"

"Two or three miles. But I don't usually run in jeans."

"You're fine. It's a short run. The back road goes down to the Gulf. It's a little over a mile. We can go there and back."

"With the dog?"

"He's not here today."

"Oh."

He shook his head. "He's a pussycat."

"Yes, well, you said that. We'll see. No comments about my height?"

"I promise. Warm up. I'll put the tools up and lock the buildings." He was striding away from her before she could say more.

Sharee stared after him, irritated at his assumption; but a moment later, she began to stretch.

Fifteen minutes after that, she realized just what a difference their heights—and her stride—did make. She forced herself to a faster pace than usual, but John loped beside her, a greyhound to her cocker spaniel.

They passed houses and parked cars along the tree-lined street. As they went by a small, forest-green house, a large pit bull hurled itself against a fence. Sharee jerked to a stop, heart pounding. The dog leaped against the fence again, barking ferociously.

"You're safe. He's behind the fence." John caught her arm and urged her on. "Once we pass, he'll calm down. He's been here a few months. Always outside when the Dodge van's there. Inside, I think, when the owner is gone. It's quiet on those days."

She slid a glance his way. "You must jog here often."

"About once a week. Near home, at Howard Park, most of the time."

Sharee nodded. They finished the first mile in silence. What a difference—jogging with someone. By herself, the time dragged. And she never felt safe listening to music. She needed to know what was going on around her. What was going on here? He'd asked her to jog. Did that mean anything? No. It couldn't. He'd planned on jogging, anyway. He was just being nice. His manners again.

She shot a sideways glance in his direction. It didn't matter—that light in his eyes, the smile, the deep set eyes. He wasn't a believer. Nothing would go on here.

They stopped before a cluster of sea oats and sea grapes on a small, undeveloped portion of land. Sharee welcomed a moment to get her breath, and she tried to catch a glimpse of the water. The foliage in front of them blocked the view. On both sides of the vacant lot, houses rose three stories. Their decks fronted the Gulf of Mexico. Sunset streaked the sky in pink and melon and orange. Half-hidden by the horizon, the sun thrust light fingers upward.

"I love the sunsets here."

He made a rumbled sound of agreement. "The east coast has beautiful sunrises, but the sunsets here are incredible."

She nodded, breathing normally again.

"Ready to head back?"

"Yes, but you go ahead. I know I'm holding you back. You're not getting out of this as much as you wanted."

"Oh, I don't know. I think I am." A smile played across his face, but his eyes were on the road.

Sharee frowned, not sure of his meaning.

As they ran by the forest-green house, she noticed that the van had disappeared and so had the dog. John had gauged that correctly.

Long, slanting shadows painted their way across the road, and the sky began its transformation from papaya to gray. A few minute later, they jogged onto the church grounds.

John pointed to his truck. "I've got water in a cooler."

They stopped in front of it, and he reached inside and took out two water bottles. "Here."

Sharee paced up and down, breathing hard. She took the bottle but gave him an inquiring look. "Thanks."

"What?" He fell into step beside her.

"I just wondered how long this…truce…would last."

"Truce?"

"Yeah, truce. Whatever."

"Well, it proved harder than expected."

"Did it?"

His mouth lifted. "Exercise in restraint. Good for the soul."

"Something you're not used to?"

She got a sideways look.

Her walking slowed. "The sun's going down. I guess I'd better head home. I enjoyed the run."

He stopped and appeared to struggle with something he wanted to say.

"Exercise in restraint?" she asked.

"Okay, that's two snide remarks from you. All promises are canceled."

"But I've got to leave, anyway." She flashed him a grin, waved the bottle at him and moved toward her SUV. "Thanks for the exercise and the water."

He lifted his in salute.

"Sharee!" Marci's voice high and abrupt stopped her in her tracks. "Wait!"

She twisted around. Light spilled from the window of the fellowship hall, and Marci ran through it.

"Look at this!" The new mother carried a doll, holding it away from her body. When she stopped in front of Sharee, she thrust the doll at her.

In the fading light, Sharee could see dark gouged eyes and a slit throat.

Chapter 6

"Look at it!" Marci's voice shook, her hand trembled.

Sharee leaned forward. It looked identical to the one she'd picked up in the field. Except red paint coated the throat around the slashed areas. Her stomach knotted.

"Let me have it, Marci." John put his hand out and extracted the doll from her shaking fingers. "Where did you find it?"

"In Joshua's car seat. I left it on the table in the fellowship hall, and someone put that…that doll in it." The distress on her face mirrored her voice.

Sharee glanced at John. This looked like *the same doll*. Was it? If so, how did it get in Marci's car seat? *What* had John done *with the other one?*

She touched Marci's shoulder. "It's someone's stupid idea of a joke." But as she said it, her eyes met John's.

"A joke?" Marci's voice rose. "This is not a joke!"

"No, it's not."

"Well, if I find out who did it…"

"Where's Joshua?"

Marci's eyes widened. "He's with Ryann and Abbey. The girls went for a walk with him. Why?"

"Nothing. Just wondering. You found it in the car seat?"

"Yes. I brought Mary for drama practice, and I have to bring Joshua because I'm nursing."

"Did you bring any of the other children?"

"Yes, Deborah and Elizabeth, but they're with Mary and the other girls in the youth room."

"You probably don't want the girls to see this." John indicated the doll. "I'll put it somewhere out of sight."

Marci nodded. "Yes, the younger girls would be upset." As John walked away, she looked at Sharee. "You think it's a prank?"

"Yes. Mean and thoughtless, but a prank." She put her arm around the other woman's shoulder, and they walked toward fellowship hall.

"Roseanne dropped us off a little while ago. I always bring the car seat inside with Joshua. I need a place to sit him. Anyway, I took him out of the car seat and with me to watch the girl's practice in the youth hall, but I left the car seat in the fellowship hall. I usually do. And then Abbey and Ryann came in. They wanted to take Joshua for a walk. When they didn't come back, I went to look for them. And... and that's when I saw the doll."

"The girls were outside? We didn't see anyone. Of course, we just returned. I'll call Ryann." Sharee tugged her phone from her jeans.

"Here they are!" Marci's voice rose when the girls rounded the corner of the fellowship hall. "Where did you go?"

"We just walked around the building. We weren't gone long."'" Abbey put the baby into Marci's outstretched arms.

Marci cradled Joshua against her chest and stroked his face. "Someone put a horrible doll in Joshua's car seat. I guess I was just worried."

"A doll?"

"Its throat was cut and it's eyes blacked out."

"That's terrible," Ryann said. Her gaze jumped to Abbey.

Sharee caught Ryann's look and frowned. "Do either of you have any idea who would do that?"

"Of course not." Abbey's quick denial was accented by Joshua's wail.

"Shh, darling." Marci bounced the baby up and down.

Abbey's scowled increased. "Look, we were bringing him back, anyway. We have to go. Come on, Ryann." She grabbed the other girl's arm.

Ryann reached over and touched Joshua's back. "I'm sorry, Mrs. Thornton." She hurried after Abbey.

John lifted an eyebrow in Sharee's direction as the girls passed him.

Marci kissed Joshua's head. "I think I'll call Roseanne and get her to pick me up early. This and the notes are getting to me."

"Did you tell Stephen yet?"

Marci shook her head. "Not yet." She shifted Joshua to her other shoulder. The baby sucked on her neck.

"Marci."

The woman frowned. "Don't worry about it, Sharee. I'll take care of it." She headed for the youth room.

Sharee watched her go. Why hadn't she told Stephen? Saying Stephen thought she was hormonal didn't add up. Marci wasn't imagining things. The notes and the doll were hard evidence.

"What notes is she talking about?"

Sharee frowned. "She's been getting harassing messages. First about what could go wrong during her pregnancy and now about what could go wrong since Joshua was born."

"No wonder she's upset. Look, I know it's getting late but walk back to the truck with me."

"Okay."

The sunset sky had pearled, and the smell of the lumber on the trailer filled her nostrils. "You've put the wood back on the trailer."

"I organized it by size. George picked it up for me and didn't think to put it on according to size."

"Oh."

"The work goes faster when we have everything we need, and it's in order."

"Ah."

He slanted a glance at her, and she peered at the sky, struggling to keep her face straight. He was a perfectionist.

"We might be able to do your control tower if the bleachers are affordable *and* not too time consuming."

"What? Really?" A feeling of delight surfaced. "I hope so! And I need to make a sign-up sheet and start calling people for help. We need volunteers for the construction, and the play, and the staging." She raised an expectant face to him.

They stopped beside his truck, and his brows drew together. "I'm helping with the sets, but don't count on anything else. And I won't be here the night of the program."

Something dropped from her chest to her stomach. "You won't?"

"No."

"But...but I thought you might do the spotlight. We have that old one, and it's heavy. It needs somebody strong, with a steady hand." He said nothing, and she felt a ball in her stomach. "It's built into a stand now, and it's almost useless that way. When I went to look at it, I knew we'd have to take it out of there. Someone needs to hold it."

"I'll look at it. I might be able to build a new stand that will work, or I'll take it out of the old one. But ask Matthew or someone else to use it the night of the program."

"I just thought..." She broke off, seeing the set of his jaw. Her stomach tightened. Sharee fought the feelings surging through her. *He wouldn't be here.* "I'm sorry. I just assumed..."

"You wear jeans to work?"

"What?"

"You've had a pair of jeans on every time you've been here—except Sunday."

She stared at him. He changed subjects with the ease of a traffic light changing colors. "Uh...yes, we all do. We decided a long time ago not to look too... well..."

"You don't want to look better than your clients?"

"We don't want anyone to feel intimidated or feel we can't relate."

"And can you?" He reached in through the window of his truck and pulled out a sheet of paper.

"Most of us can. To a degree. We might not be homeless—although some have been—but we've all had tough times, financially or otherwise."

"You enjoy what you do?"

"Yes." She raised her chin and met his eyes. The evening light accented their darkness and his dark hair. The scruffy beard was back. She swallowed, feeling his closeness and stepped away.

What was happening? She wasn't interested in him any more than he was in her. He didn't know the Lord, wasn't a Christian. She was not interested. Period.

"I'd like you to read this." John's voice halted her internal discussion. The sky behind him had paled to a dusky gray. "Let's walk to your car. You can read it once you get in."

The SUV's interior light popped on as she slid into the driver's seat.

"I find quite a bit of stuff around here. Talk about notes. Lots of notes from the youth. I found this today. Most of the time, I toss them; but this...well, see what you think."

She felt his hesitation and wondered about it. The small, scratchy writing on the paper could reflect either a boy or girl's hand.

Ryann, thanks for your friendship and listening to me. I've never talked with anyone else about the baby. My parents made us place him for adoption. My parents! Can you believe that? It still hurts. The counselor said it would get better, but who knows? A child of my own—gone. Just like that. So, yeah, I resent the new baby on the way. She gets to have babies and keep them! What if one of hers disappeared? How would she feel then?

Sharee looked up at him. "It's not signed."

"No."

"It could be Abbey. She's so miserable and angry. You saw her a little while ago?"

"Yes."

"If she did write this, it's no surprise she's taken to Ryann. They've both lost children—just in different ways."

He took the note, folded it and turned back to her.

Sharee's heart ached. "Kids go through so much these days. And that... that," she pointed at the paper, "has happened more than people realize. Children in sexual relationships they're not prepared to handle. Placing their babies for adoption or aborting them and having to live with that." She clenched her hands together. "Why can't we just do it God's way?

Can't we see He knows best?"

John said nothing. She swallowed and bit her lip.

"I'm on my soapbox, but ...at fourteen, fifteen, sixteen having to deal with all the ramifications of sex—whether physical, emotional or spiritual. They're too young. And there's too much abuse." She gave a long sigh. "I'm sorry."

"Why?"

"Because..." She didn't know how to finish. She took a long breath.

"Because you're passionate about what you believe?"

"I...yes. I am."

"Don't apologize."

She stared at him a minute then dropped her gaze. "Abbey should be getting counseling. Placing a child for adoption is a blessing to the families that can't have children. Hard for the mother, though." She put her head down a moment. "I hope someone's told her that the pregnancy centers in the area have adoption classes. Some classes you take after the baby is placed. Just to help you through it."

He put an arm on the car's door and leaned closer. "Adoption classes?"

"Yes. It helps the girls realize what a gift they've given to someone else and to their child, because so often the mom, if she's young, can't raise him or her—either financially or emotionally." Sharee cleared her throat. "Will you show the note to Pastor Alan?"

"Probably. About the dolls..." He hesitated.

"Was that the same doll?"

"As the one Cooper found? No, that's still in the tool building. I put this second one there just now."

"I wonder if Abbey did it? But if she did, how would she get the doll into the car seat without being seen?"

He shrugged.

Sharee her hand under the mat and took out her key. John frowned and shook his head. She turned the key in the ignition, and the CR-V coughed once, twice, then caught.

"Sharee." The roughness of his voice cut through the engine noise.

She turned the SUV's lights on and gave him a sheepish smile. "I'm going to get a battery. I promise."

"Just do it. You've had plenty of time."

She rolled her eyes but turned serious at the look on his face. "I will. I promise."

୶

Her plans for Wednesday evening concerned a trip to Walmart and a few teenage girls. Now she sat in her CR-V as the girls arrived for drama practice. Last week, the younger girls had practiced in the fellowship hall. This week, the high school and college-age girls had their turn. In a couple of Sundays, the youth group would take over the entire service for a day. Sharee looked forward to it.

She waited until she knew the drama practice was well underway, and then she slipped into the fellowship hall and made her way to the youth room. Someone had propped the door open. Listening from the passageway, she heard what must be the rehearsal for a skit. She hefted the giant water pistol she'd bought and stepped into the room. Three or four of the girls turned. Sharee jerked the gun up and pulled hard on the trigger. Huge sprays of water hit them. Screams followed. Hands rose to protect their faces. More screams rose as she leveraged the gun sideways. Bodies spun away from her. Grinning now, she soaked their backs, whirled and raced back down the hall.

Entering the dining hall, she sprinted through the room and flung open the door. The huge water pistol jolted against her side. She tore around the corner of the garden shed, yanked the door open, and jumped inside.

Next to a wheelbarrow, John straightened, hefting a bag of fertilizer onto his shoulder. He looked her way, brows rising.

"Hide me!" She waved the water pistol at him. "Please, hide me!"

Outside, coming in their direction, were high, shrill voices and the slap of racing feet. John reached for her, pulled her over behind the wheelbarrow, and shoved her down. A second later, a blue tarp fell over her and the wheelbarrow. It rocked as he dropped something heavy into it. Just in time.

The door rattled. Excited voices filled the room. Sharee caught her breath and tried to hear over her pounding heart. Laughter threatened to choke her.

"Have you seen Ms. J?" Ryann's voice reached her, breathless and animated.

"You're looking for her?" John asked. "Why?"

"Because she soaked us! She had the biggest water pistol you've ever seen! Really! Look at us!"

Sharee could imagine Ryann spreading her arms, showing her drenched clothing.

"And we were working on our drama!" Another voice rose in fire-alarm pitch.

John chuckled. "Well, no wonder you want to find her."

"Come on." Ryann's voice again. "Let's check the office. She's got to be somewhere." Feet brushed the ground, crowding against each other.

Sharee waited until their footsteps and voices diminished before she pushed the tarp back. John lifted it off her.

"Thank you." She stood, breathless and grinning, holding the water pistol. "Really. Thank you. Wow. That was great." She started toward the door.

He caught her arm. "I'd give it a minute, *Ms. J.* They'll probably come back this way when they don't find you."

"Oh, you're right." Laughter surfaced. She couldn't help it. "You should have seen their faces. But they got me first, you know."

"You did say you'd get even."

"Oh, yeah. They drenched me and my car last Wednesday. They deserved it."

She stood close, her head tilted up at him. He grinned. They stood that way for a minute, and then his arm caught her waist and pulled her against him. His head came down, and his mouth sought hers. The hard strength of his body spurred quick emotion in her. When he drew his head back, his eyes, warm and dancing, met hers.

The water pistol dropped from her hand, clattering to the floor. A whole set of emotions flooded her. She could do nothing but stare.

"Sorry," he said into her look. "It just seemed…appropriate."

"Oh." The word hung in the air for a moment. Nothing else came to mind. In fact, that part of her body didn't seem to work at all. Forcing her legs to move, she edged backward out of his embrace. "I…better go."

"Sharee."

Her heart flipped at the way he said her name. She moved again, opened the door, and stepped through it. One long breath later, she ducked around the corner of the building and fled.

Chapter 7

Standing in the half-light of the shed, John's feelings matched Sharee's open-eyed stare. And the difference of how she felt in his arms startled him. She weighed next to nothing, and he'd leaned pretty far down to kiss her.

Janice, on the other hand, had been tall, solid, muscled. He had liked that about Janice—liked that her stride was almost the same as his, liked the way she looked and laughed and loved. For the last three years, he hadn't thought about another woman. Hadn't wanted to. He'd only focused on getting through each day.

Unexpected pain assaulted him, stronger than he'd felt for a while. He had learned to accept the pain and let it have its way. He stood now, doing that, closing his eyes while it ballooned in his chest. When he opened his eyes, he stared straight ahead. In the dim quietness, he identified the other emotion that rose with the pain. Guilt—a new kind of guilt.

He digested it, his body tightening at the implication. He felt guilty for having kissed someone, as if he'd betrayed the vows he'd taken. And, in a sense he had. Hadn't he? No, that was ridiculous.

Yet, his mouth and arms still held Sharee's imprint. She'd tasted of peppermint. *So different...*

His chest squeezed. A minute later, he leaned over, grabbed the fertilizer, and threw it onto his shoulder. He'd had enough guilt. Enough pain and guilt. With his free hand, he tore the tarp off the wheel barrel and dumped it in the corner.

Why had she come in here, anyway?

He stepped to the door, yanked it open, and went out. She'd invaded his thoughts these last two weeks. Her indignation, her skittishness amused him. But that would stop. He'd make sure it stopped because he wanted no involvement of that kind—no involvement with her or her God.

و

Sharee climbed into her CR-V, slammed the car into reverse, backed out of the parking space and sped home.

I'm fleeing, but that's what God's Word says to do. Flee temptation.

Her response to John's kiss, to his arms around her, shook her. Although lighthearted on his part, on hers…no, lighthearted wouldn't describe that.

Dear Lord, what am I going to do? Her hands tightened on the wheel. *What will I do Saturday? It's the first work party for the program. What am I going to do?*

❧

Saturday morning, John arrived at the church an hour before the others. He stared at the framework of the two bleachers he and the other men had worked on. George Costas and Sam Byrd often gave a helping hand when he needed it. Today, the other volunteers would finish what they'd started, while he, George, and Sam began work on the "control tower." And if everything went as planned, they might have time to start painting the scenes he'd drawn on four-by-eight-foot sheets of plywood.

A memory twisted his heart. Janice returning from the store with some his sketches matted and framed. She'd displayed them above their sofa, encouraging what he classified a hobby. But like many other things in his life, he'd quit sketching. He no longer drew, no longer flew, no longer worshiped.

He dragged his thoughts back. Concentrate on the day. Today would have its own troubles. Sharee would be here.

Moving the tools from the work buildings to the field, he organized the projects in his head. Directing the work would be up to him, and he knew from experience which volunteers were skilled and at what. After a break for lunch, some volunteers would leave. Only the core workers would finish the day.

The definition of core worker fit Sharee like his Otterbox case fit his iPhone. She'd be around until the last person left. His jaw tightened. Most of the time, he admired that kind of dedication. Today, though….

Why had he kissed her?

Stupid, ridiculous impulse. He'd let down his guard from the beginning—talking about the project, seeing her enthusiasm, hearing her excitement. And he'd watched her—the way the wind tossed her hair, the way she moved and laughed. His mind went to the dress she'd worn that Sunday, the breeze tugging at her skirt, the material hugging her curves. *Don't go there.*

He chewed his lip. His response to her warmth and enthusiasm was no surprise. Three long, lonely years had made him vulnerable. And perhaps, if he'd met her somewhere else, if her commitment to God was a plaything, maybe then. But he hadn't, and it wasn't. Alan and Daneen had sung her praises in that area for the two years he'd worked here.

Today, he needed to make a statement, to make sure she understood the kiss meant nothing. Avoidance had worked well with her before. It would work again.

When she arrived along with close to twenty volunteers, he assigned everyone to the two sets of bleachers. They'd finish those today. He treated Sharee just as he treated the others. If she noticed his brusqueness, she didn't show it. She seemed preoccupied herself, and that was good.

When they accomplished more than expected in the first few hours, he reduced the bleacher crew to George, Sharee, and two other workers. Sharee used a saw, hammer and screwdriver comparably to most men. Someone had taught her well.

After instructing the others what to do for four of the scenes in the program, he and Sam moved to start the "control tower." Laughter and conversation from the workers echoed to the sounds of hammering and sawing.

John's shoulders began to relax. The problems he'd expected had not materialized.

Around noon, when Sharee, George, and the other two men backed up from the bleachers and inspected them, he couldn't help glancing their way. Sharee looked tired and disheveled, her jumble of curls in disarray; but her smile held that twist of accomplishment, even joy, that signified satisfaction. She and the men grinned at each other.

George slipped an arm around her shoulders. "They're done, Sharee. What do you think?"

"I think it's great. I can't believe we finished so quickly."

John's chest tightened. George was only a friend, but the camaraderie the two shared forced unwanted emotions through him.

One of the other men slapped George on the back. "It's almost one. Time for lunch."

"You deserve it," Sharee said. "But they haven't rung the bell yet."

"It'll be soon." George headed toward the fellowship hall with the other men. "I'm going to wash up."

Forcing his attention back to their work, John pivoted toward Sam. The man held one end of a twelve-foot four-by-four and a question in his eyes. John muttered under his breath, leaned over and grabbed the other end of the board. They headed past the bleachers.

As they went by, Sharee waved her hand at them. "Well, what do you think?"

Hands full, Sam nodded her way. "Great job. Things are going well all over. Have the men deserted you?"

"They went to wash for lunch."

"Ahhh," Sam nodded. "We'll be doing that, too, in a few minutes."

John swallowed what he might have said. Avoidance, he reminded himself, looking away from her happy grin. He felt her eyes follow him, felt the questioning. She'd understand soon.

$\approx$

At lunch, Sharee watched John fix his plate, glance around, and disappear outside to eat. He often did that, but today her shoulders dropped as the door closed behind him.

She inhaled and straightened her shoulders again. It was best. She had kept her distance today, and he seemed to do the same. But then, he was everywhere, helping. A special talent. When George's saw broke, John put a replacement in his hands two minutes later. When one of the girls proved ineffective with both hammer and screwdriver, John sent her to get paint cans and later brushes and rags from the work buildings, keeping her useful and busy. And he anticipated problems before they rose, asking her questions to make sure they were doing what she envisioned. Although his questions today were short and to the point, and he seemed preoccupied.

She missed his teasing grin. Better this way, though. She groaned inside. Yeah, sure, better.

Toward the end of the afternoon, she put her brush across a paint can, straightened and stretched her back. The scene she had chosen to paint was coming together. John had drawn some them on the boards, included a picture and suggested colors. Amazing man. How could a man have that tall, dark and handsome thing going and still have so much talent?

She shook her head and turned her focus to the other workers. A few people walked past her, brushes and paint cans in their hands. Clean-up time. George, Sam, and John stood fifty feet to her left. They'd sunk a quartet of long four-by-fours into the ground like they were fence posts and then poured concrete around them in preparation for the platform.

Sharee breathed deeply, straightened her shoulders, and walked in their direction. "You guys are wonderful. I can hardly believe what's been accomplished today."

Sam wiped his hands down the side of his jeans. "Yes. Good work. And we'll get the platform up for you sometime this week."

"I can't say thanks enough. Are you going to build steps, too?"

Sam indicated John. "Ask the boss."

John's brows drew together. "I think with the time constraints and money issues, we'll use a ladder."

"Okay."

"We'll remove it each evening. We don't want the youth climbing up there. Someone could fall off."

She hadn't thought of that. Sam's nod of agreement caught her eye, but she concentrated on John's frown. It hadn't changed.

He crossed his arms over his chest. "Look, are you planning anything else we need to know about?"

Sharee leaned back a fraction, reacting to his tone. Her mind darted back over the day. Had she added anything to his day? Any other project? Not that she remembered.

"No, I—"

"Good."

The word came clipped and final. She blinked. George's head turned, his face mirroring her surprise.

"I...uh." Her words stumbled. "I'll just wash these brushes."

"Don't bother." John's voice still carried its edge. He put his hand out. "Go home. I'll take care of them."

Sharee's eyes met his. She had planned to stay until they'd finished everything, but now... She put the brushes into his hand thinking about his difference in attitude today. She took in the detached coldness of his eyes, felt her heart twist and, without another word, turned and walked to her car.

Chapter 8

Monday had already proved a hard day at Downtown Ministries. Sharee didn't mind. The distractions and numerous clients she dealt with kept her mind off John. But her last client might change that.

Simone Timbler, a mother of three, had no electricity; and the meteorologists had predicted a cold front for the end of the week. A forecast in the mid-forties had brought her to the center. Two years ago, after a layoff at work, she and her children ended up living out of her car. Now, she had a good job and an apartment. What she didn't have was money to pay car repairs and electricity at the same time. The car repairs had come first, leaving her without money for the power bill. Then both children had succumbed to strep throat, and the co-pays for medicine and the doctor had eaten into Simone's finances again.

Now two months had passed without payment, and the power company had turned off her electricity. Simone had used long extension cords from her neighbors' homes to run her refrigerator and a light for their living room, but the prospect of cold weather had driven her back to the ministry for help.

Sharee's list of churches and nonprofits that helped Downtown Ministry's clients was long. The ministry itself did background checks and personal inquiries to make sure the clients' needs were real. Still, only a few ministries actually helped with finances. Pastor Alan and New Life Church topped that list.

When she called Pastor Alan with the explanation, he told her to come pick up a check. She hadn't doubted his willingness. He might give her difficulty over a Christmas program before agreeing, but his hand was open when it came to helping those in need.

The power company wanted the check in their hands before they turned the woman's electricity back on, so Sharee agreed to drive to the church, pick up the check and take it to the power company's offices. The checks were made out to the company, anyway, not the clients. So, no problem.

Then why had tension crept into her neck and shoulders? She moved her head back and forth, feeling the pull on her muscles, knowing the reason. The prospect of seeing John and finding that his attitude toward her had not changed left her heart beating overtime. She tried to convince herself he'd had a stressful day on Saturday, but that explanation didn't feel right.

She let out a hard breath. Don't be idiotic. John might not even be there or anywhere near the office. She'd get the check and leave immediately.

When she arrived, she headed straight to the church office and smiled at Daneen as she opened the door. The tension across her shoulders eased. Daneen was alone.

"Here you go, Sharee." The pastor's wife held out the check.

Sharee took it and put it in her purse. "You know how much I appreciate this."

Daneen returned the smile. "I'm just glad we can help. As long as God continues to furnish the funds, we'll do what we can. You know that."

"I do. I'll run this to the electric office."

"Okay. Be careful in the traffic. You look nice today."

Sharee smiled and stepped back into the sunshine. She'd dressed for their "job interview day" at work. Once a month they all dressed professionally to allow those that came to classes see how they should arrive for a job interview.

George waved from across the parking lot. Propped against the large pine tree, a number of four-by-eight-foot boards stood.

His smile and the plywood boards drew her. "Hey. You're working on scenes for the program?"

He used a paintbrush for a pointer. "Yes, we have lots to do. So, I came today to help John. I give the background two coats then he draws the scene."

"Oh." She glanced around. "Well, has he left you alone?"

"He went to get some tools and parts. When we're finished, we're going to connect these four together."

Sharee surveyed the boards, frowned then scanned them a second time.

"What's wrong, Sharee?"

"These look like inside scenes for Herod's Court. We talked Saturday about having an outside scene. I wrote that part of the drama last night."

George eyed the section he'd started painting. "You want me to wait?"

She hesitated. Would she have to see John, after all? Swallowing, she put her shoulders back. *Just get it done. The program's more important than your feelings.* "I think so. Let me talk to him. Do you know where he went?"

"Sure." He pointed with the paintbrush once more. "John went that way."

A few minutes later, Sharee found him in the tool building, hanging tools on the wall above a work bench.

"John." He straightened but didn't turn. She cleared her throat. "John?"

The look he cast over his shoulder caused her stomach to clench.

"Yes?"

"I need to talk with you a minute."

He shifted to face her, and his gaze dropped, his face mirroring surprise just before it shut down. Her gaze dropped, too. The business attire. He'd asked about her dressing in jeans every day, and here she showed up in a suit.

She stared at his frown. What had become of the man that helped her these last two weeks? He had kissed her one day and appeared to loathe her the next. She shoved aside the hurt and lifted her chin.

"Herod's court is wrong." Her words sounded abrupt and pointed. Not what she intended. His mouth drew into a thin line. She tried to recover a softer tone. "Didn't we talk about an outside scene?"

"We decided on an inside scene."

"No, an outside scene. I guess it wasn't clear."

"It wasn't."

"I'm sorry. I accept the blame, but will it take much to change?"

"Yes."

"It will?" She fought with the idea of rewriting the part of the drama she'd written last night.

"You want me to draw four new scenes?"

He had offered to do the drawings the first time. How could she ask him to do it again? She exhaled the hurt curling inside.

"No. It's fine. I shouldn't have mentioned it. Sorry."

"Good." He turned back to the work bench.

She hesitated a moment, wanting to reach out and ask what was wrong. Instead, she spun to leave, almost hitting George. Heat filled her face. Had he heard John's obvious impatience with her? She nodded and moved past him.

What is John's problem, Lord? Does he regret that kiss as much as I do?

Except she didn't regret it. In fact, it took all her determination not to relive it. Work kept her mind busy, but at home, at night…

He doesn't know the Lord. A relationship is impossible—even if he wanted one—and obviously he doesn't. She sucked in deep breaths and blinked her eyes in rapid motion. *Don't cry for some guy who can be Mr. Happy one day and Mr. Grumpy the next. Besides, how dare he show such irritation. He's the one who kissed you, not the other way around!*

Her eyes dried. She reached her car, yanked the door open, climbed in, and slammed it shut. The warm rise of anger pushed the hurt aside. In the future, if she needed to say anything to him, she'd use go-betweens. George or Sam would do fine. That should make him happy. Yeah, Mr. Happy again.

An hour later, after sending George on an errand, John scrutinized the four boards. He clenched his fists. How had he missed what she wanted? She'd accepted the blame, but it was his. Instead of listening to what she said last Saturday, he'd concentrated on making each contact with her short and curt. And he'd snapped at her today even though the blame was his.

George had caught his incredulous stare when she drove into the parking lot. He hadn't sent for her. Why was she here? Didn't she have work today? When she disappeared into the office, he'd left George working and headed for the tool building.

That should have worked, but she tracked him down. In a business suit that hugged her curves like insulation wrap hugged a hot water tank, with pink lace peeking from the jacket. And high heels. He closed his eyes, and the image was still there. He ground his teeth together.

She hadn't backed down from his anger either—not as skittish as he thought. So, he still needed to make things clear to her.

Saturday would do.

His mind raced ahead. That scenario had one big problem, and that centered on his gut reaction when he saw the hurt he'd caused. She tried to cover it Saturday and again today but hadn't succeeded. Maybe there was another way to do this. Maybe he should tell her...tell her what? About Janice? That would lead to a whole explanation. One he wasn't ready for.

He ran a hand through his hair, picturing the hurt in her eyes. Her method of coping was to retreat. Well, not entirely. She stood firm when it came to her work or her faith. He had evidence on both those scores. But she withdrew when it felt personal. He hefted the four boards and headed toward the tool building. Why the lack of confidence when it came to personal issues?

His mind went back to the first day he'd seen her. Sitting by the pond, sobbing with a depth of pain that mirrored his own. He hadn't cared about the cause that day. He'd only cared about the bottle clutched in her hand. He stood the boards against the wall and opened the shop's door. What had happened that day that sent her running to the church and out onto the grounds to cry by herself?

A man, most likely. He pushed the door inward and stopped. None of that was any of his concern. His only concern centered on finishing this project without the complications she now presented.

Chapter 9

As she climbed from the car on Saturday, Sharee grabbed a stretchy band and pulled her hair back, securing it at the back of her head. The degree of success of today's work party rested squarely with the weather and John's attitude. The meteorologists had predicted the low forties last night and that meant cool temps today, and if her personal radar gave an accurate reading, John's attitude mirrored that. His glance her way when she drove into the parking lot had not held warmth.

George approached her. "Come, I have something to show you."

"Okay, but could you do a favor for me?"

"You ask. George does."

She laughed. "You better watch out. Giving a girl rein like that could land you in trouble. But seriously… Would you let John know that in the center area, where we're planning a replica of Bethlehem, that I would like some side walls at the rear of the mock-up? Everyone from the drama will have to fit into that area while waiting for the final song. I don't want the audience to see everyone standing there."

"You do not want to discuss this with John?"

"No. I…I think it will be better coming from you."

He shot her a glance but then stepped next to some plywood boards set against the large pine. "He reworked the sketches from the other day."

Her hand went to her mouth as she stared at the boards.

"He did right this time?"

"I…ah…yes." He'd redone the boards? Guilt washed through her. "It must have taken him a long time. I…"

George waved his hand. "John likes to stay busy. If he did not want to do this, Sharee, it wouldn't be done. I will bring you some paints. He has me doing other things today, and he said if you wanted them so much, you could paint them."

"Oh, he did, did he? Well, I guess that's only fair."

"Good." He smiled and turned away.

"George?" When he turned back, she gave a weak smile. "Tell him there will be no lunch today, either. Lynn and most of the other women will be at a wedding shower. It's at 1:00, so they're deserting us for the day."

George grumbled under his breath. "Then most of the workers who come will desert us, too, at lunch time."

"I know. It's cold, and they'll definitely want to eat, so..." She shrugged and gave a sigh. What could she do?

"Don't worry, Sharee, we will get this done."

As George walked away, she tilted her head and stared at the boards. How did she process this after John had been so hostile the other day?

God, did I miss you? Are we supposed to be doing this?

About one o'clock, Sharee watched the youth group head for their cars. She waved goodbye to some them. Their laughter and hard work had helped in a big way today, but she couldn't blame them for leaving. Her stomach had growled for something to eat, too, something hot and nourishing. Other volunteers began to leave, and she debated about leaving with them. But she needed to finish the boards John had redrawn. A little longer wouldn't hurt.

She tracked down George and asked for more paint. If he felt surprise that her requests came to him today, he masked it well.

A while later, she pulled the band from her hair and shook it loose, relishing the feel of it covering her cool neck. Tilting her head, she studied the last board.

Not a bad job, Sharee. You whipped through that and did it well.

Gathering the paints and brushes, she took them to the storage shed to put away. Only George, she and John were left. She'd better leave soon.

She exited the storage shed and sent George a surprise wave as he drove past. The man was leaving already? She wanted to clarify a request she made earlier. The muscles across her shoulders tightened. Could it wait until next week?

She glanced around. John was at his truck, putting tools into the toolbox in the bed. Working up her courage, Sharee approached him, meeting his frown with a lift of her chin.

"I wanted to thank you for all your work on Herod's Court. The first one and this second one. You have a lot of talent, and...well, I'm sorry about my rudeness the other day."

His eyes opened a little, and he gave a quick, sharp nod.

"I wanted to talk with you about something else, though."

He crossed his arms and leaned against the truck, his wary look causing her stomach to clench.

"You were talking with George about the new lighting I requested earlier. I think he misunderstood what I said."

"What did he misunderstand?"

"My request about the star. The one made from strings of lights. I'm not expecting you to build anything new. I know there's enough to build already. I just wanted lights strung from one post to another to form a six-pointed star."

"We can do that."

"Parallel to the ground."

"Parallel to the ground?"

"Yes, not a vertical star, but a horizontal one. Eight feet off the ground and parallel to it."

He straightened. "Horizontal?"

"Yes. If we can put some poles in the ground at each point of the star, we can string the lights from pole to pole. Eight feet high. Parallel to the ground." When he said nothing, she bit her lip. "I...I don't think it's hard to understand."

He gave her a cold stare. "And yet George misunderstood you."

She blew out a breath. Anger at his attitude this past week simmered inside, but the hurt rested below that. A hard ball formed in her stomach. His irritability, the cold day and her hunger began to mix as if in a cement truck. Did she really want to put up with this?

"Look, just forget it. I'll talk with George later." She turned away.

He caught her arm. "Don't go storming off. I just need to get my head around this."

She yanked her arm free. "I don't care whether you get your head around it or not. I'm tired of this. Of whatever you've got your back up about."

A line formed between his brows. "If you'll tell me—"

"No. I'm not telling you anything. I don't need the hassle." She whirled away from him, and her foot twisted under her. The next moment, she landed hard on the asphalt. Her head slammed back against the truck, and pain shot through her skull.

"Hey!" John's voice echoed through the pain. "Are you okay?"

She closed her eyes and put a hand to the back of her head.

"Sharee?"

Moisture formed behind her eyes. She heard him move and felt his nearness as he squatted beside her. His hand on her arm shook her this time. *Please get me out of here, Lord.*

"Are you okay?" His voice had deepened.

"I'm fine." She rushed the words and opened her eyes. His were inches away. She squeezed hers closed again, her heart slamming hard against her chest.

His hands tightened, and he lifted her to her feet, steadying her for a moment before releasing her. She shivered but didn't know if it was from his closeness or her fall. His head tilted as if to catch her look, but she stared past him. The view of the tall pine and its gilded needles met her.

"Sharee?"

"I'm fine."

He said nothing for a moment then stepped away. "All right. Finish what you were saying then. You want a six-pointed star made only with lights, eight feet above the ground and...parallel to it?"

She swallowed and forced her concentration to his question. "Yes. I didn't think it would be much trouble, but perhaps it is."

"No, we can do it, but..." His voice changed. "Do you want the planes flying over to see it or what?"

Her eyes met his finally and saw the amusement. She stiffened. "If we turn on the lights at the end—while everyone is singing—it will add an accent to the finale and look great from the bleachers. You just need some imagination."

"*I* need some imagination?"

She pulled herself to her full five-foot-two height. "Yes."

A quirk edged the corner of his mouth. "Okay. If that's what you want." He rubbed a thumb over the stubble on his chin. "We need to make a trip to Home Depot."

"We?"

"Yes."

"I'm not going anywhere with you." Flat. Short.

One brow lifted. "Well, it's your idea, and I'm the one with no imagination. Obviously, I need your help."

"No."

"Yes." His eyes held that familiar backlight.

She shook her head then winced.

"Do you want this finished on time or not?"

"I said..."

"I heard what you said. We've had too many mistakes already. If you want to finish this on time, we don't need any more." He walked around to the driver's side of his truck. "Come on. I won't bite you."

She stared at him. "I am not..."

"Finish on time or not? It's up to you."

She hesitated, threw a look at the sky and walked to the door.

He climbed into his side, and she climbed into the other, slamming the door. She locked it, latched the seat belt, and moved as far away from him as possible. He eased out of the parking space, and as she shifted back against the seat, she caught his grin.

The man was a bully, arrogant, and egotistical. She stared straight ahead. Why had she ever thought him attractive? And why let herself be bullied into coming with him?

He pulled onto the roadway. "How's your head?"

"Fine."

He slid a glance her way. "Your standard answer. Okay. How are things at Downtown Ministries?"

"Fine." The word came as short and clipped as the first before she could stop it. He grinned once more, and she huffed and crossed her arms. After a minute, though, she dropped her head. Somewhere inside, God's Spirit was nudging her. *Be better, rise higher than the circumstances.* She'd let hurt drive her actions and words.

Before he asked another question, she cleared her throat. "This week we've seen a number of families. Usually, we see a lot of single men, but this year, more families."

"And that adds new problems, right?"

"Yes. It's harder finding a place for families, because of the restrictions for children. And, of course, they need more space…" Her voice trailed off.

On the shoulder of the highway, a woman and a young child walked. Neither had a coat. The woman wore flip-flops, the boy a pair of shorts and a t-shirt. Sharee bit her lip. *They have to be cold.*

When the truck drew alongside, she inspected the two. The boy looked about three, the girl in her late teens. They looked like many of those coming into Downtown Ministries these days.

"John, could you pull over?"

"What?"

"Pull over. Please. Now."

He pulled to the side, onto the shoulder and out of traffic, giving her a quizzical look. Sharee fumbled in her purse, grabbed a bus pass she kept for such times and yanked free a twenty-dollar bill. She jumped from the truck, and ran back down the shoulder of the road, then slowed to a walk.

"Hey," Sharee said.

The girl stopped, reached down and pulled the boy next to her.

Sharee smiled. "I wondered if you might need a ride."

The girl wiped a hand down the side of her dirty jeans. "No, we're fine."

"I work at Downtown Ministries. Do you know it?"

"Yeah, I've heard of it."

"Good." Sharee hesitated. She didn't want to offend the girl. "You know we try to help people if they're homeless or need food or clothing."

"I know. I gotta place to live."

"That's good." Sharee smiled and looked down at the toddler. His summer clothes caused her to shudder.

"Hi," she said to the boy. "My name is Sharee. What's yours?" The boy edged closer to his mother.

Sharee smiled again and looked at the girl. "I just thought you might need a ride somewhere."

"We're just going to get some food. Up the road."

"To the grocery store at the strip mall?"

"Yeah."

"We'll give you a lift."

"No, we're fine."

Fine. She was having her own words echoed back at her. So that's what it felt like. She glanced at the boy. "It's a long walk for…your son? What's his name?"

"Michael."

"I'm Sharee." The girl nodded. Sharee touched her arm. "We can drop you off. We're going that way. It's pretty cold out here." Even the mother's clothing—a sweatshirt over t-shirt and jeans—would be losing their warmth to the approaching evening.

The girl hesitated then nodded. "Well. Okay. Thank you."

Sharee handed her the money and the bus tokens. "Here. Please. Take these. Get something extra for Michael."

"Okay." The girl stuffed the money and tokens into her pocket without looking at it.

"What's your name?"

"Kaitlan. Thank you."

The three of them walked to the truck. A minute later, Sharee looked in the passenger window, eyeing John with uncertainty and praying under her breath. His truck had a bench seat, no console. Kaitlan and Michael would have plenty of room.

"John, this woman is walking to the grocery store." She pointed the way they were headed. "Do you think… would you mind…"

"Do they need a lift?" he asked.

She smiled with relief. "Yes."

"Well, they can climb up here with you."

Sharee opened the door, hesitated a minute, and then helped the girl and her son into the cab. "I'll get in the back." John started to say something, but she closed the door and walked to the back.

Big truck. She'd had trouble just climbing in the front seat. Now she reached up, scrambled onto the bumper and hauled herself into the bed. Glancing around, she scooted over next to the toolbox near the cab.

Through the back window, John glanced her way and shook his head. He pulled onto the roadway again. The wind caught her hair and whipped the shoulder-length curls about her face. She wrapped her arms against the chill and huddled lower.

Cold had stiffened her limbs by the time they arrived at the strip mall, and Sharee had to force herself to a standing position. She grimaced, reached a hand to the side of the truck and jumped down. Straightening, she ran her fingers through her hair and walked to the front.

John's voice drifted from the cab. "You're sure you have a way home? We'll be coming back this way."

"Yes, we'll take the bus. Thank you." The girl pushed the door open and stepped down. She drew the boy from the seat. "We're fine." Her gaze met Sharee's. "Thank you. For the ride and the other stuff. Weren't you cold back there?"

"A mite," Sharee massaged her arms. Her flannel shirt covering a tee was no better against the cold than the girl's clothing. "Can you get home?"

"I just told...John...that we'd catch the bus."

"Okay. Take good care of Michael."

"I will. I always do." Taking the boy's hand, she drew him toward the store.

Sharee climbed in, shivering, running her fingers through her curls again.

"Cold enough back there for you?" John headed for the highway.

Sharee glanced his way. His tone sounded somewhere between exasperation and amusement. She couldn't tell which, but she was freezing. She rubbed her shoulders.

"You never wear enough clothes." A second later, in a different tone, he added, "For the weather."

She folded her arms across her chest. He made his little comments but made no move to turn on the heat. She tried to keep her voice level, knowing, as the words came, that she'd been unsuccessful. *"Do you... think... you could turn on the heat?"*

His teeth flashed, and he reached for the switch. "I know you've brought people to church for help before, but do you do this kind of thing often?"

"What kind of thing?" she asked. She huddled against the seat, soaking in the warmth that radiated from the heater.

"Pick up hitchhikers."

"They weren't hitchhiking."

"Technically, no. I meant, do you pick up people often?"

"Sometimes." She couldn't keep the antagonism from her voice. Just because he'd given Kaitlan and Michael a lift didn't mean she'd forgotten his week of hostility.

He didn't respond at once. A mile later, though, his head turned her way. "You know, I promised I wouldn't bite you; but, if you're going to be so sarcastic, there are other things..."

She straightened a little in her seat, inspecting him and feeling a smidgen of remorse. "Look, thank you for giving them a ride. It's cold out, and the boy looked so little, and it's late. I knew they must need some help."

"I was glad to do it." He swerved off the road into a McDonald's and headed for the drive-thru. "What would you like besides hot coffee?"

"What?" She gawked at him for a moment. "I... uh... coffee will be fine."

"Cheeseburger, chicken, or salad with that?"

"No, I—"

"Come on. I'm starved. We've been working all day and neither of us stopped for lunch." He waited. When she said nothing, he added, "Unless you want me to take you to someplace more upscale?"

"Some place more...what?" And then when his words sank in, she felt a flush in her cheeks and saw the light in his eyes. She gritted her teeth.

"I'm teasing you," he said. "Please order something." The box squawked at him. "Just a minute." He turned back to her. "I liked what you did for Kaitlan and Michael, but you were foolish to sit in the back. It's freezing. The cab had plenty of room. If you didn't want to sit next to me for some reason, you could have put Michael and Kaitlan between us." When Sharee just stared at him, he said, "I'm going to order for you. Do you want a burger or chicken?"

"Cheeseburger."

He ordered three and fries, two salads, coffee, and water, and eased forward to the pay window. She sat in silence and chewed her lip. When they handed him the order, he gave her the bags, set the drinks in the cup holders, and pulled into a parking spot.

"Fix your coffee. I don't like to drive while someone's doing that."

She set the bags between them and began to fix her coffee. No wonder he's so good at organizing things. He likes giving orders.

She tasted the coffee and sighed. The warmth from the heater eased the cold in her frozen extremities, and the coffee warmed her insides.

She relaxed against the seat. "I think I would have survived sitting next to you for a short ride. But it really didn't enter my mind. I just assumed there wouldn't be room in the cab, so I got in the back."

She took another sip from her cup, and he reached into the bag and drew out a burger. He didn't open the paper, though, but studied her until she glanced his way.

Something in his expression made her straighten. "What?"

"I need to apologize for this past week." His gaze held hers. "My attitude and my behavior were deplorable. I took a personal problem out on you. I apologize for that."

She held the coffee in both hands and stared down at it. Where had that come from? She nodded, not sure what to say, not trusting her voice.

"So, was that the only reason you were avoiding me?"

She lifted her head. "What?"

You were avoiding me, using George as your go-between."

"You were avoiding me!" The words popped from her mouth.

"All right." The amusement returned. "Don't throw your coffee at me. Just drink it."

She frowned, lowered her head and took a sip. Its warmth bathed her throat. She held her face over it and sipped and breathed in the comforting aroma.

He held out a cheeseburger, and after a moment's hesitation, she took it. His guess about that scored a bullseye, anyway. Hunger chewed at her insides. She kept her concentration on the burger. Without saying anything more, he passed her one of the salads and reached for the other burger. When he offered her the fries, she shook her head. He ate all of them, finished the other salad and drank the water.

"Warmer?" He questioned a little later.

"Yes." Short and curt.

His mouth lifted. Sharee twisted and studied the McDonald's sign.

"I meant what I said before. I apologize for the past week."

The seriousness in his tone surprised her. She ducked her head, sipped from the cup again, and thought how her father always said it took a big man to apologize.

When finished, she stuffed their trash into the bag, sat back, and tried running her fingers through her hair. They caught in the numerous tangles from her ride in the back.

"It's a mess."

"I know." She glanced across at him and swallowed at the unexpected warmth in his expression. "Thank you for the coffee, and the food, and...the apology."

He nodded, shifted toward her and said, "You have very expressive eyes. Hazel, right? Pretty."

Sharee felt a flush start at her neck. Why was he being nice again? He'd apologized, but... With a quick motion, she reached up to push both hands through her curls. Her fingers slid and straightened, working out the tangles. When she dropped her hands, he reached to brush an errant strand from her face.

Every nerve in her body tensed; every muscle tightened. She drew in her breath and saw the look on his face change. Electricity jumped, arced between them. His fingers trailed along her jaw, dropped to her neck, and slid into her hair. Breathing was impossible. Her head arched backward, and her heart slammed hard against her chest.

His gaze held hers a moment before it dropped to her mouth. The hand at the back of her neck tightened, pulling her toward him even as he leaned forward. His mouth covered hers. The gentle, exploring pressure of his lips sent strokes of lightning through her.

Dear, Lord. Help me.

A second later, she put her palm against his chest and pushed. He hesitated, his fingers taut against the back of her neck; and then his mouth lifted, his hand fell away. He leaned back.

They sat in silence, their breathing filling the cab. The intensity of his look caused her to close her eyes. How did we go from constant irritation to this?

His fingers stroked her jaw again. "That's what I'm wondering about, Sharee. Your avoidance this week. Does a kiss scare you so much? Or was it my attitude?"

She tried to find the words. You're not a believer. I won't date you, can't marry you, so there's no use starting this. But nothing came from her throat. The twist in her gut stopped her.

"I...I can't..." The words stumbled out. *Wrong. Tell him, Sharee. Tell him.*

A slight inclination of his head indicated he'd heard her whisper. "I like you, Sharee. I like working with you. I'm sorry about last week. I can't explain any more than you can right now. I guess we have a stalemate." He leaned back against the seat. "Has someone hurt you before?"

"No. I mean, yes, but that's not the reason. It's..." *Lord, how can I tell him? He doesn't know you. He won't understand.*

Silence as he watched her. Then he nodded. "Okay."

He started the engine, put it in reverse and backed out. The wheels spun their own quiet tune for a few miles.

He sent her a brief glance. "I know we need to work together. So, let's forget this. For now."

In a few minutes, they drove into Home Depot. When he parked the car, he turned his head in her direction and gave a mocking salute. "So tell me, *Boss Lady*, how big is this star supposed to be?"

Chapter 10

Lunch, the following Saturday, came after a long morning of work. John picked up a paper plate and utensils and thought over all they'd accomplished. A great deal. The project would be finished on time. Good.

He filled his plate and thanked the ladies that waited behind the serving table. He winked at Lynn. She supervised the lunches whenever they had Saturday work parties. She and the other women had outdone themselves today to make up for last Saturday's absence.

After acting like a bear the week before, not just to Sharee, but to others as well, he felt like himself again. Being close-mouthed was one thing; acting harshly didn't sit well.

Silence had reigned on the drive back from Home Depot last Saturday. Hers in reaction to the name he'd given her and his ribbing in the store. She'd sat on the other side of the cab again, arms crossed.

His own thoughts had cracked and run like pool balls after the initial hit. What was he doing? He'd already made this decision. No involvement. Yet, here he went again—teasing her, kissing her, riling her.

The attraction hadn't left just because he'd wanted it to. Her vulnerability, her enthusiasm, even that stubbornness she exhibited—lifting her chin, ready to fight if needed—all of it attracted him. Balance that with the heart she had for others, and, well, what did he expect of himself? His mouth quirked as he remembered the wildness of her hair after the ride in the back of his truck. And the way the dress had fit her that day after church. He liked the whole picture.

Holding his plate now, he moved up behind her and stopped. Everyone had camped around the long table in the fellowship hall, talking and eating. Usually, he took his plate outside. He preferred that to the crowded table and endless chatter from the others. But today, his agenda differed. Today, he would make a statement.

George, on her right, gave him a hostile stare. Over the previous week when his irritation with Sharee showed, George had risen to her defense. No getting a seat there. He glanced to Sharee's left. Christy Byrd, Ryann's mom, sat next to her. Good. She would welcome him at the table.

"Do you think there's room for one more, Christy?" He asked and watched Sharee's back straighten. She had avoided him all morning.

Christy scooted over. "Of course, John. There's always room for one more."

He sat down between her and Sharee. Close quarters. His arm and leg rested against Sharee's. She stopped eating.

A number of people looked their way. His impatience with Sharee last week had been noted and shared, he knew. The fact that he chose to sit beside her today would be noticed, too. He glanced around, and the others ducked their heads and resumed eating. Pastor Alan sent him a wary and inquiring look. John raised an eyebrow at him and began to eat.

He looked to his right and noted Sharee's averted head. "So, did you explain your whole idea about this six-pointed star to Sam?"

"Yes."

"And what did he think?"

Her eyes met his. "*He* thought it was a great idea, and *he* had no trouble understanding it at all."

Beside her, George chuckled, and John looked past her at him. "You understood, too, George? About this star eight feet in the air and parallel to the ground?"

George nodded. "Yes. I guess I had it wrong before." A touch of satisfaction filled the man's voice.

John studied him. He hadn't liked John's treatment of Sharee last week, and he'd enjoy seeing Sharee put John in his place. "So, you don't think doing a night project for airplanes is a problem?"

Sharee set her iced tea down so hard it slopped out, staining the tablecloth. Across the way, Lynn sat up and stared at the spreading stain. Pastor Alan's eyes met John's.

George shot him a hostile look, but before he could answer, John turned to Lynn. "Real good cooking, Lynn."

"Thank you, John. A lot of the ladies helped today."

"I can tell. Pork chops are delicious." He elbowed Sharee. "Shall I get you some more tea?"

"No. I'm finished." She didn't hide the irritation in her voice and started to rise.

"Well, listen, if you're going to get some dessert, I would love some of that peach cobbler. Do you..." He saw her stiffen. "Do you mind bringing me some?"

She glared. He gave her his best smile. Her eyes narrowed.

She bent down to pick up her plate and cup and said under her breath. "Oh, I'll bring you some cobbler, all right."

He didn't hear the rest, but he'd be on guard when she came back. He watched her throw her paper plate and cup into the trash and walk toward the table with the desserts. The look on her face mirrored her voice.

He rose from the table as she began to heap peach cobbler into a dessert bowl He walked up behind her and slipped an arm around her, covering her hand with his. "I think that's plenty. More than five people could eat."

She jumped.

"Hey! Don't spill it." He took the bowl from her and sat it back on the table then lowered his head next to hers. "Of course, I like to eat it, not wear it."

He grinned at her expression and returned to the table. The door slammed behind him. Hmm. Some door stops were needed. He caught Pastor Alan's look and grinned. Alan shook his head but said nothing.

Once the work resumed, it took his time and thoughts; but later, as the volunteers began to leave, he glanced around to find Sharee. She stood with the hose, cleaning her brushes. He watched her a minute. She set the brushes down and washed paint from her face and arms. Ready to leave.

Picking up his tools, he headed for the truck but stopped next to Sharee on the way. "I need some bungee cords. They have them at the dollar store. Take a ride with me, and we'll go get them."

She lifted her head, holding the hose still. "You've had too much sun, or you're just plain crazy. I'm not going anywhere with you. Once last week was enough."

"Come on. Take a drive with me. Last week wasn't all bad." By the heightened color in her face, she knew exactly what he referred to.

Without a word, she dropped the hose. It spewed water over the pavement and forced him to jump out of its way. She walked to her car. John moved over to the faucet and turned off the hose, then strolled to his truck. Many of the volunteers had finished, and cars were exiting the parking lot by the minute. Lynn came from the fellowship hall and stopped by Sharee's car to talk. Sharee opened the door to signal her readiness to leave, but Lynn didn't appear to notice. More cars passed behind him. At length, Lynn hugged her and walked to her own car.

Well, he had tried the direct approach. He lifted the toolbox lid, put his tools away. He took his time. Lynn waved when she drove past him. A minute later, he heard Sharee coming; but he kept his head down, his hands busy.

Sharee snatched at his arm. "What did you do to my car?"

How had she pinned that to him so fast? "What are you talking about?"

"You know what I'm talking about! My car was fine this morning. It's been fine all week! I don't know how or when, but you did something to it. It won't even turn over."

"Well, let me look at it."

"No! Keep your hands off." She whirled and headed toward the office.

He watched her try the door, yanking on it with impatience. Alan and Daneen had left an hour earlier. She spun back toward the parking lot. George's car and two others were last to leave.

"Thanks for the help, George!" John raised his voice as he heard Sharee's shout. "See you later this week."

Sharee ran toward the parking lot as George and the other cars pulled past him and circled the building toward the main road. She stopped at the edge, her mouth drawing into a line. In a moment, she raised her head and sent him a look from narrowed eyes.

He tried but couldn't keep the smirk off his face. Disabling her car a few hours ago took no time at all. She made it easy because she never locked the car. Something they needed to talk about, like that other thing she did—picking up hitchhikers. But now, he wanted to talk her into dinner. They eyed each other a long time. At last, she sunk her hands into the pockets of her jeans and moved toward him.

"Okay, whatever you're playing at, you win. Will you fix my car?"

"Later."

"Later?"

"After we eat."

"Eat?" She demanded. "I thought you said bungee cords."

"I need some. We'll get them first and then stop at the Lucky Dill. What about it? It's almost 4:30. Close to dinner time."

Her face didn't lose its wariness. "I'll get my purse."

He cleared his throat as she turned away. She glanced at him, and he pulled her phone from his pocket. She grabbed for it, but he raised it over his head.

"You're going to look silly trying to get this from me." He had one cautious moment as he looked down at her. Janice would have spent the next thirty minutes fighting for it, and she never fought fair. He watched Sharee for a moment and relaxed. But her response surprised him.

"I could have you arrested for kidnapping."

He shook his head and grinned. "Not yet."

"All right." Her words came grudgingly. "You win again."

He pocketed her phone. Hmm. A little too easy?

"The Lucky Dill then, but I'm ordering the most expensive thing on the menu and two of those."

"You won't be able to eat half of it."

"I'm sure I can think of something to do with the rest." She turned and walked to the passenger door of his truck, opened it, and climbed into the cab.

He climbed in on his side, grabbing the seatbelt, snapping it into place, and waited.

"What?" she asked.

"Your seatbelt."

"Oh, I forgot." She pulled it across, hesitated and looked up at him with big eyes. "John?'

"Yes?"

"Could we call a truce here?"

He turned to get a better view of her face, feeling the caution again. "Okay."

"Thank you."

As he put the truck in reverse and began to back out, she put a hand on his arm. "Oh. Wait. I do need my purse." He stopped the truck. "Do you mind getting it for me?"

"Okay." When he stepped down, he let the door shut and took two steps away before shooting a glance over his shoulder.

Sharee threw the seatbelt off and jumped into the driver's seat. He whirled, covered the ground in one step and shot his hand through the open window. She jumped as he grabbed her wrist and wrestled to free herself. When he managed to pull her hands off the wheel, he caught both her wrists in one hand and yanked open the door. She struggled against him as he dragged her out.

"You didn't really think that would work, did you?" Her head came up, and he saw the defiance but also laughter.

"It almost did."

"If you'd snapped that seatbelt in, girl, I might have trusted you."

"Don't call me girl."

He laughed. She stuck her tongue out, and he pushed her back against the truck.

"Do that again." His tone dared her.

Sharee's eyes danced. They stood a moment grinning at each other before her face changed. She sobered and glanced away.

He ran his fingers along her chin and to the nape of her neck. The silken feel of it caused a groan inside, and he dropped his gaze to her mouth. She stiffened, looking like a wild horse about to run.

What was she afraid of?

He stepped back and cleared his voice. "Let me take you to dinner." He gave his best "I'm harmless" look, but she drew her head back and frowned. She wasn't buying that, not after the last week. He couldn't blame her.

"Just dinner, I promise. Well, if you behave." He strove to lighten the mood. "All bets are off if you try to take the truck again."

Silence. He leaned away, putting some space between them.

She searched his face. "All right. No bungee cords?"

"Oh. Dinner and bungee cords, if that's okay. I'll run in. You won't even have to get out. But I'll take my keys." He chanced a wink. "Wouldn't want to tempt you."

By the time they got to the dollar store, the lights were on. Twilight had dropped over them.

"Did they just get a new shipment or something?" Sharee scanned the crowded parking lot.

"Probably. I'll just be a minute."

Sharee jumped out the other side. "I'll come, too. Might find something I don't need."

He stopped himself from taking her hand as she met him in front of the truck, but as they entered the store, he winked at her before veering off to the auto and patio aisle. She went the other way. He grabbed the bungee cords and cruised past other items, eyeing the array of inexpensive tools and patio items, but he didn't skimp on tools. The bungee cords would do for what he needed, but that would be all he brought here.

Sharee stood in the next aisle over, clutching a small package in one hand while staring at a large doll with the other.

He moved next to her. "I'm ready to check out. Do you want to look some more?"

She turned, eyes wide, and then lifted the doll. It took a moment. How innocent the doll looked without the gouged eyes and slit throat.

"It's the same one, isn't it?" Her voice had changed, deepened.

He took it from her. "It looks the same. Anyone could buy it here. It's cheap, and a lot of people are in and out here every day. They could buy four or five."

Sharee shuddered. "Let's hope not. I don't want Marci finding any more of them."

He dipped his head in assent. "I think I'll buy it and compare it with the others—just to make sure."

They went to the counter together. He paid for the doll and the bungee cords and noted Sharee's purchase—a bag of soft peppermints.

When they climbed into the truck, he dropped the bags behind the seat. "Did you notice the teeth marks in the first one?"

"No, but Cooper had it in his mouth."

"Yes, but he was by my side until just before I saw you. He must have picked it up right where you were. Did he growl at you?"

"Yes."

"Hmm. If he gets a new toy or something, he's possessive of it. I'm sorry that he scared you. It was dark, and if he just found that doll and growled at you, well... I understand why you were upset."

"I wasn't upset."

He grinned. "I'm just saying he's big, it was nighttime, you were alone and he growled. Scenario for a monster movie. If you weren't scared, then you're self-preservation skills are sadly lacking. Which, by the way…"

"Oh, so you admit he's big? And I'll accept the apology, too."

He shot her a look, saw the laughter in her eyes, and told himself not to respond the way he wanted. That would send her running from him as soon he stopped the truck. She grinned as if sensing his forced restraint. At that, he gave a low growl. It caused her eyes to widen and the grin to waver.

Good. But he needed a diversion. Her mass of curls, the expressive eyes, even the paint-accented t-shirt, were distractions of the wrong kind—right now. Back to the dolls.

"Some dog chewed the doll, however. Maybe brought it to the field. Which is odd. The other doll was purposely placed in Joshua's car seat. This one…well, I wonder where it came from."

They drove in silence for a while. Sharee leaned her head back against the seat, closing her eyes. After a few minutes, though, she opened them and stared out the window.

He sent her a long look. "What is it?"

"Nothing."

He reached across and gave her hand a squeeze. "Are you tired?"

"Yes, and I know I look horrible."

He chuckled. "No, but you do have a few well-placed paint splatters."

"What? I do?" She straightened. "Where?"

"Don't worry about it. You're fine. Here we are, anyway. You're stuck with them for now."

The deli's lights welcomed them with laughter and the smell of fresh bread. A hostess led them to a room with dim lighting and small tables backed against the windows. Lights from outside twinkled against the glass.

The hostess handed them each a large menu, and Sharee bent her head, studying it. John scrutinized her. How could he get past the reserve, the fear that she evidenced? She'd been sobbing that first day they'd met. Was that the problem? A relationship gone bad? That made sense. But if so, whatever happened had left her afraid either of men in particular—and his gut tightened at the thought of what that could mean—or simply frightened of another relationship.

The waitress brought a basket of rolls with their order of sweet tea. Sharee put her hand out to take one and met John's. She snatched her hand away.

He grinned and held the basket toward her. "Don't eat all the brown knots, please."

She took one, gave him a malicious smile, and bit into it. "I think these will be my favorites."

"Ah. I'm in for competition." He took the other one and buttered it.

Sharee glanced around the room. John followed her gaze. The designer had covered the deli's walls with every conceivable view of New York City and much memorabilia.

She waved what was left of her roll at him. "Oh, New York deli."

"Nothing gets past you."

"Drop the sarcasm, or I'll eat the last of your favorite rolls."

"I've always admired women who can out-eat me."

Sharee gave him a mocking smile and reached for another knot. "They have a big menu."

"Have you been here before? I assumed you had. Popular place."

"I have, but it was a while ago. I might need to try a number of items."

"You're going to make me pay well for your company?"

"You practically kidnapped me."

He wanted to laugh, but reached into the bread basket and took the last brown knot, instead. "Well, if you plan on eating that much, you won't need this." He broke it and bit in half.

"I bet they'll bring another basket if I ask."

He glanced at the last half of the roll and with an exaggerated sigh held it out to her.

"Oh, no, I wouldn't deprive you."

"Good." He popped it into his mouth.

"Pig."

He finished the roll and downed some tea. "All right. I'll order another basketful."

"No, you won't. I'm gonna order a table full of food. If the waitress ever returns—" Sharee bit off the words. The waitress stopped next to them. Embarrassed heat ran up Sharee's neck.

"Excuse my dinner companion." John tried to control his laughter. "She's had a stressful day. In fact, I think she's ready to order one of everything."

Sharee glanced up at the waitress, who had her pencil ready and a blank expression on her face. She picked up the menu.

"I'll have a bowl of the matzo ball soup, please. Also, the hot dog and bun with sauerkraut. A salami sandwich with Swiss cheese on rye. An extra pickle and potato salad on the side. And the Jasmine salad." She took a deep breath. "Oh, and we need another basket of bread—particularly, those rolls that look like brown knots."

She glanced at John. He shook his head but smiled.

"And for dessert..."

"Dessert is free with the meal." The waitress stated.

"Free?"

"Yes, you get to pick from cheesecake or apple strudel."

"What if I want both?"

"Well, you could each get one and share."

"What if I want both for myself?"

The waitress hesitated. Her eyes started to shift to John then stopped. "I'll see if I can get both for you for free."

"No, no, that's all right." Sharee's eyes met his. "He's paying. It's quite all right."

The waitress finished writing and turned to John. "You, sir?"

John kept his face serious. "I'll take the salami and Swiss cheese also. On rye. Greek salad, dressing on the side. The cheesecake sounds fine. Do you have chocolate chip cheesecake today?"

"Yes, I'll bring you an extra-large piece."

They stayed quiet while the waitress wove through the tables toward the kitchen. Sharee gave him a wide smile, and he settled back in his chair.

"I doubt if you finish two bites of each."

"Just watch. Next time you'll think twice before messing with my car and taking me hostage."

"The Ransom of Red Chief?"

Her eyebrows rose. "The man is educated!"

He reached across the table and squeezed her hand. She tried to pull away, but he tightened his hold.

"Sharee..."

"John, I...I need to run to the ladies' room. I'll be back in a minute."

He released her hand. What could he do? Even though it sounded like an excuse, he couldn't keep her there. But as she left, she stopped their waitress and talked with her briefly before making her way to the ladies' room.

When she returned, she'd washed some paint splashes from her neck and face, combed through her unruly hair, and added lipstick.

She sat across the table from him. "I wonder if our waitress is always so good at hiding her feelings?"

"I wonder what it would take—or cost me—to get a serious conversation with you?"

She looked down at the table. He reached for her hand, tightening his grip again as she tried to pull free. When she bit her lip, he rolled her fingers into her palm and let her go.

He broke the quiet that huddled over them. "So, tell me, what did you add to your order?"

"My order?"

"I saw you stop and talk with the waitress."

"You did? Well, you'll have to wait and see."

Her voice had teased, but he didn't miss the tension there, too. He bent his head. How could he get past that defense?

"John?"

As he raised his head, he noticed a familiar figure coming through the main doorway.

"I need to tell you something." Sharee's voice held more tenseness than before. "You asked before why...why..."

"Marci just walked in."

"What?"

He indicated the front of the deli with his head.

"Mommy, I want dat! I want dat!" A child's voice, lifted in demanding tones, cut across the room.

Sharee twisted around. "It is Marci. With Lizzie and Joshua. My, she's doing a lot of running around already."

The small girl by Marci's side tugged on her mother's arm and pointed to the dessert case. Marci cradled the baby in a front sling. His hand reached for her face only to grab a length of long hair and pull. Marci grimaced and let go of the toddler's hand to extract the baby's fingers from her hair.

John pushed away from the table. "I think I'll go help. You want her to join us here?"

"Yes, that will be—" Sharee touched his arm. "Wait."

A man walked up behind Marci. He said something, and Marci glanced over her shoulder, her mouth popping open. The man smiled, leaned over and took the toddler's hand. The little girl slapped at him, laughing. A moment later, he stood again and talked with Marci.

"That's Ted Hogan, isn't it?"

"Yes."

He dropped his head to study her. "What's that tone for?"

"Nothing. I..."

John sat back down. "If it's nothing, why is your face radiating disapproval?"

Sharee put a hand to her mouth. "Is it?"

"Definitely. You don't like Ted?"

"He's been following her. She said something not long ago."

John inclined his head toward the small group. "And he's hitting on her now."

"What's his problem? She's married, and this is her seventh child. Joshua's barely a month old. I don't understand this."

John watched as they sat at a table on the other side of the room. Ted handled the toddler and managed to pull the seat out for Marci, too. In a moment, he reached to help untangle Marci's hair from Joshua's grip.

"She's still an attractive woman, Sharee. Tired and in need of help. Some men find that attractive. If a woman is needy, dependent."

"But Marci's not like that. She's not needy. She's just—overwhelmed with the new baby. I've talked with her, and it's a bit much. Neither the kids nor Stephan is much help. Stephen's a good man. He's good with... well, he's good with the older children. Not so good when they're this age."

"While Ted looks like he's made for this."

The waitress stepped next to their table. One hand held a tray of food. She set down another basket of rolls between them, then two Greek salads, followed by two plates filled with thick sandwiches, pickles, and chips. "I'll get you some more tea," she said and disappeared.

John examined Sharee's plate for a minute. She'd changed her order. He lifted his head.

"Well," she answered his unspoken question, flustered. "Well..."

"You're a wimp."

"I am not! I'm just a good person. I felt sorry for you."

"Uh huh. Sure."

"Why is it people always make you feel bad when you're trying to be nice?"

He chuckled. "Are you, at least, getting the two desserts?"

She glanced down at her plate. "Do I have to?"

Now he laughed. She looked overwhelmed herself. "We'll share as she suggested. But Sharee..."

"Yes?"

"You should have made me pay."

She said nothing for a moment, picking up her fork and eyeing the salad. Then she met his look and smiled. "As you indicated a week or so ago, there are other ways."

He lifted an eyebrow. "I'll remember that."

"Good. Do."

He stopped as he reached for the mustard, lifting the brow higher. She laughed and dug into her salad.

Chapter 11

They passed Marci's table when they left, but she didn't notice, and they didn't stop. Sharee wasn't sure what she'd say. John had glanced her way, but she shook her head. What was going on in her friend's life? Her heart squeezed when she thought of Stephen and the children. Something was wrong. Marci hadn't told Stephen about the dolls, and here she sat with Ted.

Just as they neared the exit, Ted glanced up. She knew he saw her stare, but he said nothing. Her mind churned as they walked out. Ted had parked right outside the restaurant. Sharee seethed inside. He'd probably noticed Marci going in and shot up here to follow her. She stared into the back of his car.

A baby's car seat? What was he doing with a car seat?

Not until they drove into the church parking lot did Sharee remember the problem with her Honda. She cocked her head. "What did you do to my car?"

"You cleaned the terminals, right? Well, I figured they would still be loose enough to lift off—leaving you with no power. Now, if you had a newer car…"

"Hey, don't put down my car. It runs."

He glanced sideways at her. "Most of the time?"

"Yes. I mean…until the other day."

"The other day? More like four weeks ago." His voice became serious. "I'm surprised the motor still turns over."

"I know you said it might need a battery, but it's been starting pretty well. Perhaps it was the terminals…"

His look combined impatience and something else, which Sharee could not name. She scrambled down from the truck. For all his teasing, certain things seemed to set him off. Lightheartedness gave way to seriousness as quickly as the turtles scrambled into the water when she approached the pond.

John handed her the bag of peppermints she'd bought at the dollar store and went around to lift the hood. She pulled the hood latch and waited until he stuck his head out.

"Okay. Try it."

She turned the key. It coughed once and started.

After dropping the hood, he stepped next to her door and settled his hand on the car near her shoulder. "Sharee."

His voice carried that depth to it—that seriousness that made her want to run. She tried to think of something to say.

He reached into his jeans' pocket, hauled out her phone and handed it to her. "When are we going to talk about it?"

She said nothing, knowing what he meant. When was she going to tell him why she kept pushing him away? The moment had passed in the restaurant. *Be instant in season and out of season.* As much as she didn't want to tell him, didn't want what would happen between them when she did, he deserved the truth. She took a deep breath.

"All right then." His voice cut across her thoughts. "I promised you 'dinner only' tonight, but next time…" He moved away from the window, and amusement returned to his voice. "Next time the kid gloves are off, girl." He slapped the trunk of her car, walked around his truck and climbed into the cab.

Sharee waited for a minute, glad for the darkness that hid her expression, glad for a chance to escape the explanation one more time. She backed out of the parking space and pulled forward, telling herself not to worry. She had started to tell him, but he'd stopped her.

As she went by his truck, she drew a long, uneasy breath. She knew what God said in His Word, and she wasn't doing it. Instead, she was running again, and leaving an opening for the enemy.

Okay, Lord. Okay. I'll do it next time. Right when I see him, I'll tell him. I promise.

એ

The next morning, dread still fluttered in her stomach like the erratic movement of a bat in flight. She's tossed on the mattress all night. Why hadn't she told him?

John's face filled her vision, his brown eyes warm and teasing. After the food had arrived at their table the night before, they'd talked and laughed. Nothing personal. Everything non-threatening. Only when they arrived back at her car had he broached the subject of…what? Their relationship? Is that what he wanted?

Whatever he wants, it's impossible. He doesn't know the Lord. End of debate. She pushed herself to a sitting position and raised her hand to her chest. The cry of her heart since she was little was to serve the Lord and to marry someone with whom she could do that.

In almost thirty years, she hadn't found that someone. Maybe God wanted her to remain single. She'd talked to Him about this numerous times. If He would just tell her, then she could forget the idea of marrying, of having children. Tears rose unexpectedly.

And, of course, she ran men off. They laughed at her idea of purity until they found out she was serious. Then they either got angry or simply disappeared. Others thought her work at Downtown Ministries nice but tried to finesse her into getting a "real" job. "One that paid," they said. Her's paid—just not much. Yeah, she'd run off everyone, except Dean…

Stop whining, Sharee. Stop it!

She forced a smile and walked to her closet, shuffling through the hanging clothes and stopped with her hand on the yellow dress, the one she'd worn when she'd noticed John working in the field a few Sundays back. He had liked the dress. She'd seen it in his eyes. Perhaps he'd be working during church again today. Perhaps…

Stop acting like a love-sick school girl!

She straightened, shoved the yellow dress out of the way and yanked out a dark blue one.

෴

Twelve hours later, at sunset, Lynn drove her into the church parking lot. Her Honda CR-V occupied the first space. A couple spaces down, John's truck was parked.

She stared at the Ram insignia. You're not going to let me out of this, are you, Lord? No way around it. No miracles. Just do it. She drew in her breath. All right.

Lynn turned off the car's engine. "Great Bible study at Marci's, wasn't it? Stephen has such knowledge about God's Word, and the youth enjoyed the way he told that story about Elijah and Jezebel and the prophets of Baal."

"Yes, that was good, but I wish the girls had helped Marci instead of creating a problem."

Lynn laughed. "I just loved the way you took the baby from Abbey and said neither of the girls could hold him—that you were going to take care of him for the afternoon."

"I couldn't believe how they interrupted Stephen with their quarreling."

"Besides you wanted to hold him yourself, didn't you?"

Sharee started to deny it but didn't. "He is a darling."

"Yeah, you looked like a mother hen cooing to him."

Lynn stretched and looked at the church. "Are you staying for the evening service?"

Sharee's eyes focused on John's truck. "I don't think so. Are you?"

"No, I'm heading home. No one's here yet so we can slink away before they see us." Lynn put a well-manicured hand on the wheel. "Except John, of course, and he's not going."

Sharee glanced around. "I wonder where he is."

"What's going on with you two?"

"Nothing."

"Well, why isn't it?"

"That should be obvious."

"Not to me. Over six feet, good body, totally gorgeous smile—which you seem to have brought out. After two years, at that. He likes you, Sharee. He went from ignoring you, to snapping your head off, to—whatever he's doing now. Which is…"

"Driving me crazy."

"Un huh. That's what I mean."

"Lynn…"

Lynn leaned against the car's seat, her blue eyes holding unconcealed bewilderment. "What's the problem?"

"He doesn't know the Lord. You must know that."

"Oh. Well, I know he doesn't come to church, but I thought…"

"Thought what? That because he works at a church, he's a Christian?"

"Well, yes. Are you sure?"

"Oh, yeah. I'm not the only one who's tried to talk to him about God, especially when he first came."

"Well, it's not like he's asked you to marry him or anything. Can't you just go out and have fun?"

Sharee rolled her eyes. "Just have fun doing what you know God doesn't want you to do? Just have fun and pick up the pieces later?" She shook her head. "I'm too old to just have fun anymore, girlfriend."

"Yeah, almost thirty and desperate."

"Hey! You're only two years behind."

"Exactly what I'm saying. I know. You can't afford to throw someone this hot overboard. He's obviously interested."

"Stop that!" Sharee shook her head, laughing, and climbed from the car. "You're corrupting me."

Lynn started the engine again and put the car in reverse. "Well, I'd give it a little more thought if I were you." She waved and drove toward the highway.

Sharee watched the car disappear around the bend and glanced heavenward. "Lord, you know I don't have to think about it. All I have to do is tell him."

After a minute, she walked past the bleachers, across the field, to the pond. Sunlight slanted through the treetops. Around the pond, silence settled. The fading light darkened the water. Here and there, silver rings formed on its surface where minnows tried to find supper while not becoming appetizers themselves.

She lowered herself to a soft mound next to the water's edge, glad for the old, broken cypress knees made smooth by years of wear. Sadness gathered in the pit of her stomach.

I like John, Lord. I've let that influence me. I haven't told him because I don't want to. Forgive me.

A cardinal's quick tweet sounded close, and the red flicker of its body flashed through the trees. The sun dropped behind the horizon, leaving only gray and pearl light. She hugged herself, pulling her knees up to her chest. As the minutes passed, the birds' songs disappeared. The crickets' chirping replaced them. The damp, earthy smell of the ground rose to her nostrils. The shadows lengthened, and her chin rested on her knees.

A sudden rush of footsteps startled her. Her head jerked around. From under the trees, amid the deep shadows, a figure raced toward her. She leaped to her feet, heart pounding. She could make out the shape this time. Cooper broke from the undergrowth and leaped at her.

His heavy paws hit her chest. She screamed and tumbled backward into the cold, dark water.

Chapter 12

The pond's surface closed over her head. Cold shocked her arms and legs. She flailed upwards, feet shoving against the bottom, slipping in the muck beneath her sandals. Her head broke free, and she gasped the warm air. The dog's tail slapped her as he made for shore. She jerked back, and her feet hit bottom again.

"Cooper!" John's voice came from the other side of the undergrowth. He darted around the brush and skidded to a stop before the pond.

Sharee's breath came hard and fast from the cold, but she treaded water as the dog scrambled for dry ground—better than standing in the cloying mud. Cooper clawed onto the bank and sent sprays of silver flying as he shook off. She swam forward a few feet and tried to stand again.

"Sharee?" John's voice rose an octave. "What happened?" He stepped onto the moss-covered platform and stretched his hand toward her.

The icy water plastered her hair to her head. It ran and dripped from her arm when she reached for him. Behind him, the dog wiggled and squirmed. *His dog.* Sharee glared at the animal then at John. What if she grabbed his hand and yanked him in?

John snapped upright, yanking his hand back. He'd read her like a book. Too bad.

"Good reflexes." She reached for a plant on the bank. He leaned forward again, offering his hand once more, but eyeing her warily. She slapped his hand away.

"Come on." His mouth twitched. "Let me help."

"Don't laugh at me."

"Of course not." But he didn't try to hide the grin as he reached past her hand, grabbed her arm, and dragged her out.

She stepped onto the bank, slipped, and fell hard against him. His arms went around her, but she'd knocked him off-balance, too. They teetered, swayed, then sprawled to the ground. His chest rocked her head when he laughed. She wanted to pummel him.

Lord, this is not how I planned…

The dog leaped forward, pawing at them. Sharee jerked back, trying to bury herself against John's chest.

"Get him off me. Please!"

"It's all right. You're all right." John tightened one arm and shoved the dog away with the other. "Cooper, sit! Stay!"

Sharee peered from under his arm to see the dog settling on its haunches, mouth open, tongue lapping, tail wagging.

"He's just trying to join the fun." John pushed them both to a sitting position. "Or what he thinks is fun. Are you all right?"

"Does it look like I'm all right?" Her voice shook, and her arms hugged her chest. Water dripped from her hair, running in frigid streams down her back. She shook.

"Not really." Again the amusement.

"That...that beast jumped me."

"I know it sounds crazy, but he probably just wanted to say hello."

"Hello?" Her voice squeaked.

"When dogs get excited, sometimes they jump."

"Yeah, right into people."

"Exactly." He moved his arm and brought a hand up to push wet hair from her face. "He wasn't attacking. He was saying hello. If a Chihuahua jumped on you, you would know he was greeting you. It's just that Cooper's bigger."

"Yeah. Much."

The dog poked his nose at her, and she sunk into John's chest again.

"He likes you."

"The feeling is not mutual."

"Come on." Climbing to his feet, he put a hand down to her. She glared at him. His teeth flashed white in the twilight, and he hauled her to her feet. "You're soaked."

"Gee, nothing gets past you either, Sherlock."

He unzipped his jacket. "Here."

"No. No. That's leather." She shook her head, but he removed the jacket and settled it on her shoulders. "John, no, I'm filthy."

"Filthy and freezing." He took her hand. "Come on. I've got towels at the work building."

The moon hung low in the sky but scattered shadows across their path. They stumbled once or twice crossing the field to the buildings as darkness dropped. John led her to the larger building.

"There's a shower here and hot water. You can clean up."

"Are you crazy? I'm not showering here."

"You're soaked and freezing. You can't go home like that."

"Just give me a towel."

He opened the door and hit the light switch. Her eyes darted around the room. She'd been here before. On one side, tools hung on the wall, labels attached above them. Beneath them, an empty but decent sized work table stood. On the other side, the wall and the hooks were bare. Hand tools littered the worktable.

"Alan and I share the shed."

"And you're the neat freak," Sharee muttered, still shaking.

"Yes, and be thankful. It's the reason I have clean, dry towels for you."

He led her to a bathroom in the back. "Look, the bathroom's clean. So are the towels, and here." He reached up into an open closet, grabbed a bar of soap still in the wrapper, and handed it to her. "Clean soap."

"I said…"

"I know what you said. You haven't looked at yourself. Take a shower. There's shampoo. There's a lock on the door, and," he reached into a basket of clothes sitting on top of the washing machine to drag out a pair of jeans. "These are clean, too. I keep them here in case I want a shower and clean clothes before I leave for home—or anywhere else."

The amusement in his eyes riled her. "I am not…"

"You'll have to roll the jeans up two feet. And here," he pulled a t-shirt from the basket, "this will do fine."

"John…"

"I think that's everything. Did I mention there's a lock on the door?"

"Yes, but I…"

"Cooper and I will be outside. Leave the wet towels on the floor. I'll get them." He went out and closed the door.

The man was infuriating. She stood shivering, hugging herself for warmth, teeth chattering harder now. She surveyed the room. If he did the actual cleaning, he did a good job. So, he is a neat freak then. It fit the way he worked. Her mind turned to the hot water. She gave a deep sigh and reached for the lock.

After the shower, she towel-dried her hair, and put on damp underclothes then pulled John's jeans and t-shirt over them. The t-shirt reached halfway down her thighs. She rolled the jeans at the waist and the ankles. She couldn't find a belt and rolled the jeans at her waist once more. That should keep them up.

When she straightened, she saw the dolls.

Each plastic head showed on the top shelf of the closet. No doubt what they were. But why had he kept them? She shuddered and picked up a comb, staring at the dolls as she pulled it through her hair. Did Abbey think that by harassing Marci, it somehow made it better for Ryann? Or even for herself? Crazier things happened these days.

Sharee reached for her wet shoes then dropped them back to the floor. No way. Digging through the basket, she found a pair of clean socks. Their warmth on her feet felt like holding them toward a fire. She slipped her arms into John's jacket and glanced in the mirror. *No telling what this outfit looks like.*

የ

Lights shone down the hall from the main room, but neither he nor Cooper was anywhere around. She padded through the tool room to the outside door and opened it. He leaned against the building, eyes closed, arms crossed, Cooper curled at his feet. The dog lifted his head, and she took a quick step back.

"John?"

He turned her way, one eye open.

"I...I'm sorry I took so long. I forgot about your jacket. Here." She began to pull her arms free. He peeled himself off the building.

"Keep it." Pushing her back inside, he stopped and looked down at her. A grin crossed his face. She scowled at him, daring him to say anything.

"Let me get a sweatshirt from the basket." He walked to the bathroom and returned pulling it over his head.

She bit her lip. He'd waited outside in the cold. To make her feel safe? She swallowed. "Thank you for the shower and..." She looked down at his clothes.

"You look cute." The grin returned. "I'm glad you found the socks. Come on, I'll walk you to your car."

"Oh! My clothes." She ran back to the bathroom and wrapped them in the towel she had used and returned.

"I would have taken care of them."

"Uh uh. Not my clothes." She went past him. "And if Pastor Alan came in before you did?"

Cooper rose from the ground. The large head swung her way. She stopped.

John shut off the lights, locked the door, and chuckled. "Well then, we would have some explaining to do."

The dog stepped closer, and she leaned away. "John."

"What—" The question died, and he stepped past her and shoved the dog away. "Cooper, sit."

The dog whined but sat, his eyes still on Sharee.

"I've got a leash. I can tie him up here."

"No, I...I'm fine if you're with me."

"You're shaking."

"Sorry. Too bad he's not a Chihuahua. I think I could handle that."

"Tell me what happened."

"Cooper jumped me, that's what happened. He knocked me into the pond."

"The other time. Tell me why you're afraid of dogs."

She hesitated. "It's…it's no big deal."

"Of course it is."

"I…" She put her head down. Stupid that something so long ago could still affect her.

Tell him about the other.

Her head rose. "What?"

"You were attacked at some time?"

"Yes."

Tell him why you can't date him.

"Can you tell me?"

"I…uh…" *Tell him.* "I need to tell you something else. I…"

He stroked her jaw. "Just tell me what happened."

His touch sent waves of warmth throughout her body. She took a step backward. "It was my aunt's dog. I knew him. We had visited numerous times."

"Had he bitten anyone before?"

"No. At least, he'd always seemed friendly. But I went there with friends. They petted him and went on, but when I tried to pet him, he growled. It startled me, scared me actually, and I backed away. When he growled again, I ran. He chased me and knocked me down." Her hand went to her head where the scalp rose tight and rough. "He bit me numerous times on the back of the head."

"How old were you?"

"Six."

He groaned. "I'm sorry that happened to you. I'm sure it was horrifying."

"It was."

"Did they take you to the hospital?"

"Yes." She swallowed.

"And you've been scared of dogs ever since."

"Yes. People always think their dogs are harmless. You read that in the news all the time when someone is attacked."

He glanced at Cooper. "Well, I have to admit, I think Cooper's harmless—unless someone broke into my condo or tried to harm me. That would be a whole different story."

"Yeah. And he's huge."

John laughed. "So you've said. Come on. Let's walk back. I'll keep you safe."

The moon's light bathed the path, and the cold, clear night circled them. When she shivered, he slipped his arm around her shoulders and tugged her close.

Just walking beside him stirred emotions that overwhelmed her. She had to tell him. When they got to the car, before she left...

They stopped in front of her car, and she froze. He took the bundle of clothes from her arms, setting them on the hood of the car. Other cars were parked in the parking lot now, but she couldn't see anyone. Lights from the church windows stroked the darkness. Music drifted in muted tones across the night.

He pulled on a wet strand of hair. "You see I can be trusted. Whatever the problem is, can we put it aside? Can we stop the games? You must realize I care about you."

"John, I..." Her voice trailed off as his hand went to her throat, his fingers gentle, caressing. She felt the tension between them, the electricity just as it had been the week before.

He bent his head. She tried to step back but the car stopped her, and her neck arched at his touch. She moaned, and then he was kissing her with an intensity that startled her. His hand moved from her throat, catching her around the waist and drawing her close. She could feel the whole length of him, his body warm against hers, and she began to shake with the struggle going on inside.

Her hands rose to push against his chest. "John, I can't. I..." His mouth stopped her, and her defenses dropped. She returned his kiss, bathing in the emotions surging through her. His grip tightened, but a warning—like bowling pins crashing—went through her. She shoved against him this time, her heart beating so hard that words came with difficulty. "No. Please. I can't."

Moonlight brightened both their faces, and she knew her dismay must be clear to him. *Lord, why does it have to be this way? Why?* She tried to speak again, but her voice sounded strange, and she stopped.

"What are you afraid of?" His voice was as uneven as hers. "I won't hurt you, Sharee."

"It's not that. It's..." her voice trailed off.

"It's what?" His eyes searched hers. His mouth quirked. "Are you married and not telling me?"

"Of course not."

"Then what?"

"It's because..." She struggled to find the right words and forced two more. "God says..."

Lord, how can I do this? How do I say it?

His head moved to the side, watching her. In the moonlight, she saw his brow crease. His arms dropped, and he stepped back.

"So, that's it."

"What?"

He stared down at her, his face changing the way his voice had, the withdrawal clear. He reached past her and picked up her clothes and put them into her hands.

"Well, you better go home then." He opened the car door. She could only stare. "Go ahead. Get in."

She slid into the driver's seat. He closed the door and stepped away. She set the wet clothes in the passenger seat, fumbled under the mat and pulled out her keys.

"John?"

"Go home, Sharee. Goodnight." He turned and walked back the way they had come. Cooper trotted at his heels.

Chapter 13

Sharee glanced at the homeless man in the passenger seat. Pedro Gonzalez's ready smile served as her reward for the long, hard day. He had appeared on a regular basis at the homeless shelter until six weeks ago. When she saw him today with his hand-lettered sign, she pulled off the road and offered a ride.

He tucked the "Work for food" sign under his arm and climbed into the passenger seat.

"I can take you to my church." Sharee rolled the window down as his unwashed scent reached her. "My pastor might be able to give you some work for a few hours."

She couldn't promise anything, but Pastor Alan would most likely put him to work for the rest of the day and pay him. Some homeless didn't want the work; some did. Pedro did.

"Thank you, Sherry. God bless you."

She'd quit trying to have him pronounce her name correctly. "We haven't seen you in weeks."

"I had an apartment and a job."

"You did?" A surprise, but a good one. "What happened?"

"We got an apartment, Logan and I. You know him?" Sharee nodded. "Logan and this one friend of his were collecting scrap metal. So, they asked me to help. That's how we could afford the apartment. But about a week ago this friend of his took off with the last of the money we got. So…" Pedro shrugged.

"Oh, Pedro. I'm sorry to hear that. Can you still collect metal?"

"No, he had the truck. Logan and I have no transportation."

"So, you're on the street again."

"Si`." Quiet settled inside the SUV.

Sharee turned her head as he muttered under his breath. "What?"

"I got used to the apartment, hermana. To being dry, to sleeping safe and in a bed."

Her stomach caved. "Oh, Pedro. I wish I could help. The other man took all your money?"

"Si`. But the man was trouble."

"Sounds like it."

"He wanted our help—mine and Logan's—with other things."

Sharee lifted her brows. "With what?"

Pedro hesitated. "For something illegal, although he said it wasn't. No matter, Sherry. I said no. But he offered a lot of money."

Sharee sent up a silent prayer for him, even as other thoughts crowded in. She fought them just the way she had the evening before and throughout the day.

What happened last night, Lord? Does John know? Does he understand?

As she parked the SUV, she shoved the questions aside and forced her attention to Pedro. Three o'clock. Not too late. If Pastor Alan were here, he'd help. Somehow. She and Pedro climbed from the car and walked to the office.

Minutes later, she came out, leaving Pedro with the pastor and his wife.

Her eyes went to the field. Daneen had informed her that both John and George were working today. She grabbed John's jacket and the bag with his clothes from the SUV and headed their way. She had to know what he'd meant last night when he said, "So, that's it."

She forced her shoulders back, took a deep breath and stopped in front of them, watching a minute as both men were sanding the edges of four-by-eight plywood sheets. They had cut holes that she assumed were for the spotlight and the speakers on the platform.

George glanced up, and she forced a smile. He returned the smile even as he lifted the board he held and moved to the platform, hauling it up the ladder. She held her breath until he reached the top.

She glanced at John. He continued sanding a portion of the wood. The silence stretched awkward and uneasy. After another minute, he put the board against a wooden sawhorse lined with tools and looked her way. His eyes were dark and unreadable.

Pain hit inside. "I... I... brought your jacket. Your clothes are in the bag." She held both out to him.

"Thank you." His voice sounded as unwelcoming as a guard dog on patrol. He took the jacket and the bag and looked around. He dropped the bag on the ground and threw the jacket over the sawhorse.

She stood motionless, heart pounding, her mind filled with what she wanted to say, to ask; but she found it impossible to form the words.

He lifted the board again, his gaze running down it. Without looking at her, he said, "The man who came with you—you picked him up?"

"Picked him up?"

"Yeah, is he one of your homeless cases or a hitchhiker?"

"Both. But they're people, not cases."

His eyes met hers again. "*Excuse me.* What I meant was did you pick up *this person* from the side of the road?"

"Yes, but I…"

"What you're doing is dangerous."

His anger and the hardness of his eyes shook her. She forced her shoulders back. "It isn't any of your business, you know."

"No, you're right there."

She fought against the pain. "Why are you acting like this? What did you mean last night?"

He put the board down. "You don't know? I finally understood what your problem was. You and God are a team, right? And you can't serve Him and have a relationship with me. I'm a heathen, after all. Not in your class. Right?"

Sharee sucked in her breath. He did know. Somehow. Only, he didn't understand. How could she explain that the simple prohibition against being "yoked together" with an unbeliever was better for them both? It had nothing to do with him being good enough, and yet that's how he saw it.

"John, it's not like that. Please let me explain." She put a hand out to touch him.

He moved out of reach, giving her a mocking smile. "Oh, I understand." The smile vanished. "Don't bother trying to make it sound better than it is."

"It's not what you're thinking. Please don't do this."

"Well, it's your decision. But tell me, how long were you going to let this charade go on? How long before you told me?"

"I wanted to tell you. I…I didn't know how."

"The truth, up front, would have been nice."

"I wanted to, but I…"

"Did you?" The thin smile again. "You could have at any time."

She swallowed. No, she hadn't wanted to tell him. Everything in her had recoiled from what would happen—what was happening now. She'd wanted a relationship with him more than she'd wanted to do what God said. Tears sprung to her eyes.

She should have told him at the McDonald's and saved them both this pain. As she tried to tell Lynn yesterday, she didn't date unbelievers; because, to her, dating was a step toward marriage. But, where John was concerned, she'd let her feelings reign over her commitment to God. God deserved better and so did John.

She glanced up at him, wanting to make an excuse for not telling him, but excuses were just excuses, anyway. His cold, remote look tore at her heart.

She pivoted away from him and forced herself to walk back across the field, across the parking lot. When she rounded the corner of the fellowship hall, out of sight, she stopped. A minute later, she leaned against the building, brought her hands to her face and let the hot tears spill through her fingers.

≈

John watched until she disappeared, holding down the boil inside him. Last night, when he saw the panic on her face, when she'd mentioned God, it all came together. He understood then why she kept pushing him away.

His eyes raked the skies. *Will you take away anything I care about?*

Someone grabbed his arm, yanking him around. He looked into George's irate face.

"What did you do to her?" The Greek accent, which John never noticed before, highlighted the words like a threat.

He stepped back, every muscle tensed. "What business is it of yours?"

The older man's arm moved, the fist tightening. John waited, hoping for that outlet, wanting it, but the blow never came. The man dropped his arm and spat on the ground. Surprise jerked John's head back. George turned and stalked away.

John whirled and grabbed his jacket from the sawhorse, knocking it over. The tools spilled onto the ground. He pulled on his jacket and walked away.

≈

He sat at his desk, head bowed, praying. He needed to talk with John and with Sharee. When George had burst through the door a short time ago, the man's eyes blazed and his normal complexion had reddened. Alan had asked the homeless man to wait a few minutes and moved with George into the inner office. The second meeting with George about John proved as volatile as the first.

"Pastor Alan?" Sharee hesitated by the door to his office. Her eyes were red and swollen.

A talk with his cousin jumped to the top of his priority list. He'd sent George away with Pedro, promising the homeless man a few days' work with pay. George would take him for a meal and then drive him back to the tent city where he lived. That would calm George down and keep him away from John the rest of the day.

"Have a seat, Sharee. You need to talk?" When she nodded, he reached for the phone. "Let me call Daneen. She's on her way here, anyway."

He listened and his heart tightened as Sharee and his wife quietly talked. Sharee stumbled through an explanation of her feelings for John.

"I knew God's will in this situation but didn't do it. I've hurt John, and he's upset."

Alan leaned forward. "Sharee, we can't always control our emotions. With you and John working together, this is not a total surprise. You said John's upset. Knowing John, you mean angry, don't you? I hope he didn't say anything out of line."

Sharee shook her head "No. He does angry good, though." She managed a half smile. "Perhaps someone could take over the Christmas program? I...I can't see John and I working together, and I wouldn't like to see it dropped."

He sat back and slid a look at Daneen. "You felt like God put this on your heart, didn't you?"

"Yes, but..." She stopped, swallowed. "I was thinking that I might go to another church for a while. You know, just to get away."

He rose, moved around the desk and sat on the edge. "I don't think running off will help. You've got more courage than that." When she said nothing, he leaned forward. "Have you and John ever discussed his relationship with God?"

"No. That's a closed door."

"You've never asked him what he believes?"

"It seems obvious. He doesn't."

He crossed his arms. "I asked the congregation to pray for John from the day he came. You know that. John's had a difficult struggle over the last few years with his faith."

"His faith?" Her words held disbelief.

"Yes, his faith. He's struggling. I can't tell you more than that. He's asked me not to."

"I'm not sure I understand. John said... Well, he used the word heathen. To describe himself."

"Did he? Hmm... You've stirred up feelings John hasn't dealt with for a while. He acts like he's okay, but he's hurting inside. He's angry with himself and with God." He smiled and put a hand on her shoulder. "He's taking it out on you right now. Don't run away. Be patient. God has a plan."

Sharee frowned. "A plan?"

Daneen leaned forward. "God always has a plan, Sharee. And not everything is easy. You know that. Trust God—like you always have."

She stared at the floor for a while before looking back at him. "Do you know how many times I've said that to others? Trust God. Sometimes I was so impatient with them. I mean, I thought, you're a Christian just hang in there and trust God."

"It's good advice—maybe without the impatience."

"Yeah. And here I am failing miserably at being that person I thought they should be."

"Sharee, don't beat yourself up. You messed up, but it isn't fatal. I know you're hurting, and it will be tough working with John, but I think you can do it. And maybe John needs to see you do it. See you rely on God. Maybe you need to do it, too." He gave her a small smile and walked back to his chair. "Now, a lot is going on here, and we need God's help. Let's pray."

When she left the office, Sharee scanned the parking lot as she walked to her car. Everyone had left for the day. After her talk with Pastor Alan and after prayer, things looked clearer. Nothing had changed, but, she knew she would leave whatever happened in God's hands.

Across the lot, the gray of evening had settled on the field, but in the grass, she saw a gleam of light. Next to it, some other unidentifiable item sat.

What was it? Nothing important surely. Her heart jumped. Not another doll. No, it couldn't be. But she walked angled toward the field. A minute later, she stared down at the bag of clothes she had given John two hours ago. Next to them, the sawhorse lay flipped on its side, tools scattered across the ground.

He had left his tools. On the ground.

A groan rose. *Oh, Lord. Pastor Alan was right. John's hurting, too. What all it is, I don't know. But you do. Please help him.*

She stood silent for a long time, then, with a ragged breath, she bent and picked up the tools.

Chapter 14

The engine whined but didn't turn over. Sharee tried again. For a second it sounded like it would catch then it coughed and whined once more. She snapped the key backward.

No. Not now. Not here.

When Daneen asked for the paperwork on Pedro, she'd made sure John wasn't at the church. Daneen assured her he'd left to get some things for the Christmas program. He'd told her he wouldn't be back. It was late. But when she arrived, his truck sat in its regular parking space. Her breath hitched. She didn't want to see him. Not yet. Saturday would be soon enough.

She'd dropped the papers off and ran back to the car. Now the engine wouldn't start. She turned the key once more. Whine. Click.

No. Please no. She waited a minute and tried again. Whine. Click. She gritted her teeth. *Please, Lord.*

The car door flew open. Sharee jumped and looked into John's irate eyes. He was dressed in dark slacks and an open neck shirt., and he carried a tie and brown jacket over his arm.

"You. Need. A. Battery." Each word sounded underlined. He put a hand on the top of her car and leaned forward. "I told you that. Why are you still playing with this? Don't you care about your safety?"

His eyes, less than two feet away, glared at her. She pushed his arm aside and climbed from the SUV just to put some space between them.

"I *usually* don't worry about my safety around here." She saw his brows lift as he heard the meaning of her words.

"You're being ridiculous. Why didn't you get a battery like you said?"

"It's not any of your business, remember?"

His expression froze. "So you said. But you might think about—"

George's voice cut across him. "She's right, Jergenson. It's none of your business. Sharee can take care of herself, and if she needs help, she knows whom she can ask. What's your problem?"

The men glowered at each other. Sharee's gaze slid back and forth between them.

John straightened and stepped back. "The problem is she might not be at church next time this happens." He turned to Sharee. "I told you it was the battery. Why didn't you get one?"

"I've got cables if I need them."

"Cables? Get a jump-start box, then you won't have to ask some stranger for help."

"Look, she doesn't need your advice."

"She needs somebody's advice."

Pastor Alan stepped into the circle. "The advice all around seems to be getting out of hand."

They all glanced his way. A moment of quiet followed.

Sharee stabbed clenched fists to her side. "All right, I don't need this. I can take care of myself. But John's right." She sent a glare his way. "I need a battery, and I'll get one when I have the money. In the meantime, I've got cables. All I need is a jump, so, other than that, leave me alone."

A car door slammed, and the sound of high-heeled shoes came toward them. "What is going on here?"

Sharee glanced over her shoulder. *Talk about your power suit.* Only it wasn't a suit. The black dress just skimmed the girl's body and ended two inches above her knees. It swung as she marched forward, and her black heels moved in double-time. The long straight hair swung to match her stride, and her eyes flashed with undisguised displeasure. No, the outfit didn't speak of power; the woman did.

"I asked, What's going on?" Her gaze bored into John's, shifted to Pastor Alan's, and rested on George, seeming to absorb every detail of his appearance.

John moved from Sharee's side. "Calm down, Alexis. No one needs rescuing here." He paused a moment. "Sharee's had trouble with her car. I told her she needs a new battery, but she's not listening."

The girl's eyes held his for a moment. "I...see. Okay. Does she need her car started? Can't one of you help her with that?"

"We'll help her. It's not that." John's scowl echoed in his voice. "She's had problems for a while. I've told her what to do, but she hasn't done it."

"Yeah, and with that attitude, I probably wouldn't either." The woman frowned and met Sharee's glance. "They call this helping? Ganging up on you?" She turned to the Pastor. "Isn't that what you're all about, *Pastor*? Helping people?"

"Now, Alexis..."

"Don't use that tone with me! No one needs placating, either." She looked at George. "You seem the best of the lot. Do you think you can get her car started and make sure she gets home?"

George grinned. "Yes, ma'am."

"Good." Her eyes narrowed at John. "And get her a battery." She nodded to Sharee and marched back to the Jaguar.

The three men looked at each other and back at Sharee. John scowled, walked to the woman's car and slid into the passenger seat. The Jaguar accelerated and moved off.

Sharee didn't move when the car left. Pain ricocheted through her. Who was that? And why was John so angry with her if he was seeing someone else? Dean had been deceptive, too... She had always been a mess where men were concerned.

"Alexis will have his head on a platter," Pastor Alan said with a chuckle. "She's right, you know, we need to do something about this."

"I'll take care of it."

"I know you can, but let us help." A smile crossed his face. "George will jump your car tonight. Are you going straight home? Good. If it won't start tomorrow, call. If it does, come to the church, and we'll go get a battery." She started to protest, but he cut her off. "Sharee, you would be the first one to march up to me the same way Alexis did and demand we get one for someone else. Don't let your pride get in the way."

She said nothing. She could have called her dad and asked for the money; but at almost thirty, living on her own, she hadn't wanted to admit she needed help. Talk about pride. It took a minute, but she nodded. "Okay. I'll pay you back on payday."

"No, you won't. As many of your clients as we help here, we can do something for you, too."

"Let him do it, Sharee," George said. "And accept the Lord's blessing. I'll get my car and jump this for you."

"Okay. I... Thank you." She watched as he walked toward his car. How many times would the Lord have to tell her the same thing?

Morning took a long time coming. Sharee climbed from bed and went to stare out the front window of her apartment. The stand of oak and pine trees in the middle shifted the morning light to the ground. Squirrels slipped from tree to tree. Cardinals and sparrows chirped and called. She closed her eyes and tried to inhale the peace it usually gave her.

Why had she fallen for John? And she had, no doubt about that. He'd worked there for two years. No way she saw this coming.

Of course, she'd stayed away from him after that first meeting. When he'd found her so broken and humiliated. She'd been sobbing uncontrollably, and she had the bottle of pills in her hand. The pills were from surgery she'd had a few months before to remove a cyst.

Dean's rage had exploded that day. He'd slapped her and shook her until she thought her neck would crack. When she managed to break free, she'd raced home and, in desperation, made a change of plans. She needed to go somewhere where he wouldn't find her. Hurting already, she'd grabbed the pills and left.

The church was deserted when she arrived—what she'd expected that Saturday. She ran to the pond, dropped to the damp ground and buried her head in her hands. Shock and disbelief and sobs shook her. Until John stepped from behind a tree.

She hadn't seen anyone near the water when she climbed from her SUV and didn't know him then. But he'd quickly introduced himself, explained who he was. The new maintenance man. She was familiar with the name.

He kept talking—telling her where he came from, what he thought needed doing around the grounds. She tried to interrupt, but he seemed oblivious. Only later, she knew he wasn't. He had moved to general topics and then to how people dealt with hard times. He began encouraging her that no matter what she was going through, things would get better. It was only later when he asked for the pills that she realized he thought she wanted to kill herself.

She stepped back from the window. So, humiliated still, she'd kept away from him. Until now. Something broke inside her chest. Emotions washed back and forth while she stared out the window, seeing nothing. Amazing how much she cared in such a short time.

The other thing hovered like dense fog around her. She tried to ignore it. She moved to the kitchen, took a hard-boiled egg out of the refrigerator and grabbed a banana before sitting on a stool at the counter. As she ate, her eyes lost their focus. Yep, the eight-hundred-pound gorilla in the room. The giraffe with its head through the ceiling. Or the rhino standing in the corner.

All right, I can't ignore you. You and your black Jaguar. Who are you?

Shoving down the hurt in her chest, she climbed from the stool, made her way to the bathroom and stared into the mirror. Her shoulder-length hair curled about her head in wild disarray. *Not neat and straight like hers.* Sharee grabbed a band from the basket on the counter, gathered her untamed hair at the back of her head and secured it.

Her glance fell on the end table and her Bible. Walking over, she lifted it and opened to the chapter of Hebrews she'd read last night. Her finger moved down the page, Chapter thirteen, verses five and six. "He has said, I will never leave you nor forsake you; so we may boldly say, The Lord is my helper and I will not fear."

A few minutes later, she went to her bedroom, changed into jeans, a cotton shirt, and a sweater. Grabbing her laptop and purse, she headed out the door.

She'd dealt with anger, with pain, and with tears, but her shaking hands presented a new problem. The unsigned note she picked up from the driver's seat of her CR-V trembled even as her hands did.

Car unlocked. No surprise.
Battery installed.

She knew who'd left it. Why wouldn't he leave her alone? And he objected to the unlocked car, too. No surprise there, either.

As uncivil as it sounded, she wanted to rip out the battery he'd put in, dump it back on his all-too-neat workbench, and let Pastor Alan buy her one as planned.

Work would be a welcome relief to all that battled within her now. She stepped into the SUV and slammed the door. The engine started without a hitch.

Chapter 15

Alan carried two large cups of coffee as he walked toward John's truck Wednesday morning. A cold front had moved into the region, earlier than usual for Florida. Good thing he'd listened to Daneen and put on a light jacket.

John stepped from the truck and gave him a wary look as Alan handed him the warm drink. "Greeks. Bearing gifts."

The childhood banter he and John had used when growing up came back to him with a smile. His mother was Greek, and Alan had delighted in pulling pranks on John when they were younger.

He smiled now. "Hmm. That might be closer than you think. We need to talk. Let's go sit on the bleachers." Alan led the way, and they climbed about halfway to the top before sitting a while in silence.

John sipped at the coffee. "Thanks. I needed this."

Alan nodded. He'd spent time in prayer last night and again this morning. People he cared about were hurting. The enemy had attacked on his watch, in his church; and he didn't like it. The church, ultimately, belonged to God, of course; but God had put him in a place of responsibility, and that trust was sacred.

"You've done a good job." Alan waved his cup in front of him. "With these bleachers, with everything needed for the program. It's a lot of work. I appreciate it, and I know Sharee does, too." He hesitated a moment and watched the steam rise from his cup. "So, were you looking for a fight Monday or what?"

John glanced his way, frowning, then his face cleared. "Ahh. George." He took another sip of coffee. "Good man, hard worker. I like him. I can't say he feels the same. He spat on the ground rather than hit me."

Alan looked at him in surprise, and John nodded. He said nothing, though, just studied the top of his coffee cup and let the moment pass. Another subject held his concentration. He would make the jump. "It's his second time to get in my face about you...about your treatment of Sharee."

"Second time?" John frowned. "What makes it his business, anyway? He's too old for her, and I don't get those vibes."

"As to too old, I would imagine that's all in how you look at it. But no, he's feeling protective. She has no covering here. No father. No husband. No one to look out for her. Not that she wouldn't fight that as a sexist attitude. George sees it as my place more than his. As her pastor, I see it that way, too. At the moment. I'm her covering."

John sent him a sideways glance. "And if I'm messing with her, you're coming after me?"

Pastor Alan chuckled. "Sounds like a bad western. But… are you?"

"Am I what?"

"Messing with her? Playing with her, I think George feels."

"Playing? Oh, no, I haven't been playing, but don't worry. I'll be staying away from her, as much as possible, from now on." The edge to his voice highlighted the words.

Alan fingered his cup, staring at it, repeating a silent prayer from this morning. "I didn't think you were playing. That's not your style. But…" he took a deep breath, knowing the next words might infuriate him. "George is concerned about—I believe the term was—your moral compass."

"My moral compass?" John asked, and then his eyes changed, his mouth tightened. "So he thinks I've had sex with her, is that it? And now that I've got what I wanted, I've got no use for her?"

Alan stared across the field, not answering, giving him time. John started to rise, and he put out his hand.

John shook it off. "That's not saying much about Sharee, either. Has he thought of that?"

"Sit down. He's concerned about Sharee."

"He can take his concern elsewhere. I don't need it. Sharee doesn't need it. She's fine."

"John, if you were standing where George is, you'd have come to me long ago."

They stared at each other, and then John looked away. In a minute, he lowered himself back onto the bench. "All right. You got something else?"

"Sharee's been here for eight years. I know her fairly well. She's a woman of strong convictions. Some might say to a fault. She believes in doing things right, in following God."

"You don't have to sing her praises to me. I understand exactly what you're saying."

"You used to like that in people. In fact, that's a trait you held in high esteem if I remember correctly."

"You have the past tense correct. Look, I don't know where you're going with this, but I said I'll be staying away from her. That should make both you and George happy." He set his cup down.

Alan glanced at him. "Do you like the fact that George is judging your intentions in regard to Sharee?"

"No."

"Well, you've judged Sharee in a similar way, haven't you?"

John's head came around. "Where do you get that?"

"You've judged her intentions. I'm sure she never meant to keep something from you. She got caught up in her feelings for you. But you've kept something from her, too?"

"No."

"No?"

John's face hardened. "It doesn't interfere with the relationship."

"You can't believe that. And you let her believe you don't have a relationship with God."

"What was I supposed to do? Lie? God and I no longer have a relationship."

"I didn't say it was a good one," Alan let the hint of a smile come through. "You haven't told her about yourself. That was another thing you were always big on. The truth. Omission is not truth." John said nothing, and Alan continued, "You're angry that she didn't tell you earlier that she won't date someone who's not committed to God. She should have, yes. But you should have known that, too."

"What?" John's frown sliced him, and the word skidded across the morning air.

"Yes. Daneen and I have talked about Sharee and her convictions before. Perhaps your emotions got in the way, too." John said nothing, and Alan took a last sip of his coffee. "She made her choice a long time ago. Do it God's way. And it hasn't been easy for her, but the choice is right, and you know it."

"All right." Exasperation wove through the words. "You've made your point."

"On the other hand, you didn't bother to share things about yourself. Things she has a right to know."

John rose from the bench and brushed a hand down the side of his jeans. "After this program is finished, it might be time for me to move on."

Alan stood, also, still fingering his cup. He stared across the field. "You won't have to. She's already come to me about leaving—before the program is finished."

"She would never do that. This program means too much to her."

"No, she is beating herself up for letting the situation between you two gets out of control. I might have convinced her to stay. That is, if you can keep your temper under control. Be civil. Give her some space. She's not fine. She's hurting. You haven't appreciated the depth of her feelings for you or appreciated her commitment to God—for which she's paying a price. *You're* exacting the price, cousin." The sentence dropped between them.

A hard silence followed. Alan's soundless prayer rose to heaven again.

"This conversation is finished." John swung himself over the side of the bleachers and walked away.

Alan watched him go then lifted his eyes in quiet communication. Taking a long, deep breath, he nodded and climbed down.

ھ

John stepped into the work building, moving over to the workbench, straightening the tools in an absent, automatic way.

She has no covering. She's a woman of strong convictions. You haven't told her the truth. You haven't appreciated her commitment to God. She made her choice a long time ago, and the choice is right. You know it.

He slammed the cupboard door that stood ajar. A second later, his body locked, eyes focused on his tools. Someone had put them back. He'd left them in the field on Monday. Yesterday, he'd spent the day running errands, and George had worked at his main job. Not that Alan or George would have done it.

She'd put them away Monday after he'd raked her over the coals.

He took two quick steps to the door, then out, slamming it behind him. He stood there, and the feel of the cold moonlight as he leaned against the wall three nights ago swept over him. The sound of the shower echoed loud in his ears. He shook his head to clear the memory then jerked it skyward.

"Your idea of a joke, no doubt," he said between his teeth to the God of the universe.

She's paying a price. You're exacting the price.

John shut his mind to the words and strode away.

Chapter 16

"Sharee, who is doing this?" The despair in Marci's voice slipped out. Her voice trembled. "Why are they doing it? *Again.* I haven't hurt anyone."

Sharee's hand tightened on the phone, and early morning light painted shadows on her living room wall. "I don't know, Marci. I wish I did. Where did you find it?"

"Out with the morning paper."

"You read the paper?" The only ones she knew that read the newspaper were her parents.

"Stephen does. He likes to sit and read at the end of the day."

Sharee nodded even though Marci couldn't see her. She could see Stephen doing that. It fit his laid-back personality. "What did the note say?"

"'Enjoy him while you can.'" Marci's voice broke.

Sharee heard the sob, and her heart squeezed. "Lord," she said, praying aloud, "keep Joshua safe. Comfort Marci. And please frustrate any plans this person might have. Make them stop this harassment."

Marci cleared her throat. "You think someone does have plans? That this is serious?"

Sharee hadn't thought about her prayer. It had just risen from inside. "I don't know. It's probably a prank, but prayer can't hurt. Just in case. Have you called the police?"

"Not yet. I'll talk with Stephen tonight." Marci's voice stumbled, and she sniffed. "I can't imagine someone hating me this much."

Sharee thought of Abbey. "Maybe it's just resentment. From someone who's so miserable that they can't stand to see others happy."

"I hope, but I wish they'd stop. I hear the kids stirring. I've got to go."

"All right. I'll be at work later. Call me if you need me."

"Okay."

Sharee set the phone on the counter. She should confront Abbey. Who else could it be? Even though Ryann had lost her baby six months ago, she wouldn't do this. And no one else... Bruce? Ridiculous. But was there hidden resentment there. Marci was driving—but the other woman was cited. It wasn't Marci's fault even though she felt that way at times. She'd confessed to Sharee that she and Bruce were arguing when the accident happened. Her attention wasn't where it should have been, and she carried that guilt. Still, Bruce would never do something like this. Never.

John stopped at both Home Depot and Lowe's on the way to work. He needed sturdier brackets than he had. Herod's Court and some other scenes needed fastening together, and work beckoned today like a thousand-pound leatherback pulling herself ashore to lay eggs. A heavy workload.

The long night, reliving the past, waking from the dreams, having Sharee's face and Janice's overlaid in his mind shoved him out of bed early. He'd gone for breakfast at a truck stop and then headed to the stores before making a beeline for the church.

He parked his truck and watched George and the homeless man Sharee brought in on Monday pass right in front of him. Where had the homeless man come from? Had Sharee picked him up again?

Her lack of regard for her own safety astounded him. Didn't she know what could happen? She picked up hitchhikers and gave away money when she didn't have enough of her own—to buy a battery or a coat, he suspected. His stomach felt like a swarm of hornets inside.

The two men disappeared around the building. Had Alan hired him? John slapped the steering wheel. Not his business. She'd made that clear. None of his business. Just because he'd let himself become involved…

The helplessness and the rage he'd wrestled with first with Alexis, and later with Janice, flooded him. He wouldn't sit here and do nothing—whether it was his business or not. He'd put in the battery, but if he could stop her from picking up hitchhikers…

Stepping down from the truck, he slammed the door, tramped to the office, and yanked the door open. "Alan!"

Daneen's head shot up, eyes wide. John stopped short. With an effort, he lowered his voice. "Sorry, Daneen. Is Alan around?"

The pastor stepped out of his back office and came forward, his face a question.

"Did you hire that homeless man?" John's voice climbed once more. "The one Sharee brought here?"

Pastor Alan's eyebrows rose. "I did. He said he'd work if I would pay him. I think he needs the job."

"If you hire these people, then Sharee will keep picking them up."

"Is that your concern?"

John felt his teeth grind together. "If she knows," he said in a slow, even tone, "that she can bring these people here, and you'll help them, then she'll keep doing it."

"Don't you think what she's doing is…well… admirable?"

"No. Picking up hitchhikers is crazy."

"All right." Alan dipped his head, conceding the point. "We've all tried to talk to her, but Sharee is a grown woman. She's doing what she thinks the Lord wants her to do, and she's been doing it for years. I think the girl's got a good head on her shoulders."

"She completely lacks common sense."

"From what you told me yesterday, I don't think this should concern you." The men stared at each other. "And I think you need to work off your anger—outside, Cousin."

"Don't assign that man to work with me. I'm not helping you in this madness."

"I assigned him to George. I don't think anyone wants to work with you today." The words held a touch of amusement.

John grabbed the door handle and jerked the door open. The swarm inside his stomach had doubled.

❧

Sharee unclenched her hands and rose from the chair in the pastor's office. Her heart hammered; her face filled with heat. How dare John come in like that? Telling Pastor Alan what he should do concerning her.

She stepped into the outer office. "I do not lack common sense."

Pastor Alan grinned. "I was afraid you would come tearing out here after that."

"Perhaps I should have. What right does he have to say those things? What I do with my life is my concern."

"He cares about you, Sharee. He's trying to protect you, and he's right about the hitchhikers." Pastor Alan sat on the edge of Daneen's desk and crossed his arms. "Don't give me that look. Daneen and I told you the same thing."

"Yes, and we've talked about this before." She crossed her arms. "I always pray before I pick up anyone. Besides, John has no right…" her voice trailed off. "John's your cousin?"

"Oh." Pastor Alan's glance ricocheted from Daneen to Sharee, "I let that slip? Not good. When I offered John the job, he took it on the condition I wouldn't say how I knew him…or…anything else about him. He wanted to be left alone."

"He's had great success with that until the last few months." Sharee shifted the myriad feelings inside her. "George called and asked some questions about the project. It seems that now he and John are not talking?"

She made it a question but the pastor said nothing. "My fault?"

"Sharee, they're grown men. It's not your fault."

"Well, I came to give George a copy of the diagram John drew. He's only worked on the bleachers and the platform, so he doesn't know how everything else fits together."

"They're all out there now. Pedro, too. Perhaps you could wait until John cools down? Tomorrow would be better."

"That makes sense." She paced up and down then reached over and grabbed her keys from Daneen's desk. "He has no right to interfere in my life."

She stuffed the keys into her jeans pocket, nodded to Daneen and Alan and headed out the door. Where did he get off going behind her back, trying to get Pastor Alan to quit helping people she brought here? She'd put an end to this right now.

ᴥ

John pulled some tools from his truck and walked toward the work buildings. His mind churned like waves breaking against the sand. So Alan and Daneen had talked to her, too, about the hitchhikers. How stubborn could one woman be? Didn't she know the dangers—

Sharee entered his peripheral vision. He pretended not to notice. No way was he in a mood to talk with her. He altered his course and headed a different direction.

A minute later, though, she caught up with him, swung around in front of him and stopped square in his path.

"Where do you get off coming in and demanding that Pastor Alan do something that affects my life?"

"So, you were hiding in there?"

"I wasn't hiding. When Pastor Alan heard you come in—in a rage—he told me to stay where I was. And for your information, I have plenty of common sense. I don't pick up just anybody. I tried to tell you Monday that I knew Pedro from the homeless shelter, but you wouldn't listen."

"If he's homeless, I doubt you know him."

"I do know him. And if you're not willing to help people I bring here. Fine. I'm not asking you to help. Just don't try to stop me."

He gritted his teeth. "I'm trying to stop you from getting hurt—or worse. As for helping others, you misunderstood what I said."

"I don't think so." She met his glare. "Stay out of my life."

"Picking up hitchhikers is dangerous."

"Doing what God wants is not always safe and comfortable, you know. Sometimes it's hard or painful. Sometimes—" She stopped. Bit her lip.

The anger in her eyes changed as she looked at him, and her next words came so soft he had to strain to hear them. "Following God is not always about getting what we want."

His anger settled. The sudden urge to reach out and pull her to him shook him. He forced his arms to remain at his side.

She swallowed. "I'm sorry, I didn't tell you. I just..."

"You should have."

"I should have. You're right. But do you have to be so nasty about it?" Before he could reply, she recovered and jutted her jaw. "And stay away from my car. I don't need your help. I can take care of myself." She whirled and stalked to her CR-V.

He stood, staring after her, feeling the waves inside suck backward, a riptide cratering his stomach. Her car backed out and headed around the building toward the front.

His peripheral vision worked again, and he turned his head to see George descending on him. He noticed the man's clenched fists.

John shook his head and held up both hands. "She started it this time."

The next moment, pain shot through his jaw and up the side of his face. He fell backward and hit the ground. A broad expanse of sky stretched before his eyes.

✍

Sharee rolled over, caught a glimpse of the bedside clock and grabbed her phone. Seven in the morning. Another early caller. On a Saturday.

She looked at the caller ID. Daneen? "Hello?"

"Sharee? Sorry to wake you."

"It's okay. I needed to get up, anyway. What's up?"

"John called. He had to go out of town. A family problem. He said we should cancel the work day."

"Oh." Her brain flipped to planning mode. "I'll have to call everyone. A family problem, you say? I don't know anything about John's family. Is it serious?"

"Don't know. He said he'd call when he knew something. His mom and dad both live in Orlando, but they're divorced. The dad has a new wife."

"Oh. A couple hours' drive then."

"Yes. He got a call an hour or so ago and was already on the road when I talked with him. He took Alexis."

"Alexis?" Her chest squeezed.

"Yes. He asked me to call you and the others. He gave me the list of everyone that's come. I'm just going to text everybody. Is that okay with you?"

"Oh. Yes, that's great. Thank you."

"Let's pray for John and whatever this is and for Marci and her family, too."

"For Marci?" Her voice jumped. "Why?"

"The whole family has the flu. She called right after John. She planned on dropping Matthew off to help today, but he's sick, too. She asked if you could take her place in the nursery tomorrow."

"I haven't done the nursery for a while, but I can."

"I'll send Ryann to help you."

"That would be great." Sharee felt her heart tug. Marci and family sick. John on the way to Orlando. Ryann coming to work with the babies. "Okay. Let's pray."

Chapter 17

Sharee arrived early for nursery duty the next day. From one week to the next, things could change there. She'd need to put sheets on the cribs, find the diapers, put bags in the diaper pails and countless other things. Her key from Daneen fit a number of doors, including the nursery.

She stepped through the doorway, and her breath caught. A doll lay in the middle of the floor—throat cut, eyes gouged, red paint across the neck.

Lord, no. Not again.

A minute later, she twisted her head from right to left, examining every foot of the room. Nothing else seemed disturbed. She forced herself to look at the doll. The very neatness of the room underlined the violence done to it.

No way was she going to let the children see this. She stepped into the room and lifted the doll from the floor. Other thoughts came. Maybe I shouldn't touch it. Maybe I should call the police. She hesitated. Her mind told her to wait. Something needed checking first.

Still holding the doll, she stepped back into the hall and locked the door. She eased out the side door and headed for the work buildings. She arrived to find the door closed, but it opened with a turn of the knob.

Pale, morning light shifted from the trees through two small windows. John's tools hung above one work bench; Alan's lay scattered across the other. She went past them, trying to shrug off her tensed muscles. The quiet followed her, and she breathed a sigh of relief when she came to the bathroom.

She stepped inside, flicked on the light and was immediately assaulted by memories. Her chest squeezed. A week ago. Only a week. His amusement, his concern, his kiss. All gone. She forced her attention elsewhere, glancing at the top shelf of the closet.

Nothing. Her heart skipped. Where had they gone? What had he done with them? She shoved the one she carried under her arm and stood on tiptoe to reach in as far as she could. Her hand closed around a hard object, and she tried to yank it down.

"What are you doing here?"

Sharee jumped and spun around, one hand going to her throat. John stood behind her.

"Oh!" Her breath escaped in a long gasp. "John."

The relief passed when she looked at his face, noticing the bruise that spread from his mouth up the left side of his cheek. Remembering her words on Thursday, she dropped her eyes and felt heat climb into her cheeks. She'd lost her temper, just like him.

"What are you doing here?" The words came with less forcefulness but demanded an answer.

"I…uh…I…" She broke off and lifted the doll.

His brow creased. He reached up and pulled the other dolls down one by one, then glanced again at the one she held.

"Where did you get that?"

"On the nursery room floor. I found it a few minutes ago. I wanted to see if it was one of these."

"One of these? Why would you think that?"

"Well, because…" She stopped, not sure herself.

"Did you think I put it there?"

"What? No." Their eyes met, and the silence stretched between them. She could feel a vein beating in her temple. "No, I didn't. But someone left it. I thought maybe they took it from here."

"No one but you and Alan knows they're here."

"So, this is a different one."

"It's not different."

She frowned. "Why do you say that?"

"It's identical to the others. Look at them. The same type, style, everything. Even what's been done to the throat and eyes. They're all the same. Exactly like the one we bought from the dollar store." He held that one next to the one she held.

Sharee shuttered "You're right. They're all identical. But I meant this makes three. We have three different dolls, left at different times, in different places."

"You found that in the nursery?"

"Right in the middle of the floor."

"Here, give it to me." He took it from her hand, and put them all on the shelf, pushing them out of sight again. "Let's walk over there."

"Why?"

"I want to see where it was. I don't like this."

"Especially with the notes."

"There have been others?"

"Yes." She gave him a brief description of the last one.

He shook his head, and a line between his brows appeared. "Definitely harassment."

Turning, he led the way back through the building and held the door for her. When she stepped out, he locked it.

"I don't want anyone else in here, especially now. I should have locked it before, but I only left for a minute."

"You don't want anyone to find the dolls?"

"No."

They walked in silence. Sharee bit her lip and kept her head averted. When they reached the nursery, she unlocked the door.

He stepped into the doorway after her. "You locked it. Good."

Aware of his proximity, she moved forward into the room. He caught her arm, pulling her back. "No, wait. Let me look. Just point to where it was." He dropped her arm, and she pointed. His gaze moved over the room, even as hers had. "They had a key."

"I thought so, too. The windows are closed and locked, and the door over there is locked and chained. This is the only way in. They had to have a key."

"Who has access to the keys?"

"Anyone who has ever supervised the nursery, any of the youth..." She glanced up at him and trailed off. The depth of his eyes and his nearness made her heart ache.

When she stepped away this time, he didn't stop her. Instead, he stepped back into the hall, putting distance between them.

"I'll tell Alan about this." His voice came over his shoulder as he made his way down the hall. "I don't know what can be done. Changing the locks is a little late but may help for the future." He slowed and angled toward her. "Why are you here this morning?"

"Taking Marci's place. It's her turn to supervise, but the kids are sick."

He nodded and headed for the outside door once more.

"John."

He stopped and waited. Sharee moved to his side, tilting her head to look up at him. A muscle jumped in his jaw. It highlighted the bruise near his mouth. His breath sounded ragged.

"It was Marci's baby shower the first time, and then her car seat, and now this..." She paused. "And the notes. Shouldn't we call the police?"

"She and Stephen should." Quiet settled between them again.

She touched his arm. "What happened to your face?"

His brows drew together. Without answering, he turned, walked down the hall and out the door.

Chapter 18

Sharee groaned and stood up from her desk. Seven-thirty. That's all it was. The whole night loomed before her. She had worked late after saying goodbye to her last client, and even talked with Lynn and her parents for a while, but now she faced an empty and quiet apartment. She looked at her watch, sighed, and locked the doors to the ministry's offices.

Already, the day had proved difficult. She'd struggled to keep her focus on work. John's face floated uninvited across her memory numerous times. She climbed into her SUV and put her head on the steering wheel.

As she switched on the Honda's lights, her phone rang. She dug through her purse and pulled it out. "Hello?"

"Sharee, it's Pastor Alan. Are you home?"

"Just leaving work."

"Oh. Long day."

"Yes."

"Well, I hate to give you more to do, but could you stop by Marci's on the way home?"

"Of course. Why?"

"Stephen called. Someone left another of those dolls where Marci could find it, in the car seat again, but in the car this time. And this one had its head detached."

Sharee's stomach dropped. "No. Oh, no. How's Marci?"

"As you would imagine. Upset. It was one of the girls—Mary, I think—that found it. So, we have a whole other scenario now that the children are aware of it. I didn't realize they had no idea about the other times—the first one you found in the field and the one in the nursery yesterday."

"John told you about that?"

"Yes, and the notes."

"I was going to tell her about the others in a day or two, but she hadn't told Stephen about anything. I...I thought of showing up at their place and telling them both."

"Well, I took care of it for you. And I left a message for John. I think the police will want to talk with you both."

"Oh." Too many emotions accompanied that idea. "So they called the police?"

"Yes. As soon as Stephen saw it, he called them. Pretty gruesome from the way he described it. Eyes gouged like the rest, but the head cut off completely, left next to the body. Red painted around the neck and splashed over the doll."

"Oh, Alan, how horrible. And for Mary to find it."

"I'm out of town and can't make it back there tonight. Stephen said Marci could use some support."

"I'm on my way already."

"Listen, I need to hang-up and try to get in touch with John again. I left a message, but if he's working, he might not have checked it. I told Stephen to expect you."

"Did you ever talk with Abbey about that note John found? Should I say something?"

"I tried approaching Abbey on general issues at first, but she resisted anything personal. It was not the time, or I was not the person."

"All right."

"Pray about what you should say, but remember how big that family is and who all are around. Abbey is obviously having a hard time. We don't want to make it worse for her. And Sharee…"

"Yes?"

"We don't know for sure that she wrote that note. It wasn't signed."

"Yes, you're right. Pray for us, will you?"

"I will." He hung up.

The Sheriff's cruiser was parked in front when she pulled up at Marci's. Sharee parked behind it.

As she walked up the driveway, John's truck rounded the corner and pulled in behind her car. Sharee's heart began to pound. Not already. He'd obviously received Pastor Alan's first message. She continued up the driveway but listened to the truck door slam and John's footsteps move up the drive.

She stopped in front of the door. He stopped behind her. The quiet, uncomfortable and strained, tightened around them.

"Did you knock?"

Startled, she shook her head and rapped on the door, feeling the flush creep up her neck.

A minute later, Matthew opened it and waved them into the living area. Relief flowed over her. Anything but being alone with him. When she saw Marci's face, the other concern disappeared.

Marci jumped up and ran to her, "It happened again! Another doll in the car seat, and Mary found it. "

Sharee's arms went around her. "Oh, Marci. I'm so sorry."

"It's so horrible. Why would someone do this?"

"I don't know. Somebody's trying to upset you." She held onto Marci, feeling a deep shudder shake her friend's body.

Marci held on a little longer. When she pulled away, she cleared her throat and straightened her face. "I'm okay. I just…just don't understand this."

Stephen waved at two chairs, and Sharee's stomach tightened. John sat on one, she took the other. A Sheriff's deputy sat on the sofa. Sharee forced her attention to him. A little older than John, a little heavier, with hair brushed back from his forehead. Nice looking man, she told herself. Nice looking, but not John.

Stephen had taken an overstuffed chair near him. "This is Deputy Richards."

The deputy nodded.

Stephen leaned forward, looking from one to the other of them. "Pastor Alan said you and John found other dolls like these. Is that true?'

"Yes," Sharee answered. "One in the field the night of the baby shower and the other yesterday in the nursery."

"Why didn't you tell us?"

John shifted in the chair, his eyes caught Sharee's before returning to Stephen. "Cooper found the one in the field the night of the baby shower. Sharee showed it to me, but we didn't think much about it. At the time. Yesterday, when she found the one in the nursery that was a whole different story." His gaze slid Sharee's way again. "We also found one at the dollar store on US 19 exactly like the others—not disfigured, of course. It's an easy and cheap place to get them."

The deputy began to write in the book he held. "The dollar store? Where exactly?"

"On US 19 near Tampa Road. The store has another name, but it's one of the everything's-a-dollar type stores."

Marci took Stephen's hand. "I wish I knew who was doing this. And why."

John leaned forward. "I talked with someone last night—Alexis is a lawyer—and she had an idea. Maybe someone who can't have children feels resentful at the number of children you have."

Marci jumped to her feet. "You mean, someone's doing this because we have too many children?"

"It's only an idea."

Sharee twisted her head and stared at him. Alexis? He'd discussed this with Alexis? Sharp pain squeezed her chest. Well, why not? Why shouldn't he? He could discuss it with anyone he wanted.

At her movement, John shifted her way.

She averted her eyes, staring hard at the carpet. It doesn't matter, she told herself. Marci mattered right now. And Stephen. And the kids. Who would target them like this?

"Marci." Stephen caught her hand and pulled her down beside him. "We know there are people who don't like that fact that we have a big family."

"But to do something like this is crazy."

Sharee's heart squeezed at her friend's voice.

Deputy Richards shifted on the couch. His eyes focused on John. "You said you talked with someone about this. Do you have any idea who might be doing this?"

"No." The reply was quick.

The deputy's eyes narrowed, but he shifted his gaze to Sharee. "And you?"

She glanced at John. He'd said nothing about the note he found. She shook her head. "No."

He nodded and glanced back at John. "And who is Alexis? A lawyer? Why did you find it necessary to talk with her?"

Sharee dropped her head, trying to keep her face blank.

"Alexis is my sister. I wanted an outside opinion. Hers are good, so I discussed it with her. But she's from Atlanta, down here on vacation. She has nothing to do with this. After seeing the doll yesterday, I just wanted someone to bounce it off of."

The deputy flipped the paper in his small book. "I need your full name and address. A phone number also."

Sharee heard John's voice rumble, but she was staring at the carpet. *His sister?* Her mind reviewed the times she'd seen her. Twice? Three times? Had he ever mentioned it? She would have remembered. No wonder he acted so casual about the relationship, but why hadn't he told her?

A voice penetrated her consciousness, and she raised her head to see everyone staring at her. She blinked her eyes, trying to clear the mist from them, and hauled her mind back. John studied her face. So did the deputy. What had she missed?

"It's Sherry Jones?" the deputy questioned, obviously for the second time.

"It's Shar-ree," she answered, finding her voice, and spelled the name for him.

"Okay," He jotted it down. "Can I have an address and phone number?"

She gave it to him.

"You haven't said much. Do you have something to add?"

Sharee's look jumped from the deputy to John. Why hadn't he mentioned the note? She frowned then shook her head.

"But you found the doll yesterday?"

"Yes."

"Tell me about it."

She gave him a brief summary about finding the doll, going to look for the others, seeing John, and how they'd both concluded someone needed a key to the nursery to get in.

"You went straight to these work buildings, you say. To see if the other dolls were still there? You knew where John kept them?"

"I had seen them earlier."

"You saw them?" His eyes jumped from her to John and back. "That's how you knew where they were?"

"Yes."

"When was this?"

"The previous Sunday night."

"Was anyone else with you? Did anyone else see them?"

"No."

He nodded. "What time?"

"About 7:00."

The deputy's pen ceased moving. His eyes rose. "7:00 P.M.?"

"Yes."

"You have church services on Sunday night?"

She nodded.

"But you were in these work buildings?"

She nodded, a sudden uneasiness crept up her spine—as if she'd been caught doing something she shouldn't.

"Why?"

"Because..." She hesitated and tried to start again, pushing past the emotions that rose, past the memory of John's kiss. " Because...I...we..."

John cut across her. "I took her there to dry off. She fell into the pond. I keep towels and stuff there. There's a bathroom. The dolls were in the top of the closet, and she saw them. I put them there for safe keeping."

The deputy stared at him then angled back to Sharee. "Is that right?"

"Yes, that's correct. I did wonder why he'd kept them, but now I'm glad he did. You can see them for yourself."

The deputy nodded. "Yes, I'd like to see them." When he glanced at John, John gave a brief nod of assent. He turned to Sharee once more. "Are they all mutilated like the one found today?"

Out of the corner of her eye, Sharee noticed Marci's flinch. "I haven't seen that one, but similar." She glanced at Marci and then again at the deputy. "I think Marci could use a break, and the little ones need to be put to bed. If you don't mind?"

The deputy's blue eyes narrowed, but he gave an affirmative nod.

Gratitude spread across Marci's face. "Yes, the older ones are watching the younger ones. I do need to put the little ones to bed. And talk with Mary. She was upset when she found the doll even if she answered all the questions you asked." The last sentence was thrown at the deputy as Marci stood and started across the room.

Sharee stood, too. "I'll help."

Marci and Sharee made their way to the other side of the house. The interplay of male voices followed them down the hall.

Fifteen minutes later, Sharee returned to the living area. Her eyes focused on the deputy. "Marci wants to spend some extra time with the children unless you need her." He gave one of his quick nods, and she turned to Stephen. "The little ones are in bed. All except Joshua. Mary's taking care of him."

Stephen's smile held warmth. "Thank you for coming over. Marci needed it, even for a short while." He shifted toward the deputy. "I hope you can find who's doing this."

"We'll do what we can." He turned to John. "Can I pick those dolls up tomorrow?"

"Yes. I'll be at the church all day."

Sharee slipped her hands into the pocket of her jeans, feeling for her keys and phone. If she could leave, she wouldn't have to sit next to John again. Now that she'd seen Marci and answered Deputy Richard's questions... She caught the man's gaze.

"May I leave?"

His inspection unsettled her. "Yes, but I'll walk you to your car. I have a couple more questions."

Her stomach tightened. What other questions could he have?

She focused on Stephen, "You know if you need me, if Marci needs me, I'm available. Please call."

"We will. I promise."

Sharee gave him a weak smile, wishing she could do more. She turned toward the front door and reached for the knob. Deputy Richard's hand moved past hers and opened it. She jerked her head his way. How fast could the man move?

They walked to her car. The tension across her shoulders caused an ache on each side of her head. The streetlight spread yellow light across the cars and the grass.

"You have more questions?"

"Yes. How long have you known Marci Thornton?"

"About eight years. That's when I joined the church."

"What is your relationship with her? Are you good friends?"

"Yes."

"And how long have you known John Jergenson?"

"John?"

The deputy's head dipped, but he said nothing.

"About two years."

"What is your relationship with him?"

"Why?" The question slipped from her mouth. "What has that got to do with anything?"

He studied her. "You tell me."

"I don't see…"

"Would you lie for him?"

"What?" She stared.

"Or perhaps keep something back?"

"No, I…of course not. I…" No wonder she'd felt unsettled. The deputy had honed in on the uneasiness between her and John.

When she said nothing else, he went on, "His dog found that first doll?"

"Yes."

"Where was John when the second one was found?"

"With me. We were jogging."

"Did he go anywhere before you started jogging?"

"No, I, well, he went to put his tools away. Why? What are you suggesting?"

"Am I suggesting something?"

"No. Well, yes, I think you are, but it's ridiculous."

"Why?"

"Because what reason would John have to do something like this? This is a kid's prank. Nothing more."

"Are you sure?"

"What else could it be? Someone's trying to upset Marci."

"Why?"

"Because she has too many children."

"And that's all it is?"

"What else could it be?"

"You tell me."

Sharee shook her head.

"Doesn't John have keys to all the buildings and all the doors at the church?"

"Yes, but that doesn't mean anything. So does the pastor."

"Hmm." His eyes studied her face. Sharee shifted under his gaze.

"Just a thought." He reached across and opened the car door.

She climbed in, and he leaned down at the window. "We can only hope that you're right, and these are pranks. If you think of anything else, or if there's something you need to tell me, please call. We wouldn't want anything to happen to that baby."

Sharee took a deep breath. "No, we don't."

He stepped away from the SUV. Behind them, a door slammed. The deputy's quick movement, his hand shifting to his gun, sent a jolt through her. She glanced in her rearview mirror.

John sat in his truck. Their gazes met for an instant before he started the truck. He went by them with just a nod.

Chapter 19

George, Pedro, and John passed the fellowship hall's kitchen window. Sharee craned her head, keeping them in view. They settled into work, talking and laughing.

"What are you watching?" Lynn stepped next to her.

Sharee jumped. She drew her hands from the soapy water. Their early morning congratulatory breakfast for the volunteers had gone well, and she and Lynn had almost finished the clean-up.

"Oh. No one really. Why is it that men can fight, and, the next thing you know, they're best friends?"

Lynn had enlightened her earlier—in exquisite detail— about John and George's altercation.

"It was one punch, Lynn." Sharee had pointed out. "You act like it was a championship fight or something."

"Two men fighting over you, girl. You gotta love it."

"You don't know for sure."

"I'm sure."

"Well, *I'm sure* John didn't see it coming, or there would have been a real fight."

Lynn had raised her brows, laughed and walked away.

Sharee frowned at the men outside the window now. "Women fight, and it lasts for years."

Lynn leaned forward and stared past her. "Are you upset about it or what?"

"I just want to know how it works is all."

"That I can't tell you. But the next time we get mad at each other, I'll punch you, and we'll see what happens."

Sharee managed a smile. "Yeah. Try that one. We'll see what happens all right."

"Did you know John allowed Pedro to move in with him for a few weeks and is helping him look for permanent work?"

Sharee twisted from the sink, suds and water running down her hands. "What?"

"Hey! I'll have to mop the floor again." Lynn met her look, shoving her back to the sink. "You sound surprised."

"I guess I am. Miracles do happen."

"Woo, Sharee. Snide remark. Not like you at all."

Sharee shrugged but looked toward heaven. *Sorry, Lord.* She dried her hands and clipped her watch back on her wrist. "Come on, let's go. Work outside is calling."

"Work is always calling around here lately."

Sharee waved her hand. "Quit complaining. We're almost through. Let's go."

"Slave driver."

Sharee sent her a smile and slipped out the door. She walked the edges of the field, noting the areas John had marked off. He had each set and each group of workers under control. Between the two of them, she was the superfluous one. John could do this without her. In fact, no group seemed to need her today.

Shrugging off discouragement, she returned to the fellowship hall as Lynn exited, went through the sanctuary to the storage room. She grabbed an ancient boom box she'd seen earlier and an extension cord. Time to experiment. If she had the sound system up on the platform, would the sound carry over the field as she thought? Would they need extra speakers?

She tucked both items under her arms and retraced her steps. When she entered the kitchen, she halted. John, his back to her, was pouring coffee into a tall mug. He added sugar and creamer to it, moving in slow motion, as if fatigue claimed every move. He turned from the counter and stopped just as she had.

Silence hovered, dropped, stretched. After a moment, she unlocked her legs and headed for the door.

"George said you wanted another manger."

Sharee hefted the extension cord to her other arm and angled back toward him. "I...yes. Well, Marci does. She wants somewhere to put Joshua at the end of the program, behind the wall as she shares with the audience about Jesus."

"You don't need to explain."

"I want you to understand why she's asking."

"I'm following orders. Whatever you need. Sam will start it."

Following orders. That's all he was doing. No give and take. No teasing. She swallowed the pain. Only if God moved on people's hearts would this be worthwhile. She edged toward the door.

"How is Marci doing after Monday night?"

"She's okay. Now that the shock's worn off."

"Good." He paused, inspecting her. "You seemed upset."

"No, I was...I'm fine." Biggest lie of all. She dropped her head, but the question that had plagued her all week caused her to raise it, to meet his eyes. "Why didn't you tell me that Alexis was your sister?"

"What?" His brow crinkled. "Alexis?"

"Yes."

"You didn't know?"

"How would I know?"

"Alan didn't tell you?"

"No, he didn't."

"I assumed..." A frown and a pause. He appeared to digest the information. "It bothered you?"

She opened her mouth but closed it again. It didn't matter. Not now. She looked away. Why had she asked?

"What did the deputy want?"

His change of subject threw her. "The deputy?"

"Yes. He had more questions for you?"

"Oh. Yes."

"What kind?"

The boom box and extension cord cut into her arms. She moved and set them on the back counter. Removing her watch, she rubbed her arm where the box had dug into her skin. "Nothing in particular."

"He just wanted to walk you to your car?"

She couldn't identify his tone. "He wanted to talk about—" She broke off. How could she tell him about the deputy's insinuations?

"About what?"

"Nothing." She made the word abrupt to end his questioning. *Please, Lord, I just need to get out of here.*

"You don't want to tell me?"

"No."

He said something under his breath and put his cup down on the counter. "Why are you being difficult?"

"Me?" She stared at him, mouth agape. "You're the one who's been difficult."

"We have to work together. It might be hard, but we can be civil."

"Civil? You want to be civil? Wow. That's new."

His mouth drew into a thin line. "We need to get along. At least, until this project is finished."

"Okay." She forced the word, a kaleidoscope of emotions tumbling inside. Tears threatened. "Fine. Be civil. Fine."

She whipped around, looking for the door, and fumbled with her watch. It slipped through her fingers, clattering to the floor. She turned back, stooped and snatched it up, coming within a foot of him.

"It's too much for you to be civil?" The flat evenness of his voice had changed, and his next words matched hers in tone. "You've decided what you wanted, and you've got it, haven't you? So, what's your problem? You should be feeling pretty good about yourself right now."

She caught her breath. The watch dropped from her fingers again, and she flung her hand at his face. He grabbed it. Their gazes locked. In another moment, she yanked free, whirled, and stomped out the door.

⁓

When the door slammed, John swung around and gripped the counter's edge. Well, he'd been civil all right. For about one minute. But then no one had pushed his buttons these last two years like she was doing now.

And she'd almost slapped him. A whisper of amusement slipped through him. Five-foot-two and in his face one day, trying to slap it the next.

He took a long breath, picturing her face. When he'd caught her hand, her whole body vibrated. With anger? Or with the same pain he felt?

Her words on Monday pierced deeper than she could imagine. A few years ago, people could count on him for help, to lend a hand, to be there when they needed it. But now... What could he say about his life now?

He'd invited the homeless man to stay at his condo to prove her assumptions wrong, to prove to himself that the anger he'd harbored for three years had not made a difference in who he was. But it had.

Pedro's struggle to survive, to fight his own weaknesses, to challenge society's idea of who he was slammed into John in a way he hadn't thought possible. Purpose in life had meant everything to him at one time. Pedro's purpose was just to survive. What was his these days?

He stared out the window, seeing nothing, fighting the thoughts that flooded him. He'd been fine until a few weeks ago. Sharee had caused the problem. He'd felt good working on the project. Felt good with her. Another whisper of amusement swept through. Definitely felt good holding her, kissing her.

His hands tightened on the counter's edge once more. She was so different from Janice. Body build, attitude and faith. Because of that, he hadn't thought she'd be a threat to the life he led these days, but almost everything about her attracted him—her excitement about the program, her warmth to him and to others, her commitment to what she believed, the wild hair, her mouth... He took a long breath.

And she felt the attraction, too. That knowledge cut like a double-edged sword. He clenched his jaw, chewed on the inside of his cheek, and thought about that.

When he picked up his coffee a moment later, he drank it and pondered the possibilities. As Alan had said, she'd made the right decision…according to what she knew…

No.

No. He wouldn't go there. He'd made the right decision in not telling her. He had lied to himself before, and to her, in thinking their relationship would work as is; but it wouldn't. Not unless he changed, and it would take a miracle for him to change.

He banged the cup down. She didn't need his baggage, anyway.

The air around him seemed to change, pressure made the atmosphere thick. His gaze shot upward.

"What? What do you want from me?"

But he didn't wait for an answer. He picked up her watch, tossed it onto the counter and went out the door.

Sharee waited an hour before going back, and, when she did, the fellowship hall was empty. She picked up her watch, the boom box and extension cord and headed toward the control tower. Did the platform have room for two or three people plus the needed equipment? She needed to get up there and see. If she kept her mind on the project and off John, perhaps she could keep her emotions under control.

Setting the boom box and extension cord on the bleachers, she eyed the distance from the platform to the fellowship hall. She needed a longer extension, but first she'd check out the platform.

At a noise behind her, she stepped aside. John, George, and Pedro passed and headed toward the platform. George and Pedro sent smiles and nods her way. John's eyes touched hers a brief instant and slid past. He and George climbed the ladder they'd propped against the side, and Pedro headed in the direction of John's truck.

Sharee's stomach dropped. Great. Now what am I going to do? Her eyes rested on John as he moved across the platform. Okay. I can be civil.

"Hey." She stopped at the bottom of the ladder. "I'm coming up."

George looked over the edge. "Be careful on the ladder."

She wrinkled her nose. "I've done ladders before."

John's voice, muffled, floated down to her. George laughed. Her peace evaporated. When John's head appeared over the edge, she stopped on the fourth rung and narrowed her eyes.

"Since you're so good with ladders, can you give Pedro a hand with the tools?"

The look she gave him would have melted steel, but he had moved out of sight. She edged down the ladder.

"Sharee."

She turned and glanced up.

His head appeared again. "Fasten the tool belt around your waist before you come up. It will stabilize your center of gravity."

She glared. Always full of advice. Pedro stepped next to her, slinging one tool belt over his shoulder. He handed one to her. His own hung around his waist.

She threw the belt over her shoulder as he had done and noted its heaviness. Well, that should weigh down my center of gravity. She paused another minute, braced herself, and mounted the ladder. At the top, the ladder just ended. They'd made no railing, and she could use one to climb onto the platform. *Great.* She'd need both hands to haul herself up.

John and George were working on the half wall at the other side. Well, she wasn't about to ask for help, anyway.

She yanked the tool belt from her shoulder and flung it onto the platform. Immediately, she rocked sideways. Heart jerking, she scrambled to right herself. Shoving her feet against the inside of the ladder, she grabbed at the platform's edge. Her fingers scraped for a hold but found none. She teetered and gasped.

Both men whirled, then jumped for her. Too late. As their hands shot out, hers flew up in the air, whirling wide; and she fell.

Her mind stammered in disbelief. Instantaneous impressions followed— the sensation of falling, the thought of her body's impact, despair for the Christmas program. All cut off as she slammed into something beneath her, something that gave way and collapsed. The impression of hands digging into her side, and a man's grunt and explosion of air melded together with a second impact. Her head flew back and pain slammed across her body. The hands fell away, blackness shadowed the edges of her vision, and then the sky above her closed.

Chapter 20

Her eyes opened. The blue expanse above moved and shifted. She tried to swallow, to breathe, but her body didn't respond. Her heart jerked. She struggled to sit up but her body again ignored her command. Beneath her, something that was jammed into her back shifted. A spate of Spanish words buffeted the air. Hands fumbled at her waist, took hold, and moved her aside, flat on the ground. The pain eased.

"Estas bien…Sherry?" Pedro wheezed.

She could not talk or breathe. She flapped her hands, staring at Pedro, eyes pleading for his help.

The sound of pounding feet came through the ground. Excited words circled her. Lynn's voice, high and startled, broke through the others. People crowded close. She lost Pedro's face and shoved her hands to her throat, trying to swallow again, to breathe. John pushed aside the others and leaned over her. George shoved in behind him, his face sharp with anxiety.

"*Sharee?*" John's voice sounded strange.

She curled her hands to her chest.

"Don't move, Sharee." Lynn dropped down next to her. A sea of legs surrounded them.

"*You're chest?*" His eyes had caught her movement.

"She's had the breath knocked out of her, I bet." George's voice came from over their heads.

Sharee heard the words and choked. Air expanded her chest slightly. *Thank you, God.*

Ryann leaned forward. "I'll get Pastor Alan and Daneen. She's a nurse." Her head disappeared from Sharee's gaze.

Someone asked Pedro a question. She heard an affirmative reply and concentrated on drawing in air and pushing down the panic. Faces swirled in front of her.

"Sharee." John's face appeared again. "Can you speak?" Her hand made its way to her throat. "No? Can you breathe? Are you hurting someplace?"

She caught a quick breath and saw him hear it.

"Good." He glanced up. "Did someone call 911?"

Sharee grabbed his arm and shook her head.

He frowned. "You have no idea how badly you might be hurt."

Lynn bent forward. "She could be okay."

"I think we need the paramedics here." He pulled its phone from its holder.

Sam put a hand on his arm. "Pedro caught her. Broke her fall."

John darted a startled look past her to Pedro. "You caught her?"

Pedro pulled himself to a sitting position and gave a lopsided grin. "Si`."

"You're okay? Como estas`?"

"Bien."

John nodded and turned back to Sharee. "Are you in pain anywhere? Any sharp pain?"

She tried to push up. "No."

"Wait." John touched her shoulder. "Don't be in a hurry. Try moving your feet, your legs first."

"Do as he says, Sharee. Give yourself a minute." Lynn touched her hand. "You should have seen Pedro leap down from that ladder and catch you!"

Sharee turned her head snail-speed again and gave Pedro a lopsided smile. "Gracias…Pedro."

His glance at Sharee showed apology. "I feel like I caught a ton of bricks."

Patchy laughter followed, and the tension eased.

John's frown returned as she pushed upward again. His hand caught her arm and helped her to an upright position. "Just sit for a moment. Make sure you're okay." He slipped his phone back in its holster and sat next to her.

Pastor Alan and Daneen pushed through the crowd.

"Sharee?" Daneen knelt beside her. "How are you?"

"I think I'm okay."

"Pedro?"

"Bien, bien."

"Pedro broke my fall. He caught me."

"Thank God. Anything hurt?"

"Just sore."

Pedro climbed to his feet. Sharee looked up at him and took the hand he held out to her. John stood and put a hand out too. She took both and let them draw her to her feet. Everyone clapped.

"Pedro's the hero of the day," someone said.

"Yea, he is."

John's arm slipped around her. "Your face is pale."

"I'm okay."

"You could have been badly injured."

"I should have listened to you. I'm too stubborn."

"No, I should have had a railing up there. Something for you to hold on to."

"It was my fault."

His mouth curled. "Let's argue about it, shall we?"

She tilted her head back, and her heart slammed at the warmth she saw in his eyes.

"Both of you," Daneen said and pointed first at Sharee then at Pedro, "come to the office for a while and just sit. Please. I want to make sure you're okay. I don't want anyone fainting out here."

Sharee looked her way. "No one's going to faint."

"You never know about Pedro," George put in with amusement.

People laughed. Daneen put her hand out and caught Sharee's and pulled her to her side, heading toward the office. The group broke apart to let them pass. Pedro and Pastor Alan followed.

John stared after them. The volunteers drifted back to their projects.

My hand is not shortened that I cannot save.

His eyes rose. The verse had popped into his head with such force it seemed audible.

"Thank you." Gratefulness washed through him. But when he lifted his gaze again, he sighed. "That is why I don't understand. Where were you before?"

Where were you when I made the worlds?

John shook his head. God's words to Job were the same as God's words to him now. Whether or not they came directly from God or out of the recesses of John's memory, the question still stood. Who am I to question?

Another moment passed and familiar anger surged through him. *I'm your child.*

His hands clenched. The feelings he'd felt while he scrambled down the ladder surged over him again. He hadn't seen, hadn't known that Pedro caught her. A miracle.

The thought stopped him. Pedro had caught her. He recognized the irony, after railing against Sharee for picking him up and against Alan for giving him a job.

His eyes looked upward a third time. *You do it good when you do it.*

John stood in the middle of the field. People talked and laughed once again, but around him, everything stilled. Silence settled as if he stood on the planet alone. Minutes passed. The communication went deep into his soul.

Pressure built inside him. His resistance made a wall, but the pressure robbed him of breath. *What do you want from me?* But he heard nothing, just the pressure inside slowly filling him.

"All right!" The words exploded from him. "Okay. All right. For now."

Feeling release, he turned and strode across the field to the office. He yanked the door open. His glance swept the room and found Sharee. Her head moved in his direction, her face white, her eyes large and dark against her skin. She looked fragile and delicate. The leap of his heart caught him off guard.

"She's okay," Pastor Alan said. "They both are. God is good."

John forced his attention to Pedro. "Pedro? You're doing well?"

The man smiled. "I'm okay, except I'm getting restless with the Pastor's wife making me sit here when I need to be working."

"Some people would take advantage of that."

"I need to work," he said. "I'm not getting paid to sit here."

Sharee stood. "He's right. We've got a lot to do yet."

John tried to control the frown that rose at her words. Would she ever learn to take of herself? "Sharee, sit out a while. You don't need to..." He saw her face change, her body stiffen and he broke off. Stubborn would fit her as a middle name.

"I'm fine. I'm going back to work."

"Well, stay off the ladder until I get a railing up there."

"I'll be careful."

"Careful?" Did she think he'd let her go up there again without making the platform safe? "No one's going up there until George and I have a railing in place."

Sharee glared at him, the frail look vanishing.

"That's only common sense after what just happened."

Her eyes widened, and she pushed past him out the door. He raised his brows, and then the words he'd used hit him. He went after her.

"Sharee." He knew she heard him, but she continued walking. "Sharee, come on." Obviously, references to her common sense had the same effect as references to her height. He struggled with his laughter. "It wasn't meant the way it sounded."

She rounded on him. "Don't laugh at me."

At her look, he swallowed the amusement. "If I'd put a railing up there, you wouldn't have fallen. You can't expect me to let you or anyone else go back up there until I've done that."

She started walking again. When she reached the parking lot, he caught her arm. She whirled to face him, trying to free herself; but he caught the other arm, too.

He just wanted her safe, off the platform until he fixed the problem. "Listen, will you? If anything had happened to you, it would have been my fault. I don't want to live with that." He paused, washed with memory. "You have no idea what that's like."

Her jaw tightened.

"Come on." He tried coaxing her. "You know it makes sense."

"All right. Just don't treat me like...like..."

"Like what? Like I care?"

"No, that's not..."

"Because I think you know that." He dropped his hands, studying her. What would she say if he told her? He again felt the cold dread and disbelief as he scrambled down the ladder. The fear. He knew the tenuousness of life even if she didn't, the fact that it could be stolen from you in an instant. He had to try.

"I need to tell you something."

"What?"

"If you knew I had a relationship with Christ, would it make a difference?"

Her head rose, and her eyes widened. "Are you saying you do?"

"Yes."

"You do?" She straightened. "But when?"

"When I was seventeen."

"Seventeen?"

"Yes."

"You accepted Jesus at seventeen?"

"Yes."

Her head moved back. The brows furrowed. "But..."

"It was real."

"But...I don't understand. Why didn't you tell me?" Her voice climbed. "Why hide it?"

"I didn't hide it. I..." He stumbled, trying to find the right words.

"This doesn't make sense."

"Let me explain."

She leaned away from him. "You pretended not to be a Christian?"

"I didn't pretend."

"Then you're not a Christian."

"No. I mean, yes, I am."

"So, you let me believe, everyone believe for two years..." She stepped back. A line appeared between her brows. "What are you playing at?"

His mind raced over the last few weeks, and he had a sudden, blinding awareness of how it might seem to her. "It's not what you're thinking."

"That you lied to me, to everyone?"

He flinched at her words. He'd always prided himself on telling the truth, and maybe that had caused the problem. His pride. He hadn't wanted anyone to know, hadn't wanted the questions or the judgment. And he hadn't seen omission the same as lying.

"You were so angry with me the other day. You didn't mention being a Christian then. And if you wanted to be together, you could have."

"No, I…"

She whirled and headed across the parking lot.

He caught her before she got to the other side and pulled her around. "Please. Listen to me. I told Alan that I wouldn't lie to you. That I wouldn't tell you I had a relationship with God when I wasn't talking to Him, when I didn't want to hear from Him."

"So you're talking to Him now?"

"No, that's not it, that's—"

"I didn't think so." She twisted away and headed in the direction of her car.

He followed. When she grabbed the door handle, he stabbed his hand against the door, holding it closed.

"Let go!"

"Sharee, listen."

"Get away from me."

"I accepted Christ after Alexis was raped."

She stilled. His arm dropped.

"I've never denied Christ," he spoke to her back. "I haven't lived for Him over the last few years, but I've never denied Him. Never denied what He did." Her back still faced him. "Let me explain. Please."

She made a slow circle and faced him. "All right. Go ahead." Her arms crossed over her chest.

He drew a long breath, glanced toward the field where a number of people had stopped work and were watching them. "Not now. Not here."

Hurt shone in her eyes. He reached for her, but she sidestepped his hand and straightened her shoulders.

"When you're ready to tell me." She moved past him, away from her car, away from him, back into the field.

How could he tell her? About Alexis? About Janice? Unexpected pain caught in his chest. Would he ever get past it? She accused him of hiding his faith. What would she think if he told her everything? Could he stand the accusation in her eyes then? His own was enough.

*

She'd never known how people could ruin a work of art until now. How they could slash a painting or topple a statue on purpose. Until now. Looking at the detailed scene John had drawn, all she wanted to do was toss the can of paint on it and walk away.

He had lied to her. And not just to her, but everyone. If what he said now was true, and how could she trust that?

She lifted the paint brush and made a deliberate stroke in the right place. She stood back and stared at the drawing. A few red splashes would just add color...

No.

She stuck the brush back into the paint, lifted it and drew it carefully across the line John had drawn. She filled in the areas according to the picture he'd taped in the corner. He told everyone to use their own creativity. The pictures were for inspiration only. His perfectionism did not mask a need to control.

Not like Dean's. Her dad had tried to warn her, but Dean's constant attention, constant smile and constant explanations had concealed a need to manipulate, to have power. She hadn't seen it until he hit her. Instead of scaring her back into submission, it woke her to his need to control.

No, John's actions were different. But deception was deception. What could he say that would change that? Her chest hurt.

Glancing around, she noticed that John had returned to work. Her painting stopped, and she studied him from a distance. *What was in his life, Lord, to deny you? To pretend he didn't know you? And where will we go from here?* Her hand closed over another small can of paint. She dipped the brush again.

When a car horn honked later, she put the paint can down and massaged her shoulders. The tightness through them and her neck imitated the stitching on a football. Marci waved to her from the parking lot. Sharee put down the brush and the can, glad for a reprieve. Some other workers waved as they headed in, and she glanced at her watch. Four o'clock already. Quitting time.

Joshua gurgled in the back seat. His bright eyes focused on her, and a toothless grin appeared. The tension lifted. She leaned through the car's window and ran a finger over his bare feet. He kicked and grinned more.

"His skin is so soft, Marci."

"Baby soft with baby smells."

"When do I get to babysit?"

"You really want to?"

"You know I do. Some night when you and Stephen can get out. As long as I can get him away from the girls."

Marci laughed. "That might be a problem."

Roseanne waved as she passed them and headed for her van.

Sharee nodded in Roseanne's direction. "She's been out here each Saturday, and now she wants to act in part of the drama."

"Well, I'm glad she's here." Marci reached into the back seat and gave Joshua a teether toy. "She moved here after a nasty divorce and knows no one. I think she's lonely."

Sharee watched Roseanne climb into her van and head out the back drive. "Hmm. Well, it's good she's joined in. We need the help. But changing the subject, how are you doing?"

"Better. I panicked the other day, but I'm not going to let this throw me. If someone is resentful of the number of children I have, I can't help that."

"Good for you. I'm glad to hear it. Are you here to pick up Matt?"

"Yes. And Ryann."

"I think they went to clean up, which is what I need to do, too." She waved and strolled back to the field.

Her board stood alone. The others, along with the volunteers, were gone. Sharee pounded the lids on her paint cans and headed in. Boy, they'd exited the scene like locusts cleaning the countryside. Ryann, Matthew, and Abbey came out as she went in. Ryann gave her a wink.

When she returned to the parking lot, Marci waved and drove past her, Matthew and Ryann sat in the back with Joshua. Abbey pulled away in her own car, and a couple of cars followed hers. George, Sam, and Pedro left in George's truck.

John's truck bucked to a stop near her board. He climbed down and lifted it into the truck bed. The muscles across her shoulders bunched once more. The reprieve hadn't lasted long. Suddenly, the explanation she wanted sent fingers of dread shooting through her.

She skirted the drive and headed for her CR-V.

The truck motor gunned and a moment later, he stopped the truck beside her. "Don't run off."

She turned. Her heart hit an erratic beat. "Why?"

"We need to talk."

"We've done that."

"All right. I need to talk."

"I...I've been thinking. Whatever your reason for this charade, I can't think it will...that it will make any difference. I..." How could she say it?

His eyes darkened. "You said you would listen."

She bit her lip. Her whole chest cavity ached. "John, I..."

He leaned across the cab and threw open the door. "Please."

Which was a word Dean had never used. She swallowed hard and nodded and climbed into the truck.

Chapter 21

They drove in silence to Howard Park. John parked on the causeway, climbed down and went to put money in a box. Sharee remembered the time when parking cost nothing. Now you had to pay for sunshine and sand. John put the ticket on the truck's windshield and slid back into the truck. Neither spoke.

She stared out her window. The sun's descent into the Gulf waters sent rays of pale blue throughout the apricot sky. And closer to the water's edge, shore birds fled the incoming waves only to turn and chase them back as they receded. The tide's give and take echoed her own life. Would there ever be a time of stability? A place where she could say, "Yes, this is where the Lord wants me, and this is the one the Lord wants me with?"

John cleared his throat and rested a hand on the steering wheel. "Are you feeling okay? Any repercussions from your fall?"

"No." She stared out the window still. Repercussions? The words he used sometimes threw her. Like his reference to literature at the deli. Not that she didn't think he was intelligent. Something just didn't fit. Her stomach tightened. Obviously, things didn't.

"I'm fine. A little sore and stiff, but okay."

"Amazing."

She turned his way, met his look. "Yes."

A muscle jumped in his jaw. Dark stubble covered his chin, the deep set eyes were shuttered. She said a silent prayer before turning to watch a pair of kite surfers not far from shore. The wind filled the sails and flung the surfers across the gray waters.

He shifted his position. "Sharee, when you fell today…"

"And Pedro caught me."

"Yes, and Pedro caught you." The irony in his voice let her know he understood the significance. "God stepped out of heaven and did a miracle."

"I know."

"Do you?" He studied her and nodded. "Then you'll understand. It's why I said I'd give Him a second chance."

She stared. "You're giving God a second chance?" She tried to keep her voice level. How do you tell the God that made you, the God of all creation that you'll give Him a second chance?

"Yes." He let the quiet hover again. "And I would like a second chance, too. After I explain."

She hesitated. She couldn't promise that. No matter what her heart wanted. "We'll see."

He locked eyes with her but didn't argue. Instead, he turned and stared out the front windshield. "Alexis got her driver's license on her sixteenth birthday like so many other teens, only Mom and Dad had a banquet that night, so she wasn't supposed to use the car. She decided to take it for a spin, anyway. She wanted me to go, but I wouldn't. I'm a year older, and I didn't want to jeopardize *my* ability to use the car. So, she went...alone." He paused, and his mouth tightened. "I told her that when I drove it earlier, I had trouble starting it; but it started fine for her. Dad said later that it needed a new battery. He planned to get one the next day."

His head came back her way. Understanding went through her. A new battery. Like her own. His insistence about the battery, his frustration about it had something to do with his sister. Something had happened to his sister. Her stomach felt cold. Knowing what it was made his anger all the more understandable.

"Go on."

"When she didn't come back, I called her friends. Those I knew. No one had seen her. I went out looking and found the car. She'd gone to a hangout near school. Talked with some friends who had to leave, and when she finished her food and went to leave herself, the car wouldn't start. The place had emptied out while she'd played on her phone, but a man there offered to help. After they had the hood up, he grabbed her, covered her mouth and dragged her off into the woods." John's voice became harsh. His eyes met hers. "He stuffed something into her mouth and raped her. Not thirty yards away."

Sharee made an involuntary sound. His eyes shifted past her, and he stared out the window again.

"The man threatened to kill her. He had a knife. When he finished, though, she managed to pull the cloth out of her mouth and scream. She began to fight him. Dad had always told her that if someone was going to kill her anyway, she might as well fight and try to save herself." A glint of amusement came through the heaviness of his voice. "She's a mean fighter. I know. Anyway, the man panicked and ran."

"Thank God."

His eyes slid her way. "Yes. I felt that way later."

"You thought it was your fault." Her words whispered along with the wind.

A line appeared between his brows. His jaw tightened. "If I had been with her, it would not have happened."

"You can't blame yourself. The man…the man that did this, he's to blame. Did they ever catch him?"

"No." Above them, the cries of the gulls sounded again.

"How did you find her?"

"She found me. At least, when I got there and saw the car, she'd managed to get her clothes on—torn and dirty. The ice cream place had closed, and so she waited." The regret in his voice hurt her. "She said she knew I'd come."

Sharee touched him. Her fingers resting on his arm. "I'm sorry, John. I don't know what to say, except what a horrible thing…to have that happen to your sister."

"I was so angry. I needed answers. Someone managed to get me and Alexis to church. I found what I needed there. I found Christ."

"And Alexis?"

"Alexis has never quite recovered. The police investigation made it worse."

"Oh, no."

"It was invasive and embarrassing." His eyes narrowed. "And all detectives aren't compassionate or trained in how to interrogate a traumatized young woman. It's why she became a lawyer. To be an advocate for those who've been abused or assaulted. For all general purposes, Alexis hates men. And Jesus is a man."

Sharee groaned. "She's so beautiful and full of fire. I know it must hurt you to see that."

He said nothing, and she considered what he'd said. "But there's more, isn't there? If Alexis's rape drove you to God, then something else drove you away."

"Yes."

She waited.

"My wife died three years ago."

Sharee's mouth opened; nothing came out. *Wife? He'd been married? And his wife died. Oh, Lord.*

He made a motion with his hand that stopped her from saying anything. "We met right after college. She'd just become a Christian. Her excitement about Jesus made everything new again. I'd been saved for five years by then and felt close to God, but her enthusiasm re-ignited the passion." His words sounded strained. He paused and crossed his arms across his chest. "You asked once what I did before I came here. Well, Janice and I had slipped back into the world. We were enjoying ourselves, not really doing anything wrong, per se, and still going to church, but just not on the right course. Know what I mean?"

Sharee nodded.

"That had just hit home, and we began praying together again, asking God to bring us back to Him when she died. We had five years together."

Her heart dropped. Oh, Lord. "How…"

His eyes slipped away, focused on something past her. "We were flying in a small, single-engine plane along the coast, and the engine quit. Just quit. I couldn't do a thing. Janice died in the plane crash. In less than thirty feet of water."

"Oh, John…I…I'm sorry."

"I was the pilot."

Her head jerked. "You?"

A long pause. His gaze didn't shift. "Someone had given us the plane, an older one, and we were both excited about it and decided to take it up." He drew a breath. "They said later it was engine failure, not pilot error; but the truth is, I never should have flown it without a thorough preflight checkup. I did a cursory one."

His pain came in waves across the cab like a physical object that she could touch. "I'm so sorry, John."

"Nothing made sense then. Not God. Not my Christianity." His voice hardened. "If God is all knowing and all powerful, where was He?"

Oh, Lord, no wonder he's such a loner. He's hurt, Lord. Still guilty and hurt and angry. What can I say?

"Don't say anything."

Had he read her mind?

"Everyone said everything they could think of at the time. They thought they could help. They couldn't. People said it was a miracle I survived. Did they even know what they were saying? What about Janice? Didn't she deserve a miracle? I should have died, not her."

A moment later, he threw open his door. "Let's walk for a few minutes."

She climbed down on her side. He offered his hand. Startled, she put hers out, and they walked down to the water's edge, hand-in-hand. The waves rushed forward, washing the sand, lapping at their feet. The sun's glow had faded, and the water's rush and pull had slowed. Most of the birds were gone. The dark comma of a kite caught the wind and pulled the board and its passenger past them.

"I didn't tell anyone here." His words mixed with the wind, and she had to strain to hear them. "I asked Alan not to. I wanted to find someplace where I didn't have to talk about it, where I didn't have to look into the eyes of those who knew, and where I didn't have to hear the platitudes."

Another kite surfer went past, the sail's bold colors accenting the darkening sky. She shivered and scooted closer to him. He glanced down, hesitated, and put his arm around her.

"Sharee, I should have told you sooner. You had every right to know." He moved to catch her look. "When I kissed you that first time, I felt guilty."

"Guilty? Why?"

"Unfaithful."

"Unfaithful?" She didn't understand then clarity hit. "To your wife, you mean?" *After three years.*

"Yes. To Janice."

To Janice. He'd said the name before. *Lord...*

"You're a pilot?"

"I was. I gave it up. Haven't flown since." The muted rush and withdrawal of the waves echoed in his tone. "I couldn't believe how I felt that day. I knew it was ridiculous, but that didn't help. I couldn't deal with it. So, I blamed you."

"It's okay. I...it doesn't matter now." She fingered her watch. *After college. Five years together. Three years ago. He must be just a year or so older than she was. Yet, he seemed older. So, he'd come here—injured— seeking a place to hide.* Something stirred in her heart. *No, that was wrong. God brought him here to heal, whether he knew it or not.*

"John, I thought you'd never attended college. In the truck at McDonald's that day—"

"I made it sound that way, didn't I?" He shook his head. "Sorry. Carrying on the charade. Look, there's something else."

She flinched. More? Her head ached already. "What?"

He paused, studying her. "No. It can wait."

"Are you sure?"

"Yes."

She pushed windblown hair from her face. "I don't want to find out something later that I should know now."

He tilted his head, his eyes never leaving hers. "It can wait, but if you're not sure—"

"No, I'm fine. If you say so."

He caught her hand again and led the way back to the truck. When they settled inside, he rubbed warmth into her arms, his eyes locking into hers now as they hadn't before. "What are you thinking?"

"I don't know. Nothing, right now."

He dropped his hands and pulled out the key. "I should have told you before. Alan told me I should."

He cranked the truck, and they headed out of the park. The quiet settled again. Her mind raced over what he'd said. She understood now. This she could forgive.

But what about the new problem? The one she'd never foreseen or expected. *It sounded like John was still in love with his wife.*

Chapter 22

"Dad?" Had she woken him?

"Yes, honey." His voice came stronger now and with affection. "How are you doing?"

"Did I call too late?"

"Sharee, you can never call too late. We've told you that before."

"I know, but..." Being an only child had benefits. The open door policy—anytime, anywhere—counted as a major one.

"I take it this is not just a hello call."

He always knew. She threw off the embarrassment of asking advice at her age. She needed Godly counsel.

"That's a good guess. How's mom?"

"She's doing well, but she is in bed. Did you want to talk with her?"

"No, no. I wanted to talk with you."

He chuckled. "Not having trouble with the car anymore, I hope."

"No. Actually, I have a new battery."

"Good."

"A man put it in for me."

The slightest pause. "Somebody we know?"

"No."

"Somebody we'd want to know?"

She inhaled. "Somebody I think I want to know...better."

The hesitation, this time, was longer. For good reason. Last time had been hard on them, too. "Okay, honey. So, he knows something about cars. Do you want to tell me a little more about him?"

"Yes, I do."

He listened without interrupting to her abbreviated account of the Christmas program and John and what John had told her today.

When she finished, he said, "I have a few questions."

Of Course. "What are they?"

"You said he's angry with God about what happened to his wife?"

"Yes."

"That's a pretty normal response, but you were surprised by his marriage? You hadn't known?"

"No, I didn't know. He's never mentioned it, but he's been pretty much a loner since he came. And he's in his early thirties, so I guess it shouldn't be such a surprise." Her voice trailed off.

"It sounds like you're afraid you may get hurt."

Hard to admit. "Yes."

"Because he hasn't been open with you? Or because he hasn't had time to heal?"

"Both. It sounds selfish, doesn't it?"

"Or cautious. Sharee, he gave you a lot of information today. For a reason. He must care for you."

The same word John had used. "He says he does." She hesitated.

"Yes?"

How could she say what she felt? John's guilt and obvious distress over his wife's death in her mind translated to a deep love. And, right or wrong, that felt threatening. "He must have loved his wife very much."

"And that worries you?" Her dad took a long breath. "You can't be afraid to trust again, to take a chance; but you don't need to rush things either. This…John…has kept things from you, but we can both see why. You need to let God lead, honey. It's when we want our way more than his that we get into trouble. Take one step at a time. See what God says. And remember, as much as you don't want to get hurt, here is a man devastated by a tragedy he cannot understand. Give him some grace."

The words sunk into her with a feeling of revelation. *Give him some grace.* All I've done is think of myself. *Oh, Lord.*

After she had put down the phone, she bowed her head in prayer.

Now, as she pulled into the church parking lot, she felt God's peace. The day's brightness, the mid-seventies temperature and the weight lifted from her shoulders caused a smile inside. She walked quickly up the sidewalk, her skirt brushing against her legs, her heels tapping the concrete, and glanced at the main entrance.

John stood on the porch, his back to one of the pillars. He'd dressed in black slacks and a dark coffee-colored shirt that matched his hair. No tie. Someone had stopped to shake his hand, and she saw the gentle twist of his mouth. Other members of the congregation stopped also. Some talked and laughed, others just shook his hand.

A jolt went through her. He'd come to church. Her smile widened to a grin. It took courage to come and even more to stand outside while everyone entered.

Their eyes met, and her heart leaped at the warmth that entered his expression. The noise of her heels followed her when she mounted the steps and stopped in front of him. She tilted her head back. His look was deep and searching. After a moment, a smile started at the corner of his mouth, and he took her arm.

"I suppose that you sit down front?"

"Well, you're right there."

He groaned. "Not on the first row, I hope."

She laughed and steered him into the sanctuary, "Not quite."

Someone greeted him and then someone else. It took a few minutes to get to their seats.

Bruce stopped his wheelchair next to them. "Well, you do like to create a stir, don't you?"

John grimaced then let his mouth relax. "I suppose they've all been praying for me since I came."

Bruce laughed, "Yep, you've been on many prayer lists. With Miss Eleanor praying for you, though," he nodded toward a thin older woman sitting on the first row, "you didn't have a chance."

John returned Bruce's grin. "Yeah, I assumed she would be a problem. Little old ladies and their prayers are a powerful combination."

Bruce glanced at Sharee and leaned closer, "Well, to tell you the truth, you had double trouble with Sharee in the mix, too." He winked at her, turned his wheelchair around and moved off.

"Hey, Mr. J, glad to see ya!" One of the boys from the youth group passed and high-fived him.

Voices quieted while people found their seats. The music group mounted the platform. Sharee caught John's sideways glance. How did he feel? She put a hand on his arm.

He covered it with his. "You look nice. I like the dress and the heels." He leaned his head close to hers. "Makes you almost as tall as a normal person." The corners of his eyes crinkled.

Sharee scowled. "Just watch it." She sat up straighter, crossing her legs, trying to look indignant. "You might have to pay for that remark."

"I got off pretty easy at the deli."

"A mistake that won't be repeated. A weak moment on my part."

His mouth lifted. The music started, and they both stood.

Pastor Alan came through the side door to the platform. His gaze passed over the congregation and jumped back to John. He paused in mid-stride. The choir began to sing. He glanced at Sharee and winked.

"*Amazing grace, how sweet the sound...*" Sharee closed her eyes and thanked God for all He'd done and sent up a silent prayer for John.

She settled back in her chair after the worship time and felt John's hand encircle hers.

Pastor Alan stepped to the podium. "My talk today is entitled, 'Perfect Love Casts Out Fear.'"

Her fear had kept her from telling John the truth about dating. And look at the situation now. She inhaled deeply, let herself feel his hand on hers. If things could just stay this perfect...

I need this kind of love, Lord. Your love. Because at the back of my mind, I wonder if this can last. No other relationship has. Help me to trust you.

She turned her attention back to the pastor.

"Fear of others, of situations, of what people think, all those and more keep us from serving God in the way we should." Pastor Alan held up his Bible. "But the Word of God tells us that perfect love casts out fear. God wants us to understand and to know what is the breadth, length, depth, and height of His love for us. He loves you with an everlasting love. Think about it."

John squeezed her hand. "I'm going to leave when he closes in prayer. Come with me."

After a slight hesitation, she inclined her head. He wanted to leave—or escape—as soon as he could; so the fact that he'd come to church didn't indicate wholesale surrender to God. She bit her lip.

In a few minutes, when Pastor Alan asked everyone to bow their heads, she slipped out of her seat, alongside John, and walked to the back and out the door to the parking lot.

"What did you think?" Sharee asked.

John lifted a brow. "I'm glad I came, but don't expect too much, too soon. God and I are still making our way."

She nodded and lifted a quick prayer to heaven.

He cocked his head. "Alexis is driving back to Atlanta today. She's picking me up in a few minutes—for lunch. Come with us."

"I...uh...no, I can't."

"Does it have to do with Alexis? Does that still bother you?"

"Of course not." She bit her lip. It did, somehow.

He pulled on a curl near her cheek. "I'm sorry you didn't know. But if you were a little jealous..."

"I was not jealous!"

His smile stretched, and she punched his arm.

Ryann and Abbey passed them. Ryann waved. "Great to have you in church, Mr. J."

More people poured out of the church, filling the sidewalks and parking lot.

"Unexpected pleasure," Sharee said, sotto voce.

"Was it?" John's hand caught her arm and drew her close. "Change your mind then. Go with us."

"I can't, really. I promised Miss Eleanor that I would have lunch with her. She and Lynn and I have a Bible study afterward."

"Ah. Competition from an 85-year-old widow is new."

A black Jaguar pulled up next to them.

"Time to make my escape." John tugged her over to the car. "Let me introduce you." The driver's side window slid down. "Alexis, I want you to meet Sharee Jones, the slave driver who's created so much work for me and the other volunteers."

Sharee's mouth dropped open, and she snatched her arm free.

Alexis laughed. "Just ignore him. His teasing's over the top sometimes." She flicked John an amused grin. It showed a remarkable resemblance between the two.

John gave her a rueful smile and moved to the passenger side of the car. He glanced over the top at Sharee. "We should be finished with all the sets this weekend. You can begin planning rehearsals."

"Okay."

"I'll call you." He slipped into the car. Alexis waved, and they headed for the highway.

She watched the car disappear and wondered if he'd call tonight. Turning, she almost collided with Ted Hogan.

"So, you and John, huh? Who would have guessed?"

The unpleasantness in his voice caused her to take a step back.

"Real shocker seeing him in church. Thought he had a big problem with God. But since you two have something going, maybe that's not the case?"

Sharee felt her frown. Why did his comments bother her? "I'm not sure that's your concern, Ted."

"That's the exact point I wanted to make. It's not your concern or his to wonder what Marci and I were doing at the deli."

She'd forgotten about it. "Do you mean wondering about why you followed her there?"

He stepped closer, lowering his voice. "Marci has enough problems. She doesn't need you spreading any gossip. You got it?"

"Got what?" She wanted to say that Ted might be Marci's biggest problem but didn't. The man was intimidating.

"Don't spread any rumors. She's struggled with this pregnancy. She didn't want this baby. She's got enough to deal with."

"What do you mean, didn't want this pregnancy? She and Stephen are thrilled with Joshua."

Ted's face tightened. "Marci didn't want any more children. She told me that. She feels guilty about what happened."

"Guilty?"

A group of people filed by them.

"Hey, Sharee, good to see John this morning." Christy Byrd waved at her.

Sharee waved back.

Ted looked around then leaned toward her. "Just don't say anything about me and Marci, and I won't say anything about you and John in the tool building the other night."

"What are you talking about?"

"I saw you both go in, and later you came out in his clothes, and he was all over you at the car."

Sharee's eyes widened. He'd watched them? For how long? "Where do you—"

He gave a sharp bark of laughter. "You thought no one saw?"

"Your mind's in the gutter."

"Maybe it is, but—"

"Hey, girlfriend, what's up?" Lynn's voice cut across his.

"Nothing." Ted's mouth tightened. "Just remember what I said, Sharee." He walked away.

Lynn jerked her head Ted's way. "Everything okay?"

Sharee watched until Ted disappeared among the cars. "I'm not quite sure."

⁂

Two days later, she stretched back against her high-back chair at work, tilting her head from side to side and loosening her neck. Only Tuesday, she sighed. Today's work foreshadowed a long week. Her eyes moved across the desk to the clock. 4:30 P.M. She reached into a candy jar for a soft peppermint. Last night, she'd stayed late to finish; and, judging from the stack of papers on her desk now, it would be the same tonight.

When the phone rang, she groaned. The receptionist had left early for a dental appointment, and the other counselors had clients.

She lifted the receiver. "Downtown Ministries, Sharee speaking."

"Hey."

Just the one word, but her heart jumped. "Hey."

"I'm sure the Lucky Dill has free cheesecake tonight, but you have to order dinner and a drink to get it."

Her breath caught in her throat, and it took a second to respond. "Really? Are you trying to tempt me with free dessert?"

"Well, if you want two, this time, I guess I'll have to pay for it, but you'll owe me."

She sat up, biting back the first thing that came to mind. She hesitated.

"Sharee?"

"Y...yes?"

"I'll pick you up at your place around 7:00?" The words held a trace of uncertainty.

"All...right." Her voice caught between the words. *Stop it. Act your age.*

"Your cell phone?"

"Yes?"

"I need the number."

"Okay."

He waited a minute then laughed, "I've missed you, too."

"You are so arrogant." But her voice belied the words.

"Not where you're concerned." A slight pause. "Seven o'clock?"

"Yes."

"Good. See you then."

She heard the click on the other end and put down the phone. Strong, unexpected emotions washed over her. She jumped to her feet and did a quick dance. He had waited two days to call—two long days. She'd wondered about that last night. But she'd waited. He'd said he would call.

A minute later, she shook herself. He had wanted her phone number, and she'd been so...so spaced that she hadn't given it to him. No wonder he laughed.

She reached for a stack of papers, her energy renewed. So much for working late. Her mind raced, thinking of things she needed to do when she got home. *Bathe, wash her hair, change clothes... What would she wear?*

Chapter 23

Whoa. The word popped across his mind when she opened the door. The mass of auburn curls twisted and twirled around her face and dropped onto her shoulders. Her eyes seemed bigger and darker than usual, and the pink t-shirt, highlighted with a touch of lace, hugged her in a way he wouldn't mind imitating. The faint scent of her fragrance stroked him.

"Hi," she said.

He cleared his throat and reached out to stretch the curl by her cheek. "Hi. You look... delicious."

She smiled, but her eyes dropped. Just one compliment disconcerted her. "You're ready?"

"Yes. Let me get my purse."

He watched her walk to the end table, pick up her handbag, and turn his way. Something seemed different tonight, and it took a moment for him to understand it. The tautness that characterized their relationship in the preceding weeks had disappeared. A quick, inward response to that washed through him. Taking her hand, he led the way to the truck and helped her climb into the cab.

He'd used the right word. Climb. A step stool would have helped, but he knew she'd take his head off if he mentioned it. Teasing her about her height brought interesting reactions.

He started to close the door when she threw him a meaningful look. It hit home. The other times she'd climbed into his truck, she'd done it without his help.

"I'm not always a bully."

Her mouth stretched. "Glad to hear it."

The faint scent of her perfume stroked him once more, and the light in her eyes almost stripped his control. He hesitated, feeling again the desire to wrap her in his arms. *No. Later.* He closed the door.

The deli contained fewer people than usual, and the noise level followed the numbers. Conversation would be easier, and that seemed important. Saturday's ups and downs needed to be erased, and her trust in him re-established. Although the welcome in her eyes when she opened the door had told him a lot.

The waitress sat them in a back section at a small table. John ordered a Greek salad, Matzo Ball soup, and roast beef with Swiss on rye then listened with attention to Sharee's order of comfort food—a Blue-Plate special of meatloaf, mashed potatoes, salad, and rolls. They both decided on the pumpkin cheesecake for dessert.

After the waitress left, he pointed to the basket on the table, offering her a second brown knot. Two had disappeared soon after the basket appeared.

"Your turn." He indicated the soft roll.

As she reached for it, however, he caught her hand and turned it over, drawing his thumb across her palm. She tried to pull away, but he tightened his grip. The color started on her neck, spreading upward; and he shook his head, giving her hand a squeeze and letting go.

"You blush easily." He reached into the basket, took the brown knot, and handed it to her. "I'll be good." He forced his mind from the things he wanted to say and asked himself what would be important to her. "How's work coming?"

She took a moment before she answered. "It's coming. We're busy."

"Why?" When she said nothing, he added with a grin, "Not an idle question. I might want a second date."

She looked down again but then back at him. "Some people don't think the work I do—with the homeless—is important work."

He'd been right about the defiance. "Why is that?"

"Because there're so many differing opinions on the homeless. Why they're homeless, and what to do about it. *Everybody* has an opinion, but not many people want to help."

He nodded, taking the half roll she'd broken off and handed him.

"I just feel it's what God has called me to right now. I don't know all the why's, and I don't have all the answers for the people I see, but I have to do something."

"So you said before. That's your gift. Mercy."

She looked startled. "Mercy?"

"Does that surprise you? Mercy is a wonderful gift—to receive or to give."

"So many people think we should be tough. You know, tough love and all that."

"They think that the homeless should help themselves, and you shouldn't interfere?"

"Yeah, something like that. As I said, there are many differing opinions. You hear some of them louder and more often than others."

"It shouldn't matter, you know, what other people think. It only matters that you're doing what you feel God told you to do." He caught her look and sat back, giving a mocking smile. "That from me? Well, it's true."

They ate in silence for a few minutes then he leaned over. "Sharee, I think what you do with the homeless is wonderful. The fact that I did not want you picking up hitchhikers has nothing to do with helping people. There just must be some other way."

She said nothing.

"You think that I don't care about others?"

She bit her lip. "You were so impatient that day. About Pedro. It surprised me when I heard you'd asked him to stay at your place. And you do have a work ethic."

"A work ethic?"

"Yes."

"Hmm. Never thought about it."

"I believe in work, too. It's not that at all. It's that I also believe in helping others. A lot of people don't think the two are compatible."

The waitress came and set down their plates, bringing more sweet tea and water, asking if they needed anything else.

"No. Thank you." John surveyed Sharee's plate with a smile. "So, the last two days have been hard?"

"Yes, they have."

He hesitated a minute. "You say a blessing when you're out?"

"It's okay. I say my own silently."

He watched her bow her head. Had she prayed last time? If so, he hadn't noticed.

In a few seconds, she raised her head. "I included you. By the way, how's Pedro doing?" Without waiting for a reply, she lifted her fork. "I don't do this all the time, you know. Usually, I'm a pretty healthy eater, but today...."

He stopped in the middle of picking up his sandwich and sat back. His glance went over her food again. "Meatloaf, mashed potatoes, fried chicken, apple pie, and what else?"

"For comfort food? Oh, I would include spaghetti and meatballs, too. Strawberry shortcake, homemade biscuits." She tilted her head, and he felt her scrutiny. "How's Pedro?"

"You want to finish eating first?"

She put down her fork and shook her head. He'd seen the questioning look. He wasn't going to be able to get around it.

"I had hoped by this weekend to have something better to say."

"So tell me."

"He never came home last Saturday. He went to George's to eat, and then he asked George to take him to see some friends. He wanted to tell them...how he saved you, how he caught you. George thought that was okay, but we haven't seen him since. It's why I didn't call yesterday. We went looking for him, went to the friend's home." He stopped, watching her, wondering how she would take it.

"John." Her face and tone changed. She straightened. "I do this for a living, remember? Have been doing it for years. I know Pedro—even if you think I don't. I know the problems he deals with—mostly. Is he drinking again?"

Revelation hit him. Her tone and demeanor showed a professionalism that echoed even in the way she held herself. And she didn't seem as surprised or devastated as he'd expected.

"Yes. According to his friends, he was so proud of himself that he had to have a drink. And that led to others. They haven't seen him since."

"He's on the street somewhere."

He saw her concern; and she bowed her head, offering a short, soft prayer for him.

Her eyes came back to his. "You gave him a place to stay and helped him look for a permanent job. That's much more than most people do."

"I don't think I could have done anything else after you blasted me." His smile took the sting out of the words. "I guess I'm not used to thinking of myself as uncaring or having others think it or say it so bluntly. A lot has changed in three years…since Janice died."

"John, I'm sorry about the things I said. I lost my temper."

"I guess I needed it." A regretful smile. "About Pedro. I really began to like him. I must say, I don't understand. Things were going well for him. He'd cleaned himself up, had gone out a number of times to look for a job. He had food when he came home."

"It's not your fault, you know. You did the best thing for him—food, a place to stay and a chance to get clean. It's up to him to do the rest. I believe in mercy. I just said that. I also know a time comes when it's up to them or, in this case, *him*. We can't make Pedro's decisions for him or for any of the others. We can point the way, encourage them, give them all the tools they need to make the right choices; but they have to do it themselves—and continue to do it. Just as we do. Pedro did it for a week or so. Maybe next time, he'll do it longer."

He shifted back in the chair. She did know what she was doing. The girl's life radiated contradictions—professionalism in her work, strength in her faith, and both those intertwined with a personal vulnerability that left him wanting to protect her.

He let the smile move to his eyes. "Eat your comfort food before I get up and come over there and kiss you. In front of everyone."

"Don't you dare." Sharee dropped her eyes from his and snatched up her fork.

Later, he took her hand as they left the building. The temperature outside had dropped. Thanksgiving and Christmas advertisements winked at them.

His reaction to her differed in many ways to those he'd had with Janice. Janice's physical height and strength along with her outgoing, Type A personality had allowed him to watch—with love and amusement—from the sidelines as she made her way through life. When she stumbled in her relationships (and that often happened with her take charge character), she'd bring her confusion and hurt to him; and he'd give her any wisdom he had then point her back to Christ. They'd had a good marriage. He'd never needed or wanted a subservient wife.

But something had changed when Janice died. Her death, along with the feeling of helplessness that engulfed him, had destroyed his attitude of invulnerability. Life had a different feel to it now. He admired Sharee's faith, had admired it, he realized, for some time. He respected the strength it gave her. But the protectiveness that rose in him, that need to shield and guard, those were new attitudes to him. And her crazy lifestyle and seeming carelessness about her own safety didn't help.

He offered his hand as she stepped up into the truck. "Next week's Thanksgiving. You're going home?"

"Yes. For the week."

"The week?" Surprise. He backed the truck out and slid a glance her way.

"Yes. What about you?"

"I'll go Thanksgiving Day. Maybe stay overnight." A moment later, he added, "For the first time in three years. I just couldn't do Thanksgiving when Janice died. I made Christmas, but juggling between two families and trying to cope with the loss… Well, some things were easier being away."

"They'll be glad, then, that you're making it this year?"

"Neither of my parents is real big on the holidays, but yes, I think they will."

"John?"

"Yes?"

"If some tragedy happened in my life, my parents would be the first people I would run to. I certainly would be with them through the holidays."

"I understand. You're close." The sounds of the highway filled the truck. "We were, too, growing up. After Alexis and I went to college, things seemed to fall apart. Dad had an affair. The divorce came soon after. And the remarriage a couple years after that." He leaned forward to turn on the heater. "Not something I ever want to go through again or put my children through—no matter what their age."

Sharee inclined her head, and they rode in silence for a while.

"You do the whole Thanksgiving thing?" he asked.

"Turkey and dressing and lots of family? Yes. And a game of tag football afterward. What about you?"

"Different. We'll go out to eat unless one of my mother's sisters decides to do the traditional thing. We'll go over to her house if so."

"Are you making fun of me?"

He shook his head. "No. I'm the black sheep in the family. I like tradition. My parents always liked doing something different—some kind of wilderness trip that we'd all take. Alexis is the same these days."

"Oh."

"Do you need a whole week to celebrate Thanksgiving?"

"I guess not, but I always go home. Why?"

"'Why,' the girl asks."

"Yes."

He looked at the light ahead. It had just turned red. "You want to know why?" He brought the truck to a sliding stop, pulled her to him and found her mouth.

He meant it to be a quick kiss, but her response brought another one from him. When a horn sounded, Sharee jumped and pulled free. He feather-touched her cheek, put the truck in drive, and went through the now-green light. A car sped past them with another honk.

John glanced her way. She looked flushed in the passing streetlights. His whole body had moved into overdrive. *Go easy.*

He touched her hand. "As crazy as this relationship has been, I still thought you might miss me."

"I might. Unless you embarrass me to death first."

He chuckled. "I'll behave."

As they pulled into her complex, the truck's lights swept past the apartment doors, and John stopped a few spaces down from her apartment. He reached over the back of the seat, plucked something from behind it, and dropped it into her lap.

She looked down. "Peppermints?"

"I needed something at the store and saw them. The soft kind. You seem to like them."

"I do. Thank you." She unwrapped one and offered it to him. He shook his head, and she put it into her mouth.

"I thought of a different way of tasting them." He couldn't help the grin.

"You're incorrigible."

"That's a hundred dollar word."

"I'm sure you think you're worth it." Her voice held laughter.

"Does that mean you're not asking me in?"

"Yes. No, I mean. No, I'm not asking you in."

Long breath. "Well, no surprise there. Just my luck I picked a committed Christian. However…" His eyes dropped to her mouth, and he bent his head toward hers.

"John." She flattened her hands against his chest and pushed him away. Her face had changed.

He stared. "What? What did I say?"

"I'm serious. I…you need to know before this goes any further. If you're asking what I think, well, I'm not inviting you…or anyone else in…until I'm married."

He heard the difference in her voice and sat back. Had he really asked that? He'd just promised to behave. Five years of marriage and three of self-imposed exile, no wonder he'd forgotten how to act. Dating was different.

"Sharee, I'm teasing you."

He felt her examination. The look in her eyes was uncertain. "Were you?"

"Yes. I understand what you're saying, and I expected that answer. It doesn't change anything. I'm not running off."

"Really?" She swallowed the rest of the peppermint, her eyes intent on his.

"Really." For a lot of men, he knew, it would change everything. If they came back at all, it would be to test her resolve; and from the look on her face, she'd met some those.

"Really," he repeated, thinking about the seventeen-year-old boy whose sister was raped. Before that, he'd decided that he would not graduate high school a virgin. He'd started a quest to find the right girl. But all his determination disintegrated with Alexis' rape. His salvation soon after, and his youth pastor's teaching on purity left an enduring impression. He understood Sharee's stance. He had married as a virgin himself, enduring teasing and harassment from his friends for a number of years before that. However, it had made the wedding night and honeymoon a thrilling extravaganza. He had brought no remorse, no guilt, no other faces or bodies into their lovemaking.

At length, she relaxed and settled back. "Okay." Her eyes narrowed at something over his shoulder. "What's on my door?"

"Your door?" He switched on the truck's lights.

Sharee sucked in her breath, and John shot his head around. A second later, he shoved the truck door open and leaped to the pavement. Sharee scrambled after him. He grabbed the object from her door and yanked it free. Something metallic hit the pavement.

The doll's head fell away from a red, gaping throat, and its black, gouged eyes stared up at them.

Chapter 24

Sharee clutched John's arm. "Who's doing this?"

"I don't know, but I'd sure like to find out." He felt heat rising inside him. "And why you? Are you sure the other one—in the nursery—wasn't meant for you?"

"No, how could that be? No one but Marci knew I would be there."

"Marci and the children and Stephen. Anyone else?"

"No one. Marci's family all had the flu, but none of them would do this."

"They could have mentioned it to someone." To anyone. Friends at school. Other church members. Why was she a target now?

"Should we call Deputy Richards?"

"Probably."

"John, why were you keeping them?"

"The dolls?"

"Yes."

"I'm not sure. I thought if something were to happen…"

"Please, no."

"I know. We'll hope it doesn't. I'll call Deputy Richards on the way home. There's nothing else we can do." He glanced at the sidewalk then leaned to pick a shiny object from the concrete. He turned it over. "A magnetic hook. Look, open up, and let me check out your apartment."

"Why?"

"Just being careful."

"You think someone's inside? How would they get in?"

"I'm being overcautious, but it would make me feel better."

"It's just a prank. No one's done anything but leave the dolls."

"And the notes. Humor me."

She put the key in the door. He slipped inside while she watched from the doorway. Her apartment was modest. The inspection took only a few minutes.

"It's fine." He wished he'd thought of a way to check her apartment without alarming her. "Okay. Lock the door, and don't let anyone in that you don't kno—" he cut off the last word.

A mosquito buzzed past, and she eased the door closed. "It's someone we do know, isn't it?"

"Well, use that common sense you brag about and be careful." The doll being left on her door didn't sit well with him. It didn't follow the pattern of the others. Had she annoyed whoever was doing this? Was it a warning?

"Do you think it's Abbey?"

"Not sure, but if it is, why you? Is she angry with you?"

"She could be. We had a run-in at Marci's shower, but after reading that note you found..." The words faded. "What if it's not her?"

"Then someone has a sick sense of humor. Lock up." He opened the door and stepped back through the doorway. "I'll call you tomorrow."

She nodded and sent one last glance his way before closing the door again.

John waited until the sound of the bolt sliding into place ceased. A few miles down the road, he remembered he still didn't have her phone number. He fought the urge to turn around.

Glancing upwards, he whispered his first request in three years, *"Keep her safe...please."*

✣

Sharee arrived at work early the next morning, glad the long night had ended. When she walked into the Downtown Ministries offices, the phone's musical bleep swelled in her ears. The receptionist had a phone to her ear already. The girl pointed to the other line, and Sharee scooted into her office and lifted the receiver.

"Good morning. Downtown Min—"

"What's your phone number?"

She pulled the phone away, staring at it in surprise, then put it to her ear again. "You just called it."

"Your cell number."

"And how are you this morning?" She made her voice warm and sweet, trying to keep the smile hidden.

"Your number," John said. "I almost came back last night for it."

"Did you?" She forced a serious tone. She had thought about it, too. Neither of them had the other's number. "I'm surprised you weren't at my door first thing this morning." She thought she heard a growl and glanced at the phone again, grinning.

"I thought about it. *Your phone number.*"

She reeled it off. "Please don't lose it." She didn't bother to hide the amusement this time. "We don't want to go through this again."

Definitely a growl. "You're asking for trouble."

"No. I could be if you were here, but you're not."

Quiet settled. "You're enjoying this, aren't you?"

"That you were worried about me? I guess I am. It's nice to know you care."

"And you didn't know that?"

"I did, it's just—"

"Because there are some things I could do if you need to know." His voice deepened.

"No," she said, reacting to the change.

"Some very definite things..."

"John." He'd turned the tables on her.

"If I were there."

Heat fled up her face. "John. I'm at work." She watched the receptionist motion to her. A girl in cut-off jeans and a dirty t-shirt stood at the other woman's desk. "I have a client."

"All right, babe." His voice was warm with laughter.

Her heart did a quick somersault. *Babe?*

"I guess I have what I called for. But..." He let the word hang a moment then said softly, "I wish I were there."

Phones were great, but they nowhere near took the place of an in-person, right-now, arms-around, eyes-on date. And Tuesday to Friday had stretched John's patience. He'd almost stopped by the ministry offices on Thursday but forced himself to wait. She'd worked late each night this week.

"I can't get away again until Friday. It's the holidays." Her voice over the phone did not sound nearly as frustrated as he felt. "And the cold weather up north. We always have more homeless this time of year. They migrate."

"Like birds?"

She laughed. "You could say that. It's too cold up north, so many come south. It will even out in a month or so."

"A month? You mean you'll be working late each week for a month?" And she'd be spending a week at home over Thanksgiving.

She laughed again. "Maybe not every night."

He didn't remember what he'd said to that, but he managed to get a promise from her to be ready by 6:00 on Friday. And Friday was here.

When he knocked on the door, she yanked it open and beamed as if she'd just won a race. Warmth flooded him, and he wrapped her in a bear hug.

"A woman who can be on time is worth millions."

"That is such a gender put-down. My mother would say you're a chauvinist."

"Would she?"

"Without a doubt. Where are we going?"

"A surprise. You'll have to wait and see."

She made a face at him, walked to an end table and grabbed her purse. He took notice of the powder blue t-shirt, the jean shorts and the bare legs. He'd told her the night would only require casual dress. The imprint of a flower rested just above her ankle. From it, a vine scrolled upwards about two inches.

"You have a tattoo."

"What?" She glanced down and turned her foot. The slim silver flip-flop highlighted the gray and crimson flower. "You don't like it?"

"My whole image of you just crumbled—the whole conservative traditionalist idea—dead." Her mouth opened but nothing came out, and he laughed. "I like it."

"Do you?"

He pulled up the left sleeve of his t-shirt. She moved forward to look at it. A line of script was tattooed in a circle just above his bicep.

"'Snatch others from the fire and save them,'" he quoted and dropped the sleeve back down. "Jude 23."

"I'm impressed." Her eyes lifted to meet his. So, he had been serious about his faith at one time.

He drove along Pinellas Avenue and down the Intracoastal Waterway. The sun glittered on the waters. When they reached Clearwater Beach, he circumnavigated the roundabout and parked few blocks from Crabby Bill's.

They were seated in front of a big glass window. The view past the street and the pier showcased the sun hovering above the Gulf waters. Its heated blaze sent pale salmon fingers into the cyan sky.

"You've been here before I'm sure. Do you want the conch fritters or gator?" He grinned at her widened eyes. "They're both good."

"Conch fritters or gator?" Sharee's voice squeaked. "I'm thinking of something a little more traditional."

"Were you? Me, too." He held her gaze for a moment.

When she dropped her focus to the table, he reached over and enclosed her hand using a gentle pressure to bring her eyes back to him.

"Sharee…"

The waiter appeared placing the menus before them; and he stopped, not sure what he wanted to say, only knowing that something strong happened each time they were together.

He couldn't prevent himself from pursuing it, but wondered what it might cost him. He'd said okay to God, not because he trusted Him; but because he wanted her, and that might be a grenade that would blow up in his face.

~

Sharee shivered, and John's arm slipped around her shoulders as they strolled across the street to the beach. The pier stretched far out into the Gulf, showcasing the white sand on either side. Artist and mimes and break-dancers had gathered and used it as a stage.

"Thank you for dinner, and for bringing me here. I always forget how unique this place is."

John drew her along the pier. Below them, the breaking waves curled and crashed, rolling onto the damp sands. The smell of the sea circled them. Vendor stands lined each side, their distinctive wares bathed in the sun's last rays. John urged her over to the guardrails.

On the sand below, two men twirled fire sticks, and a large crowd had gathered. Fire swirled and leaped as they tossed the sticks into the air.

After a few minutes, John took her hand once more, and they continued along the pier. Now and then, they paused to admire the crafts and trinkets for sale. John purchased a gemstone necklace.

"Tourmaline. This one matches your hair and your eyes."

"It's beautiful."

"I won't say the obvious, but the thought is there." He fastened it around her neck, his fingers lingering, caressing, and then dropping to her shoulders to turn her around to face him once more.

Her heart slammed at his look. The endless parade of tourists shifted in waves around them, background noise to what he seemed to say with his eyes. When, at last, he dropped his hands, and she could breathe again, he drew her back down the pier and onto the beach.

They ran along the sand, away from the crowds, barefoot, holding their shoes, laughing as they escaped the rush and surge of the incoming waves. She was breathless when they stopped. He watched her for a moment. When her breath slowed, she smiled up at him. He pulled her into his arms, his kiss as gentle as the moonlight touching the waters.

Finally, he turned her and they stared out across the charcoaled water, the silver tops rolling to shore.

Sharee leaned her head back against his chest. "God does such good work."

John grunted but said nothing.

She straightened, twisted in his arms, and looked up at him. "You know

God's the most important thing in my life."

He gave a short nod.

"We talk about everything else, John. When are we going to talk about Him?"

His face changed and his stance. "Give it some time, Sharee."

She had given it some time. How much more time, she wanted to know? But she didn't say anything. Instead, she just nodded, her stomach hollowing, and wondered.

Chapter 25

Sharee pulled a holiday sweater over her red t-shirt and blue jeans, eyeing her reflection in the mirror. That walk on the beach a month ago was in seventy-degree weather. Today, the first real taste of winter had blown into the area with temperatures hovering in the sixties. It would drop lower tonight.

She pulled her hair into a ponytail. No use doing anything else with it. The humidity after the rain today would cause it to curl and frizz even more than usual. Wild, John had described it, with his ever-present amusement, and that description fit tonight.

She sent a prayer of thankfulness to God. No more dolls or notes had appeared since the one left on her door. Whoever had played the ill-intentioned pranks had quit. Deputy Richards had met with John and took possession of the dolls after the last call. Now the Sheriff's department could deal with them if needed.

She directed her thoughts to the night's rehearsal—their last rehearsal. Tomorrow, they would do it for real. The following Saturday they'd do it once more. She gave a deep sigh. Why, when you looked forward to something with so much anticipation, could you look forward to its end with just that much delight?

Her phone chirped. She grabbed her purse and headed for the door, tugging out the phone and balancing it as she locked her door.

"Where RU?" the text read. "Things need attention here."

"On the way." She texted the reply and stuffed the phone back into her purse.

She climbed into the CR-V and thought about last Saturday's visit to Howard Park—and Matthew Thornton. What a surprise seeing him there among a bunch of women. And he'd been just as surprised to see them.

Of course, they were doing what had become their weekly jog, running along the Gulf of Mexico, taking in the sun, sand and waves. Matthew, on the other hand, was giving classes in car seat installment and safety.

When she waved, Matthew's eyes rounded; but he waved back and said something to one of the women before jogging over to them.

"Hi, Ms. J., Mr. J." His smile looked awkward.

"Hey, Matthew." Sharee glanced past him at the women he'd left climbing into a van.

"I'm here with a group from the Pregnancy Center." Matt indicated the others with his head. "I teach car seat installment and safety."

"You do? That's great." Sharee glanced at the women again. "We have classes, too, at Downtown Ministries. You teach at the park?"

"Well, it's a way to get everyone to come. We come, do the class then have a picnic. We leave the babies at the center with babysitters. It's a nice outing for the moms. When we get back, they install the free car seats in their cars, and we're done."

"You volunteer?" John asked.

"Yes."

"Good job."

Matt gave an uneven smile. "Well, I'd better go before they leave me." He nodded and headed back to the van.

Sharee watched Matt clamber on board the bus. "Did that surprise you, too?"

John gave a slight nod. "Especially the group he's with."

"I took Ryann to the Pregnancy Center when she told me about her pregnancy."

He slanted his head at her. "She told you before she told her parents?"

"Yes. Her nerves and her fear kept her from telling them right away. The Pregnancy Center is Christian. I wanted her to be sure, to have an accurate test, and get good advice. She brought Matthew with her, not the boyfriend."

"Ah."

The boyfriend disappeared as soon as Ryann told him."

"Around for the fun, but not for the responsibility. You were right about responsibility. Too many of us men, young and old, shelve their responsibility in these areas."

The van pulled out, and they walked to John's truck.

"It was such a tragedy when Ryann lost the baby."

"And now Matthew is on the scene."

"Yes."

Sharee brought her focus back to the present. And maybe with Matthew on the scene, Ryann would look beyond her loss to the future. As she turned in at the church, she prayed for God's presence and His anointing in the rehearsal tonight.

The lights in the fellowship hall and the six-pointed star over the field glowed with welcome. The actors filled the drive that ran between the hall and the field, most in costume, ready for practice. The areas formed by the six-pointed star glistened in the lights. She climbed from the car and stared out over the field. Everything looked ready.

She'd never mentioned the spotlight again, but somehow John ended up shouldering it through rehearsals. Matthew shadowed him once or twice as back-up. Sam Byrd volunteered to read the scriptures during each scene, and Christy offered to work the sound system. Lynn, as usual, had volunteered to provide baked goods for after the performance. Her hand-picked assistants were inside decorating the large dining room for tomorrow night.

She grinned, turned around and looked to her left. The animal pens John had built housed the donkey and three sheep Ryann's uncle had provided. She could see the donkey's head over the stall wall.

Turing back around, she headed to the control tower. John stood near the edge at the top of the ladder and watched her ascend. He stood next to the ladder anytime she climbed up these days. She smiled at him, and he took her hand and pulled her close.

"You made it. Some of the actors were wondering if you'd run out on us."

"Right. You mean they wish I had then they could all do the parts like they want to."

"Yep. That would be my guess. You run a tight ship, boss lady."

She wrinkled up her nose at him, and he laughed.

Sam and Christy Byrd joined them. Christy went right to the sound equipment, checking it. John had the spotlight, a barrel-shaped older model about three feet long, resting on a stand. During the production, he hefted it to his shoulder, using its light to follow the characters as they moved from scene to scene.

Sharee looked out over the field. "Is it too wet, do you think?"

"The ground's still damp," Sam said, "but everyone should be okay. And tomorrow will be great. Dry temps in the low sixties. Cool, but great for this. George is keeping an eye on the electrical things. He'll be on hand if needed."

"Everything's in order?"

Sam nodded. "We're ready."

"Shall we call the group to order down there?" John inquired.

"Yes. Ask everyone to take their places. We're going through the whole thing. Any questions can wait until the end. I'll give you a cue to start." She dropped his hand and eased down the ladder.

When she stepped to the ground, Roseanne bounded out of the darkness. "Sharee, where have you been? I can't find the headpiece to this costume. Someone's taken it."

"You don't know where it is?"

"That's what I said, isn't it?"

"All the costumes were together. Maybe someone took the wrong one."

"I've asked everyone."

"We're about to start. Do without it for now. We'll look for it later."

"And where's Marci and Stephen and the baby? I haven't seen them."

"They're here, I'm sure. Someone would have told me if they weren't."

"But you just got here. I don't know how you plan on doing this if you aren't here on time."

"Roseanne…"

She heard John making the announcement for everyone to get in their places. Matthew stepped next to her holding a donkey on its lead and splattered mud on them.

Roseanne jumped back. "Get that animal away from me!" She whirled and disappeared around the bleachers.

Matthew chuckled and disappeared into the darkness. Sharee jumped at the sound of wheels on the wet pavement behind her.

"Didn't mean to startle you," Bruce rolled up next to her.

"That's okay. Can you get around all right with everything so wet?"

"Yeah, I've stuck to the paths we've made for the star. But I wanted to talk with you. I'm having second thoughts about this."

"You are? Why?"

"You don't need me, and there are no wheelchairs at this time in history."

Sharee couldn't identify his tone of voice; but his face, lit by the star's lights, seemed taught, drawn. "That's beside the point."

"Not for me."

She bit her lip. "That came out wrong. I don't think anyone will be thinking whether there were wheelchairs or not. Your part plays off King Herod and allows the audience to know what Herod is thinking. It's important."

"I don't think so. You show it when he washes his hands—of everything."

"But…"

Look, Sharee, I don't want to do this."

Lynn stepped from the darkness beyond them. "Sharee, I think you need to…"

"Wait a minute, Lynn. Bruce and I were talking."

"Oh."

"No, we're through," Bruce edged the chair backward.

"Sharee," John stepped forward. "We've been calling you over the loud speaker."

"Can you give me a minute?" Her voice arced.

He stopped, moving his head back a little.

She touched his arm. "I'm sorry. It's just everybody is… Bruce, please wait."

"Sharee," Lynn pushed in next to her. "Ryann is …"

"Lynn!"

"Look, I'm leaving." Bruce shoved hard on the wheels of his chair and disappeared into the dark.

"Bruce…"

Lynn put her hand on Sharee's arm. "Let him go, Sharee. It's the anniversary."

"What anniversary?" She tried to keep the exasperation from her voice. Next to her, John chuckled. She glared at him.

"His accident. Two years ago."

"Oh."

John glanced back over his shoulder. "Yeah, that's right."

"And it's been a rough two years. His whole life has changed." Lynn gazed after him. "And Marci is having a hard time, too. She feels guilty having another baby. Why should God bless her when so many others are hurting?"

"She said that to you? Then Ted was right."

"If he said she was down, yes. But he's used it to get close to her."

John stepped forward. "I think we should ditch the discussion for now. Everyone is waiting."

Lynn turned. "Yeah. I just wanted to tell Sharee about Ryann. She's sitting in the bleachers, crying. And Abbey is adding wood to the fireplace or whatever that term is. Sharee, you need to talk with Ryann."

"I don't think this is the time."

"Something needs to be done. And John could talk with Abbey. Separate those two." Lynn moved away, disappearing into the darkness.

Sharee shook her head and sighed. "All right." She glanced John's way, and he nodded. They headed for the bleachers.

"Ryann?" She climbed to the top, ignored Abbey's grimace and sat down next to Ryann. "What are you doing here? I thought you weren't coming."

"But it's Christmas. I've worked on the sets and watched the practices, and I can sing at the end."

"But you decided it was too much."

"I changed my mind."

"Then why are you upset?"

"I just started thinking about my baby. Marci has Joshua and six other children. I have no one."

"Ryann, I don't have all the answers. No one does, but come talk with Pastor Alan." She stood and sent a look to Abbey. "Abbey, you need to get into place for rehearsal. John's at the bottom of the bleachers. Go with him, please."

"I'm staying with Ryann."

Sharee shook her head. "I'll take care of Ryann. Sometimes, our best intentions are not what's best for the person involved. Right now, Ryann needs to talk with someone else." Sharee helped Ryann start down the bleachers.

John faced Abbey as she stepped from the bleachers. "Abbey, why don't you and I walk and talk until Sharee gets back? We have a couple of minutes before everything starts."

Abbey frowned, but as Sharee turned away with Ryann, she noticed that the teen fell in step with John. Good.

Sharee put her arm around Ryann's shoulders, and they moved toward the church office. When she opened the door, Pastor Alan and Daneen looked their way. George turned in his seat.

Pastor Alan smiled and nodded. "Glad you got here." Then he glanced at Ryann and back to Sharee, frowning. Sharee slid her eyes Ryann's way and nodded.

"George, do you mind if we finish this later?" The pastor let his voice trail off, looking at the other man.

George turned their way. "Oh, no. Fine. We'll talk later." He went past them.

Pastor Alan pulled out a chair. "Ryann, you're having a hard time?"

The girl nodded and began to cry. Sharee edged backward and out the door.

Chapter 26

Sharee sat on the bleachers and watched the cars pull away into the dark. Practice had ended later than planned, but now the voices, the commotion had faded. Quiet settled over the field. Moonlight flooded it.

What a long night. She smiled and bowed her head. *But the anointing, Lord, and your presence. Thank you!* She gathered the peace around her. Her heart bowed, too.

Something hit the bleachers with a thud. Sharee jerked her head up. Ted Hogan had dropped onto the seat beside her. He directed a long frown in her direction.

"It's cold tonight." His voice echoed the look on his face. "It's too cold and too wet for Marci and Joshua to be here."

"What?"

"You should have stopped practice and let them go home."

Sharee forced herself not to react. She cleared her throat. "Both Marci and Stephen asked to do this. If either wanted to quit or go home or take Joshua inside, I'm sure they would have done just that."

"Stephen never thinks about her."

"Stephen loves her."

"Marci needs someone who listens, who will take care of her. I told you before she never wanted this baby. It's upset her."

"She loves Joshua. She and Stephen and Joshua will do just fine. You're really out of line here, you know."

"Did you know that Marci and I were engaged?"

Sharee stared and let herself process what he'd said. Why would he bring that to her attention now? Was he still in love with Marci? When he'd returned to church a year ago, was it because of Marci?

"Ted, Marci, and Stephen have been married for *sixteen* years. If you were engaged, it was a long time ago. Let it go. "

"She didn't want this baby, and she's depressed because of it. It's Stephen's fault. She'd be happier without this baby."

"Some women are depressed after a baby is born. They're tired, their bodies and hormones are out of kilter, but she and Stephen will handle that. Whatever you had with Marci was over years ago."

Ted jumped to his feet, his eyes narrowing. Sharee met his look. For a moment she thought he would say something else, but he turned and disappeared into the dark. She stared after him then lowered her head into her hands.

"Well," Lynn's voice came from behind her, "is he deluded or what? Does he think Marci is going to leave Stephen for him or something?" She sat down next to Sharee. "I can't believe he had the nerve to say all that. You need to be careful around him."

"I'm not worried about Ted."

Lynn elbowed Sharee. "Well, I was here in case you needed reinforcements, anyway."

Sharee chuckled. "And what did you plan to do if I did?"

John stepped into the light. "She had back-up if needed. Sam and I could hear from the platform."

Sharee sent them both a smile. "I don't see Ted as a threat to me. Now, to Marci…"

John put his foot on the bleachers and leaned toward her. "Lynn's right. You need to be careful around Ted."

"I don't even want to think about him right now. Between Bruce and Ryann and Roseanne, I have enough to worry about."

Lynn put a hand to her mouth and yawned. "Yeah, and I need sleep bad. See you guys tomorrow." She strolled toward the parking lot.

John sat next to Sharee. He stretched his legs out and leaned back against the seat behind him. "So, what did you think?"

"About the program?" Her voice warmed, quickened. "The sets look fabulous, and everyone knew what they were doing."

"Yeah. It went well."

" And…and God's Spirit was here. Could you tell?"

"Yes, I could tell." His voice sounded flat.

Sharee tried to see his expression, squinting in the moonlight. She'd prayed that God would touch him during the program, but his flat tone told her the wall between him and God still stood. Emptiness invaded her stomach.

"John?"

"Yes?"

She needed an answer to the question that had circled her mind over the last few weeks. It might upset him, but she couldn't help that.

"You accepted Jesus as your Savior?"

"I told you that."

"You told me you did, but you didn't tell me about it." She left it open like a question. An audible intake of his breath followed. The emptiness in her stomach moved upward, changing to pain in her chest.

"After what happened to Alexis, I needed some answers. I told you. I found them at church. Yes, I accepted Jesus as Savior."

"What does that mean to you?"

"You know what I'm saying."

"No. Not exactly."

"All right. Look. You want to know if I know what I'm talking about? Is that it?" When she said nothing, he continued in that same clipped voice, "I know I'm a sinner. My life—as I know and you well know—is far from perfect. I could never make it to heaven on my own. But Jesus' death atoned for my sins. I'm reconciled to God through His blood. He gave His life for me and for the sins of the whole world. All I need do, all anyone needs to do, is believe and accept it. I have."

Thankfulness washed over her. She had wondered if what he had told her was real. *Thank you, Jesus.*

An uncomfortable silence settled between them. Even with his knowledge, his acceptance of Jesus' sacrifice, she knew his anger and guilt had created a barrier between him and God. Would he ever be over it? Would they ever have that love for God in common?

"John?"

"What?" The one word acted as a warning.

She changed her mind and asked instead, "Did you and Abbey talk?"

"Yes."

"About anything important?"

"I didn't mention the letter, if that's what you're asking; but I did use my marriage…and Janice's death…to let her know that I understood how Ryann felt about her loss."

"You told Abbey about Janice?" She couldn't keep the surprise from her voice.

"Yes."

"But…that…" The words trailed off. He'd told someone else, someone who might tell others. Wow.

"She wanted to know why God allows things. I don't have those answers. I told her that and just let her talk."

Tears closed her throat, her chest ached—for him, for Abbey, for Ryann. She turned her head away. In a minute, she said, "Thank you for doing that."

"She's dealing with a lot."

"Can you tell me?"

"I think so. She didn't ask me to keep it quiet. "Her mom died about a year and a half ago. Of cancer. It was a long battle. Then her dad remarried six months later. She thinks they were having an affair while her mom struggled with the cancer. Needless to say, she's unhappy. Angry with her dad and her step-mom. Mad at God that her mom died."

"Understandable."

"She came to church because her mom always wanted her to go, but she wouldn't before. When she came, Ryann reached out to her, but when Ryann lost the baby, Abbey couldn't handle it. She's mad at God again and anyone else who gets in her way."

Sharee folded her hands and propped her chin on them. "All of this is hard. So, Abbey's taken an offense for Ryann just because Marci has so many children. Yet, she asks to babysit all the time."

"Some things don't make sense."

"It was hard for you, wasn't it? Sharing about Janice."

He said nothing. They both stared across the field. A cool wind stirred the black cypress. The moon, not yet full, painted night shadows across the ground.

Sharee moved to see him better. "I don't understand, you know."

His breath expelled. "I knew you weren't going to leave it."

"John, how can I? We talk about everything but God. And tonight, God moved in such a beautiful way, and you said you knew. When you say that you've accepted Jesus as your Savior then how can you..." She touched his arm. "How can you be so resistant?"

He pulled free. "Leave it, Sharee."

"I can't." She swallowed against the tears. "You've been back in church this month, and yet you act like nothing has changed. You're still angry at God."

He stood, but she caught his hand. He glanced down at her, the line of his mouth hard.

"Please."

He hesitated a moment then sat, staring straight ahead.

"John, I felt so honored that you shared what you did with me about Janice but..."

"But you want more."

"No, I just want you to forgive yourself."

"Forgive myself; forgive God. So easy to say."

Yes, it was easy for her. She recognized that. She'd never dealt with the loss of a loved one. But God was still God, whether they liked what happened in their lives or not. Her hands clasped and unclasped. Multi-colored Christmas lights flickered from the street behind through the stand of cypress. It was Christmas. God had set His plan for the world into action one starry night, and He had a plan for John, too.

John shifted on the bleachers. "You asked me if I knew Jesus as Savior, and I said yes. But what you're really asking is—*Is he Lord?*"

She twisted toward him, frowning, "Is he Lord?"

"Yes, that's what you want. It's not enough that I make him Savior. He has to be Lord. *Sovereign Lord.* You want it, and He wants it, too."

Understanding engulfed her. Yes. He has to be Savior *and* Lord.

John's voice when he continued sounded guttural. "I told you before that I knew you were a committed Christian. I joked about you asking me in that night. I expected the answer you gave. Any other answer would have shocked me because you're committed to God. And that's what you want from me." He paused. "And that's what I don't know that I can give."

In another moment, he stood up and drew her to her feet. They made their way down the bleachers, the night air enveloping them, and an unfamiliar heaviness between them. Sharee shivered.

When they stepped to the ground, he pulled her around. "I want you, Sharee, but without all these strings."

"You mean like God wants you?" She felt the tightening of his body, and she moved her hand to touch his jaw, her eyes filling with tears. "I love you," she whispered.

His mouth twisted. A second later, his hand went to the back of her head and tugged free the band that held her hair. She felt it fall around her shoulders. They stood for a long minute, the moonlight bright on both their faces; and then he pulled her to him, his mouth coming down hard, insistent, passionately on hers. Sharee's mouth answered his.

When he released her, her own arms tightened. His eyes searched her face, and then he took her hands and pulled them down.

"We'll talk," he said, his voice rough, unsteady, "after the program tomorrow and then...we'll see."

Chapter 27

Who is this King of Glory? Sharee heard the scripture in her head as the Christmas program neared the end the next evening. She stood, holding her hands together below her chin, experiencing the pain from last night mixed with the joy pouring through her right now.

Who do you say that I am?, Jesus asked his disciples. You are the Christ, the Son of the living God, Peter had answered.

"You're King and Savior and Lord," Sharee said aloud, remembering well John's words from the previous night, knowing what he meant, and remembering her own struggle later.

She'd arrived home after their discussion, closed the door and dropped to her knees, not even turning on a light. Her heart cried to God, and His Spirit seemed to fill the apartment. She lay on her face, silent and still in that presence.

Am I your Lord? Will you serve me and no other?

She knew what He asked. Would she surrender John? Or did John mean more to her than God? Would she stop pretending that what she and John had was enough? She loved him, and yet... John wanted to be loved without strings, without someone pushing him for more. And she wanted more. John had seen it, known it, even when she hadn't. She wanted someone with whom she could love and serve God. But John would have to change, to give up his anger and hurt before that would happen; and if he didn't, what would they have?

Her heart tore.

She had to give John to God. From the first, she'd ignored what she knew was right. John said she was a committed Christian, but when it came to him, her commitment floundered.

Lord, I am such a hypocrite. I can see what others are doing wrong, but I can't see myself. Pain broke across her chest, flooding it. She drew deep breaths, trying to ease the emotion.

She needed to surrender John to God, to let go. She had to tell John it wouldn't work. Unless he walked away himself. That was what he'd meant by that rough, "We'll see." She knew it. Her throat ached with tears. She had no strength to do what was needed.

Dropping her head to the floor once again, she fought with her heart and cried for strength. She must be willing.

"Here." She mumbled the word between sobs and lifted her hands—as if John were in them—to God. "He's yours. Take him."

Her heart had felt fractured last night, and tonight it felt broken again. The voices of the program's last song rose into the night sky. People made their way to where Pastor Alan and Daneen stood. Some of the actors prayed with others. Her heart began to mend. No matter what she and John decided, tonight God's blessings poured out, tonight people were accepting God's gift of salvation.

Joy mixed with her pain.

She glanced at the team at the center of the star and warmth flowed through her, easing her brokenness. The scene shimmered in light.

Their song seemed to weave the very presence of God into the air around them. She stared across the field, and the light on the chorus shimmered again then shook. After a moment, she glanced at the control tower. The spotlight was shaking.

ಲ

John felt the intense presence of God even more than Sharee. He fought the desire to kneel down. He'd known from the moment he heard about the project that it would cause him problems. When Alan first mentioned it, he put him off. Then when Alan approached him a second time, John decided to confront it head-on—by helping with the building aspect. He'd help all he could beforehand, but he would not be here the night the program took place. Even as the relationship with Sharee moved forward these last few weeks, he never told her otherwise. She assumed differently, of course. But from the beginning, he'd prepared Matthew to take over. Yet, right now, here he stood. Not Matthew. Him.

Sharee's question hit at the heart of the problem. His resistance toward God's advances would fill the proverbial book. But how could he forgive himself or God? His anger at his maker was real, but the anger at himself had created a tsunami that threatened to overtake him.

Friends had given them the plane, and Janice's excitement pushed him to take it up. He had done a cursory exam—he had, the one many people had dubbed a perfectionist. And the first time he'd slacked off... No...the second time.

The pain slicing through his heart almost bowed him. If he'd gone with Alexis that night, if he'd checked the plane properly... *His responsibility.* Both times. His.

The weight of the spotlight rested on his shoulder, almost unbearably heavy. In four weeks of practice, it had never felt like this. He stood with his feet apart, his right hand tight on the light. The agonizing weight shot pain through his neck and shoulder.

The sound of the plane's engine filled his mind again. He relived the confusion, hearing the engines sputter and spit and stop. Janice's scream. The memories of panic and loss rushed through him, and afterward, the loneliness and grief. The guilt.

Emotions dammed up too long tore loose—breaking, exploding. The hand holding the light shook.

Let me take it, son. It's an unbearable weight for you, but not for me.

John shook his head. He clenched his teeth. The presence of God swept like warm liquid through him. Intense love caused his hands and every fiber of his being to shake.

Let go, son. Let me take it.

John stumbled backward, and someone lifted the spotlight from his shoulder. He turned, staring into Sam's eyes. Did he know? John lurched sideways and looked around. Christy sat on a bench, next to the table with the sound system. Her eyes met his, compassion spilling forth. Did they know what he'd done? How he'd failed those he loved?

His legs were not going to hold him much longer. Christy moved over, and he dropped onto the bench, leaning forward, putting his head in his hands, fighting the overwhelming pain. He could hear Christy's whispered prayer although specific words were unclear. She laid her hand on his back, and electricity shot through him. He jerked at the shock and began to sob.

It didn't matter who knew anymore. The only thing that mattered was the pain washing through him and out of him like a flood. The thought came again—how could he forgive himself? And he realized that God—the God he'd held in such contempt—was making a way.

Jesus came to heal the brokenhearted, to set the captives free. And he had been captive—of his own pain and anger and guilt.

ॐ

The singing ended, and silence hung over the field. Then in joyous appreciation, people began to clap and praise God. Sharee stood next to the bleachers, tears flowing, joy bubbling from within. She held any other thought back for a minute, wanting just to worship. Thankfulness washed over her. She stood still and reveled in his presence. The God of the universe stepping out of heaven, as John had said before, doing a miracle for them.

John. She glanced up at the control tower, the ache awakening in her chest.

People began to file down the bleachers, talking, laughing. Many had come from Downtown Ministries, many from the neighborhood. They filed past her, and she smiled at each one. Lynn and the others waited in the fellowship hall for the influx of hungry people. Someone told her how wonderful and blessed they felt, and Sharee pointed to heaven. She watched the bleachers empty, watched the actors and singers in the middle of the field move around hugging each other.

Everyone had done a great job. Even Ted Hogan, playing Herod, proved outstanding. Bruce, coming at the last minute, shined as one of Herod's chief priests.

She glanced up again at the control tower and hesitated. John always came down last, but neither Sam nor Christy had descended yet. She leaned against a section of the bleachers, waiting, embracing the warmth in her heart. At last, she pushed away from the support and began to walk toward the platform. Was something wrong?

She mounted the first few steps. Voices drifted across the field again, raised, nervous. The anxious tones stopped her. Something had changed. With her hand on the eighth rung, she turned and stared at the center of the star. Toward Bethlehem. Someone ran her way.

Sharee clung to the ladder, waiting, heart suspended.

The girl ran straight to her.

"Mary, what is it?" Sharee called even before the girl reached her.

Mary grabbed hold of the ladder, head back, looking up. "Mom can't find Joshua. She's looked everywhere and can't find him." The girl sucked in air. "He was in the manger while we sang, but no one knows where he is. Ms. J, he's gone!"

Chapter 28

How many people does it take to find a baby?

Sharee sent up the desperate plea to God. Her exhaustion and discouragement were compounded by the cold, wet night. She shivered, splaying the flashlight's beam over the trees and underbrush in front of her. When the Sheriff's deputies arrived, they'd questioned Marci and the others before searching the church grounds and this deserted piece of land next to it. She, John, and Lynn, were combing the area again, and through the darkness, the flashlights of other searchers bounced off scrub pines and palmettos and wild holly. Hundreds of volunteers had arrived since the Amber Alert had gone out.

She leaned a shaking hand against a tree. They'd put out the Amber Alert even though they didn't know the perpetrator. The situation, they said, looked dire.

When K-9 units arrived, she'd pinned her hopes on the dogs; but the perpetrator had outsmarted them. The dogs tracked the baby to the back part of the field and then the scent vanished.

Lynn and John had stopped next to her. Sounds from other searchers echoed through the darkness. Their lights and voices and the moonlight imparted an unreal feeling to the area.

She raised her arm into the flashlight's narrow wash of light and looked at her watch. Eight hours since Joshua's disappearance. She glanced back. The Christmas lights from the enormous six-pointed star mocked her as well as the floodlights filling that area. Peace on Earth, good will to men? Would there be any peace until they found Joshua?

Sharee closed her eyes, and the image of the first mutilated doll burst across her mind. She jerked, eyes flying open and tried to keep her balance on muddy ground. John grabbed her arm. A moment later, he caught a wet branch as it snapped back at them. Cold rain splattered their faces.

Sharee tugged her arm free, wiped the rain from her eyes and glanced his way. John rubbed a hand across his face and met her look, but she ducked her head. Too much pain there. Too much pain everywhere.

Ted's voice drifted back to them. "Sorry."

Thank God Ted had joined them a little while ago; they needed all the help they could get. She started forward again, stepping over the undergrowth, avoiding the vines that twisted upward, grabbing anything in their way.

A quick gasp from behind caught her attention, and she glanced over her shoulder. Lynn's gunmetal quilted parka glistened with moisture, and mud covered her stylish high-heeled boots. The blonde hair hung soaked and dripping, except for one strand caught in a long-fingered branch. Lynn yanked it free.

"You okay?" Sharee shoved her own wet hair away from her face then clutched her arms to her chest. The jeans and sweatshirt she wore offered no better protection than Lynn's clothing.

"I'm okay. I just..." She stared past Sharee's shoulders, and her eyes widened.

Sharee jerked around, shooting the flashlight's beam across dark foliage in front of her. Lights and faces floated, ghostlike, among the trees. John swung his tactical flash in that direction. Pastor Alan and others from the church put up arms to shield their eyes from his light, and he dropped its beam to the ground.

"We're going in for a while," Pastor Alan said. "Come with us."

Ted appeared next to the others. "Are you crazy? We can't stop now."

"We're not quitting, but it's been a long night. We all need a break and something warm."

"Go ahead." Ted's voice hardened. "I'm staying."

The pastor waved at the three other people with him. "Go ahead. I'll come with you. We're not giving up, Ted. Daybreak's an hour away, and we'll be able to see then." His glance met Sharee's and jumped to Lynn. He frowned and sent a look John's way before following the others.

The edge of John's light caught her before she could straighten. It moved and trapped Lynn in its glare. "Alan's right. You're both done in. We could use a break."

"Go in if you want, Jergenson." Ted waved his light at him. "I got here later than the rest of you, anyway. I'm staying."

"You can't stay." Sharee heard the exhaustion in her voice and grimaced. "The deputy told us to stay in groups. If we go in, you have to come."

"I don't care what he said."

"They don't want anyone out here by themselves."

"Too bad."

"They wondered where you were earlier, Ted. This will be suspicious. They're not playing."

Ted muttered under his breath and disappeared back into the brush. John shook his head, flipped his light to the path back and nodded at Sharee.

"Let's head in."

Sharee sighed and helped Lynn around a patch of mud. The strength to argue had disappeared.

When they reached the open field near the church, Sharee saw other groups sitting on the bleachers.

"Can't we go in?" Lynn's words escaped through chattering teeth.

"I wonder if they're using the fellowship hall as a command center or something." Sharee dropped onto the nearby bleachers. "Pastor Alan's not here. He probably went to check things out."

Lynn eased down near her, snuggling down into her parka.

Sharee stared at the lights from the enormous star. If she hadn't insisted on the Christmas program, if she hadn't allowed Joshua to be baby Jesus, if she hadn't gone through with the whole thing, Joshua would be here now. She shoved wet curls from her face.

How could this happen, Lord? How? Her body trembled.

John lowered himself beside her. She avoided his eyes and his scrutiny and stared down at her folded hands. He feather-touched her back. She swallowed, resisting the urge to turn to him, to bury her face against his shoulder.

After a moment, he straightened, and she followed his gaze to the second set of bleachers. Ryann Byrd, surrounded by some other teens, huddled on the top row. She'd acted in the program tonight, but how had the baby's kidnapping affected her?

Sharee noticed another figure at the far end of the bleachers. Deputy Richards stood, feet spread and arms crossed. He stared at Ryann and the group surrounding her. His brow wrinkled. Then he turned, his gaze flickering past each huddled group until they reached Sharee. He looked from her to John and back, and in the light from the Christmas star, she saw his eyes narrow.

᠀

John bent his head, listening. Sharee's whispered prayer sounded like scripture.

"...hear my cry, O God, attend unto my prayer, from the ends of the earth, I will cry unto you... make haste to help us, O Lord. Make haste...

He raised his eyes and watched the first softening in the sky. Morning was close, and he was glad. The long night's search had proved fruitless. They needed daylight.

He tilted his head in Sharee's direction. "It's not your fault."

She jerked erect on the bleachers. "How can it not be? It was my idea. This whole thing." She swung her hand out to the Christmas set-ups.

"You can't blame yourself."

"We knew about those dolls. I knew someone wanted to get Marci. When Marci asked about Joshua, I should have said no."

"Sharee, no matter what you thought, you couldn't have known. We couldn't have known. The police knew about the dolls, too, remember? No one had any idea this might happen."

"John, what if..."

She didn't finish, but he knew what she thought. "Where is your faith when you need it?" He touched her face, pushing the damp curls back.

"I don't know. I'm so scared for Joshua. And God's presence was here—*at least, I thought so*—last night, during the program."

"It was."

"But how could this happen?"

"I don't know." He had no answers—none for his own situation, none for hers. Something inside him had changed, though. He'd come out of a tunnel of darkness, the hardness across his shoulders had lifted. Should he tell her? With all that was happening, he couldn't. Not now.

She made an abrupt move, twisted toward him, and buried her face against his shoulder. He raised his hand and caressed her hair as she cried. *Lord, help her.*

Even if he wanted to explain what had happened last night, could he? He focused on God. *This child, Lord. Bring this child back safe and unharmed. Your hand is not shortened, you said...then, Lord, save him. I will serve you again. I will give you my life...for his.*

He tightened his arm around Sharee's shoulders and bent and kissed the top of her head.

ↄ

An hour later, Sharee watched the steam rise from her coffee and sighed. How had she let herself fall apart like that? John had left when they said the fellowship hall was open. He wanted to talk with Alan, he said. She wouldn't think of his tenderness. Couldn't.

Someone must have given permission for the searchers to come into the hall. Here and there other people sat. Ornaments still decorated the tables for the celebration of the Christmas program. She tried not to sigh again.

Across the table, Lynn added more vanilla crème to her cup. She passed it to Sharee. "Have some?"

"No. But thank you for waiting with me. They don't seem in a hurry."

Deputy Richards had come over a few moments before to let her know the detectives wanted to talk with her again.

Lynn made a grumbling noise. She had combed her hair and fixed her makeup. Sharee felt the first small smile in hours lift her mouth. If she could see herself in a mirror…

"Why do they want to talk to you?" Lynn stirred her coffee. "They've asked each of us the same questions a zillion times."

"I don't know." She caught sight of Deputy Richards making his way through the scattered tables. She stood and leaned closer to Lynn. "But I guess I'll find out. Go home, friend, and get some rest."

"Like you're really going to go home."

"When the rest of us fall out, we'll need a second shift."

"I'll think about it."

Sharee turned to the deputy. "I'm ready." She didn't know what made her do it, maybe the whole weight of what had happened needed lightening, but she held out her hands crossed at the wrists as if he would handcuff her.

He frowned, but Lynn chuckled, and he glanced her way. A spark of amusement showed in the blue eyes.

"We've set aside another room," he said to Sharee. "If you'll follow me."

When she stepped inside the former youth room, she threw a quick glance around it. Someone had pulled chairs from the stacks along the wall and added two card tables against the nearest wall. One of the detectives waved her to a chair at the closest table. Another detective sat at the other table, a notebook resting on his knee.

Sharee sat. "This is my third time."

The man grunted, and Deputy Richards leaned against the second table. He crossed his arms over his chest. Already, coffee cups littered the table's surface.

"We'd like to go over some things, Ms. Jones." The older detective ran a hand through thick red hair. His look of exhaustion mimicked her own. "Tell us again why you decided to have a manger built for the last building."

"Marci wanted to share with the audience about Jesus. And she felt it would be easier if she didn't have Joshua to hold."

The detectives glanced at each other. "Okay. What do you know about Ted Hogan and his relationship to Marci Thornton?"

Sharee pulled her head back. "There isn't one on her part. Ted's imagination, though, is…lively."

The detective in the corner scribbled in a small notebook; the other shifted in his seat, watching her. His red hair mirrored the coloring in his face.

"Hogan stated that Mrs. Thornton is depressed. In fact, it's his contention that she never wanted this child in the first place, that this idea of having so many children was not hers at all but her husband's. Is that true?"

Sharee remembered the detective's name now. O'Shay. Detective O'Shay. "Ted said that to me, Detective, but it's not true. At least, not to my knowledge."

"You don't think Marci Thornton is depressed?"

"She might be, but many women are after having a baby—from exhaustion and hormone imbalances. Baby blues, they call it. You've heard of it, surely."

The detective's eyes narrowed. "What can you tell us about the accident that killed a child and crippled Bruce Tomlin?

Sharee's chin dropped. "Who told you about that? And what does it have to do with anything?"

"When we asked if anyone held a grudge against Marci Thornton, you didn't think about Bruce Tomlin? He headed the list you gave us of those that left immediately after the program."

"But Bruce is in a wheelchair, and he would never..."

"We need to be the ones to eliminate suspects, Ms. Jones, not you."

Her eyes flew to Deputy Richards. Could they possibly think Bruce could do this? That was ridiculous. How would he do it, anyway?

"Tell us about the homeless man you brought here to get a job."

"Pedro?" She couldn't keep the astonishment out of her voice. "Now you think Pedro had something to do with this?"

The other detective consulted his notes. "A number of people mentioned him."

Detective O'Shay leaned forward. "And you didn't."

"He did come for a while last night, but I don't know when he left."

"He wasn't here when the deputies arrived last night. When you were asked for a list of those that left during or after the program, you didn't think of him either?"

"No, I—"

"George Costas said Pedro Gonzalez mentioned knowing someone who put babies on the market."

"What?"

"The black market, Ms. Jones. Illegal baby sellers. Did he ever mention that to you?"

"Of course not! But Pedro would never do that. In fact, he said—"

"He said what?"

"Well, I...nothing. It has nothing to do with this."

"Please let us make that decision."

"But..." Her focus settled on Deputy Richards again, and he nodded. Sharee cleared her throat. Did they think she was keeping things back?

"Well, he said someone offered him a lot of money to do something illegal. But he told him no."

"And did he tell you what this illegal activity was?"

"No."

"No?"

"No."

"He seems to be a special friend of yours."

"I know him. I work with a lot of homeless people. I guess he's a friend. Not a special friend, but a friend. Yeah."

"You pick him up when he's hitchhiking?"

"Yes."

"You don't think that's dangerous?"

She jumped to her feet. "Look, I've got enough mothers around here. Just because I pick someone up doesn't mean I'd keep information from you if I thought it was important. If you've got any other complaints about my list, tell me. If not, I'm leaving."

Deputy Richards coughed into his hand. Michael O'Shay shot him a look through narrowed lids then twisted back to Sharee. "If you can think of anyone else you left out of the list, Ms. Jones, please tell us. Remember everyone's a suspect."

"I'm a suspect?"

"Everyone's a suspect, Ms. Jones."

Coming back into the fellowship hall, she scanned the room for Lynn; and when she didn't see her, she made her way to Pastor Alan's office. Reporters had descended on the place earlier and had stuck microphones in all their faces. She avoided them now by skirting through a back hallway and out the side door.

She twisted the knob on the office door only to find it locked, but John looked out the window and threw open the door for her. She hesitated, but he grabbed her arm and dragged her inside before relocking the door.

"We're taking a reprieve." Pastor Alan sat at the desk across from Daneen. "So, we've locked out the media."

Sharee dropped into a chair and told them about the detective's questions. "I wonder how they knew about Marci and Bruce, who told them, and why.

Daneen leaned across her desk. "Everything's bound to come out, Sharee. Roseanne told the detectives about Ted and Marci."

"But I thought Roseanne went home, too. She always goes home as soon as rehearsal is over. Checks on her dog. He gets out of the fence sometimes."

"She did, but she came back. Someone called her, I think. She came and talked to the detectives. Ted didn't. He joined you and John and Lynn while you were searching the lot next door, but it wasn't until later that the deputies caught up with him. Someone pointed him out to them. They weren't happy."

"Oh. He acted like he'd talked to them earlier."

John spun a chair around and straddled it. "I think that's what he wanted us to believe."

"What about Matthew?"

"He turned up during the initial search, remember? But they really grilled Ryann, which riled Matthew. He had some words with one of the detectives."

"Do they really think Ryann had something to do with it?" Sharee's voice rose, and she closed her eyes.

"No stone unturned, Darling."

Her eyes flew open but dropped when they met his. The concern there caused her heart to stammer. How could she deal with this and Joshua's kidnapping, too?

Lord, you promised not to give us more than we could bear.

Pastor Alan leaned his elbows on the desk. "They asked me about their relationship, too." He looked at John and Sharee. "Which I didn't know anything about. Between the two of you and the youth pastor, I usually know who's going with whom. How was I supposed to know they were a couple if no one bothered to tell me?"

John picked up a sandwich from a plate on Daneen's desk. "I don't think it's official yet."

"Did they ask about Abbey?" Sharee looked from John to Pastor Alan.

"No." The pastor made a heavy movement with his shoulders. "But I have to tell them about that note. It's not a confidential matter. It's a note John found. And it could be evidence." He shook his head. "I will not tell them who we think it is. We could be wrong. That will be up to them to figure out or find out from Ryann. The note, however, might be important. The baby's safety and return are central now." He rose from the chair. "John? You want to come with me?"

He moved over to his desk, pulled the drawer open, moved some things around, and drew out a piece of paper. "They'll probably ask for you, anyway, since you found it."

John finished the sandwich and pushed his chair back. "Yeah, sure. Deputy Richards will be glad to hear this. He thought I'd kept something back earlier, anyway."

Sharee glanced up. "He thought I did, too. That's why he followed me to my car that night."

"Was it? I thought he had other ideas."

"Like what?" She studied his face. "Oh, that's ridiculous."

"It was a hard night. Like others lately."

Silence filled the office. Sharee tore her eyes away from his to stare out the window. Pastor Alan cleared his throat.

John turned and moved toward the door. "Let's get this over with."

They left, closing and locking the door on their way out. Sharee lowered her head, staring at her hands for a while.

"Anything you want to talk about?" Daneen asked.

Sharee shook her head. "No. No, the important thing is Joshua. They have to find him, Daneen."

The pastor's wife nodded. "We're trusting God for that. That's all we can do now."

"I don't understand. The program seemed to go so well. How did this happen?"

"Satan comes immediately to steal the Word. We had a lot of people give their lives to Christ last night."

"But if I'd known this was going to happen..."

"You said you felt like God was leading you."

"I did." She tried to keep her voice from cracking. *I did, Lord. I thought you led me to do it. But I was wrong. I had to be wrong.*

"Sharee, hang on to God. Don't let go."

"Things happen we don't understand. People keep talking about it, but I've never had anything to deal with like this. John has, but—"

"John told you about Janice?"

"Yes."

Daneen's face lit. "Praise God. We wondered if he had when he started coming to church, but he didn't say anything."

"He keeps a lot bottled up."

"Yes, but lancing a boil is the best way to deal with it."

"Well, he did."

"A big step. So, what's wrong?"

Sharee rubbed her fingers across her forehead. "Me."

Daneen scooted closer. "Trust God. With John and with Joshua. Faith is a powerful weapon." She hugged Sharee. "I'm going to go find Marci now. I think she and Stephen both need some encouragement."

"Okay. I'll go to the sanctuary and pray."

"Try to avoid the media."

"I will. They're probably following John and Pastor Alan, anyway."

"Thank goodness the police have made the fellowship hall off-limits to them. Let's keep the door locked here, too." Daneen touched Sharee's shoulder and went out.

Sharee followed her, locking the door, and skirting around the TV crews, the police, and the searchers. She slipped into the sanctuary and knelt at the altar.

Peace descended as she let the prayers tumble the doubt from her shoulders. She inhaled deep into her lungs and forced her muscles to relax. Behind her, the sanctuary door opened. She moved her head.

Christy Byrd walked down the aisle. The lines around the woman's eyes looked deep, but she smiled. Sharee rose to her feet.

"The police have interviewed Ryann twice about her miscarriage, and now they've asked to interview her again."

Sharee reached to hug her. "I'm sorry, Christy. It must be horrible to have them question her. They mean well—they're trying to find Joshua—but it's tough."

"Ryann's just devastated." Christy's voice cracked. "As much as when she lost her own."

Sharee tightened her hug. "I wish there was something I could do."

Christy sniffed and straightened. "Miss Eleanor called to say those on the prayer team are praying for a miracle."

Sharee's gaze met the other woman's. "That's what we need."

"Yes."

"Listen, have you seen Bruce today? Bruce left early last night, and no one's seen him since."

"No, but I know the deputies are looking for him. It seems he's a prime suspect."

"I gathered that, but that's crazy. Is there anyone else who left the grounds after the program? Anyone that wasn't here when we first noticed Joshua was missing?"

"That's why the police questioned Ryann for so long. She left right at the end of the last song because she wanted to be alone. She came here to the sanctuary. She said something warm spread over her during the program, and she knew that her baby was okay."

"Really?"

"Yes. She felt peace, but she wanted to be alone, so she came here. No one saw her when they came looking later. She told the detectives she just laid across the seats in one row and didn't get up when people came through. Of course, she didn't know what was going on."

"What about Abbey? I know she disappeared, too."

"She was looking for Ryann and went home when she couldn't find her. And Matthew left, too."

"Was he looking for Ryann?"

"I think so. I'm not sure, though. Look, I think I better get back to the fellowship hall. I want to be there for Ryann."

Sharee followed her up the aisle and out the sanctuary door. Her eyes traveled over the patrol cars, news vans, and other automobiles lining the parking lot. Fewer than before. Good. She surveyed the scene in front of her. People milled about the parking lot.

A row of cars lined the parking lot. Besides the work buildings, Sharee noticed the back of a car parked off the pavement. In all respects, hidden from view. It's distinctive color identified it, though. She knew the owner.

Between her and the car, perhaps twenty or thirty people filled the parking lot. On her left, a group of trees and bushes grew and covered the ground up to the office. She left the church steps, sauntered over to them and circled around the back of the office. Passing behind the work buildings, she emerged near the end of the property. The old oaks, hung with Spanish moss, spilled dappled shadows across the ground.

Quiet filled the property here. Only bird songs and buzzing insects broke the silence. Sharee slipped over to the empty car and checked the back seat. The car seat still sat in the back. Something bothered her about it. Or was it another one? Another one out of place? Where was that?

She brought her mind back to the one in front of her. Why would Ted Hogan have a car seat? And why had he parked here, away from everyone else? She stood, eyes unfocused, thinking.

"What are you doing?"

Sharee jumped, whirling around. Ted stood three feet from her, eyes narrowed, fists clenched by his side.

Chapter 29

"Nothing," she said. "I...uh...nothing." She couldn't think past the obvious.

Ted studied her for a moment. "The car seat? You're wondering about the car seat. Is that it?"

"Yes."

"I told you before, this is none of your business."

"Well, I..."

"You're what?" He sneered. "Wondering if I had something to do with Joshua's disappearance? You really think I would do that? Hurt Marci that way?"

"Then what are you doing with the car seat?"

"None of your business. I told you before. My business and Marci's are not yours to worry about." He stepped forward. "You got that?"

Sharee backed up against the car. His mouth lifted on one side, and he stepped forward again.

A twig snapped to their right. Sharee jerked her head around, heart jumping.

John stood at the corner of the building. The shadows played over his face, but his eyes were intent on Ted. No one spoke.

Ted moved first, thrusting his hands into his pockets. "Your girlfriend seems to be playing detective. Why don't you set her straight and tell her I had no earthly reason to kidnap Joshua?"

They stood looking at each other. John put his hand out to Sharee. She crossed the grass to his side and caught his hand.

Ted gave a sharp laugh, whirled and strode away. They watched until he disappeared. A light breeze rustled the oaks and stirred the Spanish moss.

"Are you okay?" John's voice held a peculiar note.

She cleared her throat. "Yes."

"What was that about?"

"I just saw his car over here—kind of hidden—and I remembered I saw a car seat in it when we ate at the deli. I just wondered if he still had it."

"You think Ted had something to do with this?"

"I don't know. He said all those things about Marci not wanting Joshua.

But he's the one that resents the baby."

"You *were* playing detective."

"I didn't think about it. I just wondered."

"You didn't think?" The words jumped. "We're supposed to stay in groups. What are doing wandering around alone?"

She pulled her hand free. "Don't lecture me."

"Believe me, I'd like to do more than lecture."

A retort jumped to her lips but died at the concern she saw in his eyes.

"I saw you go past the window in the toolshed and wondered where you were headed. Sharee, someone kidnapped a baby." His voice emphasized the last sentence.

"I know."

"Well, stay away from Ted, will you? And don't go out alone."

She gave a mocking salute. "Aye. Aye."

"Good."

His mouth lifted when she scowled, and then his hand encircled hers. He turned her toward the parking lot. Sunlight spilled over the area. The news media had vanished.

"Go home and get some rest," John urged. "You must be exhausted."

"I can't."

"You can. No one's asking you to give up. Just get some rest."

"I won't be able to sleep."

"I went out with another search party but had to come back because I wasn't helping—just going through the motions. I'll find a place to crash soon, but you should go home. Come back later. We'll both be able to help once we've had some sleep."

"John, I can't."

"Do I have to lock you up someplace?" Gentle amusement laced the words.

Her heart ached at the warmth in his eyes. The heaviness that she was trying to keep at bay swept over her. She bit her lip and turned from his gaze.

His arm slipped around her shoulders, and he pulled her close. She stiffened. Why did he act like Friday night never happened?

"We need to talk." His voice had deepened.

What would she say? That unless he changed, it could never work between them? "No. Not now. Not until Joshua's found."

"I have something to tell you."

"No." She tugged free of his arm and tried to contain the emotions that surged through her. The last thing she wanted to do was to talk. She spun away, but he caught her arm and turned her around, frowning. She dropped her eyes from his gaze. "Not now. Please."

The quiet stretched and became uncomfortable before he answered. "Okay. Your way then. Later."

Her strength evaporated as if draining into the ground. Later. She didn't want later either. Fatigue flowed through every limb. Her watch showed 3:00 P.M. *Maybe I do need some rest.*

He guided her toward her car. "Go home. Get some sleep." He leaned over to open the SUV's door.

She hesitated. How could she leave? They hadn't found Joshua. Would they find him? Her heart shrunk, leaving an empty feeling inside. Why had she agreed to use him as Baby Jesus? *Idiot.* She should have insisted on a doll. Tears blurred her eyes, pooled, and overflowed.

"Don't, Sharee." John caught her shoulders. He held her against the car, his mouth touching the top of her head. She clung to him, telling herself how stupid she was for doing it.

"Don't," he said again. "It's not your fault. Don't beat yourself up."

A flash of light startled them, then another. John's head wrenched around. Sharee raised hers. The flash went off a third time. A man with a camera grinned at them and moved away. She noticed other cars arriving, people milling around behind him. Wherever they had gone, the media was back.

John reached past her, and tugged the car door open once more, giving her a gentle shove. "Take off before we have to deal with this stuff again."

She slid in and started the car. Every muscle ached. She looked up at him, and he reached inside to run a finger down her cheek.

Raised voices washed over them. The man with the camera, and then others, scurried toward a car pulling into a parking space. She and John watched until a familiar figure thrust his way through the media frenzy. Cameras flashed. People shouted questions. Sharee stared open-mouthed.

Matthew Thornton, face set, eyes staring straight ahead, ignored the questions and the popping camera lights and headed toward the fellowship hall. Deputy Richards held the door open and Matthew disappeared inside.

Chapter 30

Sharee managed to still the tears for the ride back, putting aside thoughts of John and Joshua and Matthew. Her mind went back over last night. Everything appeared to go well. The Lord's presence seemed so strong. What happened?

Out of the corner of her eye, she glimpsed someone walking. She moved her head to see in the rearview mirror. *Pedro?* She jerked to the left and, at the next turn, headed back. She found the next turn, came back up his side of the highway and drove onto the shoulder.

He ran to the side of the car and looked at her. "Sherry!"

"Pedro, what are you doing here?"

"Walking, hermana. What else?"

"But where did you go last night?"

"Last night? I saw you and John were busy, so I headed out."

"But you stayed for the program?"

"No. I thought I might help at first." He shrugged. "But I have to get on the road early, anyway."

"But…" Something felt wrong. *What—*

"Are you going to give Pedro a ride?"

"Oh, yes. Get in. Where do you want to go?"

Pedro slid into the passenger seat. A stale odor filled the car. "It is cold out today, do you think so?"

Sharee coughed and steered onto the road. "I haven't thought about it. Pedro. Until last night, we hadn't seen you for a while. Not since we started practice on the program. And I didn't get a chance to talk with you before the program."

"You were busy, hermana."

"Do you know what happened last night?"

"About the program?"

"No, about the baby. Joshua."

"The baby?"

"After the program. Joshua disappeared." Pedro gave her a strange look, and Sharee realized he had no idea who Joshua was. "Baby Jesus disappeared."

Some time passed before he spoke. "Someone took Baby Jesus?"

"Si`." She explained about Joshua, the dolls, the search parties, the detectives' questions and her own.

"Sherry, are you trying to figure out who took Joshua?"

"I guess so."

"You do not trust the deputies and these detectives?"

"Of course, I do. But Marci doesn't deserve this. No one deserves to have their baby taken. She and Stephen go out of their way to help others." Guilt pierced her. "And I planned the program. I let them bring Joshua." Is this how John felt? This overwhelming sense of wanting to redo all that had been done?

I want to move time back, Lord. To change what's happened. "I have to do something, Pedro. I have to."

His dark eyes studied her. "And John has no protest?"

"John?"

"He does not mind you trying to find this kidnapper?"

Her eyes met Pedro's again. How much had he learned about John in the time they'd spent together? She gave him a half smile.

"He sent me home to get some rest."

They rode in silence a while longer. *Marci is my friend, Lord. I've got to do something. Let me do something. Show me what to do.*

"So no one knows you are being the detective?" Pedro asked.

"No, I…"

"You think someone took the baby to get back at your friend?"

"Did I say that? Yes, I think so. You didn't want to watch the program last night? You helped so much with building everything."

He glanced her way. "I needed to find a place to sleep before it got late."

"But John would have…"

"With John, there would be strings this time."

"He doesn't like strings either, Pedro." She thrust aside the quick drop in her heart. "A number of people left after the program last night. Like Bruce, for instance."

"Bruce?"

"He's in the wheelchair."

Pedro nodded now. "I see him. He go past me very fast last night. Headed toward US 19."

"You saw him? After the program? But I thought you left early."

"Well," he shrugged. "It was cold. I kept walking. There's a place I know." His voice stopped.

She knew there were places the homeless would not tell outsiders about—an empty office building, perhaps. Not legal, but warm during cold snaps.

"Bruce went past you?"

He nodded. "I have seen his van before. He is at Anderson Park."

"Now?"

He looked at her in surprise. "I do not mean now. I mean many times at dusk when I have been there. He comes to—what do you say—to think."

"To meditate?"

"Meditate. Si."

"Well, Pedro, we're just gonna stop by there and see."

"You will take me to the church in Tarpon Springs later?"

"Yes, Pedro, I promise, just let me drive through Anderson Park. It's up here a few miles. Not far, you know. In Tarpon Springs, you said?"

"They will take me in tonight. It will be cold again. I could not get there last night. They might have hot food, also."

Dear Lord, she thought, he talks as if his life is normal, and sometimes I forget it's anything but. Forgive me.

"Perhaps your pastor, he hire me again?"

"I can't speak for Pastor Alan, Pedro, but you know I can get you something to eat. Do you have a blanket for tonight? Something warm?"

"It is okay, Sherry. Don't worry. On nights like tonight, the church, she is good."

The church consists of people, not a building. We are the church, the body of Christ.

"Sherry," Pedro interrupted, "you are awake, yes?"

"What? Oh." She yanked the wheel to the right and bumped over the entry into Anderson Park.

The pine and twisted oaks, the fern and palmetto, had always brought her peace. Her shoulders relaxed as she drove forward. A hundred memories of Lake Tarpon, the hardwoods, the wetlands and the animals—alligators, cormorants, turtles, and other animals—flooded her. If Bruce came here to meditate, she could understand and relate.

They'd soon spot his van if he were here. The Park's hundred acres took less than fifteen minutes to drive through. Down near the lake, she saw the small one-family picnic areas that edged the water, half-hidden by cypress and fern. To her left, boat docks and parking spaces for trucks and trailers gave easy access to watercraft.

"Does Bruce have a favorite place to park?" she asked.

"All over. He is a loner, I think. He finds a place where no people are." Then he pointed past her, out her window. "There, I think."

She slammed the brakes and wrenched the wheel to the left, following the drive to the boat docks. Bruce had parked close to the water. She could see him in his wheelchair at the end of one dock.

"Pedro?"

He shook his head, "No, Sherry, you go. Talk with him. I wait here."

"Okay." She jumped out and walked onto the dock. What would she say? Where did you go last night?

Just before she reached him, he turned his head. He looked unkempt, and for a minute, a wave of uncertainty, of caution, passed over her. What if... Then he smiled, and she shook off the unsettled feeling.

"Hey," she said.

"Hey, yourself." His smile widened. "Where did you come from?"

"I came looking for you."

His eyes showed surprise. "Looking for me?"

She sat down on the dock and gazed up at him. "You disappeared last night after the program, and no one's seen you since."

"I didn't know anyone would miss me. I've been here."

"Here? You mean all day?"

"No, I mean since last night." He turned his eyes back to the lake. "I needed to be alone. Just me and God."

She stared at the lake, too, quiet for a minute. "You were here all night? They let you stay?"

"No, they didn't let me. I managed to avoid the roundup. You know, like when they're closing, and you need to go." He frowned. "I probably do some strange things these days, but last night...last night God spoke to me during the program. I couldn't talk with anyone. I needed to be alone."

Sharee took a long breath, focusing her eyes on the lake for a minute. "Bruce, you don't know about Joshua?"

"Joshua?"

"Marci's baby."

"Yes. What about him?"

"He's missing."

"Missing?" His head swiveled in her direction.

"Yeah, missing. Somebody...somebody kidnapped him. Right after the program. The Sheriff's department is at the church. We've had major search parties. Everything."

He moved his wheelchair. "Marci's baby is missing?" When Sharee inclined her head, he said, "You're not kidding?" And a moment later, "I can't believe it. How's Marci? And Stephen?"

"About what you would expect. Frantic."

He started to turn his wheelchair then waited for her to move. "I need to get back." They headed toward the parking area. "You came to tell me? That was thoughtful."

She hesitated. "The detectives wanted to know where you were and why you left last night."

He rolled his wheelchair forward, moving off the dock and to his van.

He stopped at the back of his van and stared up at her. "Why should that concern them?"

"They're looking for anyone who left early last night."

"They think I might have kidnapped Joshua? Are they crazy?"

"They just want to ask you some questions."

"Why would I take Joshua?" Then his look hardened. "Oh, I get it. I'm getting back at Marci for the accident."

"I didn't say…"

"You didn't have too." His voice grated. "Well, who else could it be? Aren't I the best candidate? The paraplegic. The wheelchair-bound man. Bitter and vengeful."

"Bruce, no one said that."

"But everyone's thinking it." He nodded toward her SUV. "I see you brought reinforcements. That was smart. Hello, Pedro. So you knew where to find me?"

"I didn't bring reinforcements. Pedro just needed a ride."

His eyes focused again on her, dark now, and he asked softly, "So, who else knows you came to look for me? Anyone?"

Chapter 31

"Who else?" Bruce asked again.

"Uh, no one."

"Not a good answer. You better think this through before you go confronting kidnap suspects. Or is it murder I'm supposed to have done? Look, I'm going back. Stay out of my way, so I don't run you over. On accident, of course."

Sharee jumped out of the way when the back doors swung open, and he rolled inside. She went to her SUV. Bruce backed out a moment later and drove past.

Her heart ached for him, but anger surged, too. Kill the messenger, will you? She backed out in turn, and in a minute, turned north onto US 19.

"Pedro, you said Bruce went by you last night."

"Yes, Sherry."

"Then how did he get into the park? He said something about being here all night, but we know that can't be true…"

"You think Bruce is the kidnapper?"

"I don't know what I think."

"If he took the baby, Sherry, where is the baby now?"

"I don't know, Pedro. That is why I am so scared."

"Babies bring good money."

Her head twisted his way. "What?"

"You had not thought about that? Babies bring good money. People want them. Especially when they cannot have their own."

Her hands tightened on the wheel. "George mentioned that."

"Aye. He and I discussed it when I work there. It is something to think about. I think of it first thing." An uneasy silence fell between them, but another mile or two down the road, Pedro asked, "You will drop me at the church, Sherry?"

"Yes, but isn't it early?"

"I have things…that need to be done. Drop me off. Never worry. I will be fine."

She dropped him at the side door, made a loop in the drive, and hit the brakes. Should she go home or back to the church?

Her mind juggled the information she knew about the accident. The accident. Bruce hadn't worn his seat belt, and the police cited the other driver; but did he harbor bitterness toward Marci? Would he do something this horrible to get back at her? He had knocked Marci down with his wheelchair. An accident, or was it? He said God moved during the program last night, and he wanted to be alone, but he'd lied to her. The "roundup" as he called it happened at dusk, at closing time. But he wasn't there at closing time. How did he get in after dark? If he did get in then. Even now, he said he needed to get back to church. Or had he just said that? Because he needed to leave in a hurry? What if he came to the park, to the lake last night for a reason? Not Joshua... She recoiled from the thought.

She needed time to think and pray. She put the car in drive and edged forward onto US 19 once more. A few miles down the road, she pulled into a McDonald's drive-thru, ordered a small coke and parked. She sat and thought and prayed.

Pedro's story didn't make sense, either. He said he'd left the program early, but then he saw Bruce leaving at the end of it, and he mentioned about babies bringing good money. Why would he say that?

Someone needed motive and opportunity. Opportunity limited itself to those acting in the program last night. Or did it? Someone might have snuck into the back of the set while the spotlight highlighted the players in front. But then, they would have to know where the baby would be and that everyone else would be occupied beforehand. That severely limited the suspects.

Who had a grudge against Marci? That's what the disfigured dolls and notes indicated. Had someone planned to kidnap the baby all along?

Bruce had motive and opportunity, but how would he get Joshua to his van without being seen? Impossible. Unless... Could the baggy costume he'd chosen hide a baby in his lap? And no one saw him leave last night. He just disappeared.

What about Ryann? Could Ryann's pain have evolved to such a point that kidnapping Joshua seemed a solution? Her story about being in the sanctuary while the others sought high and low for the baby seemed farfetched. But if so, where was the baby now? Surely, she'd have left with the baby.

And Abbey? She'd disappeared after the program, too. Could she have taken the baby someplace? Sharee's breath caught. What if they were in it together? Ryann and Abbey? She pondered it for a while then shook her head.

Ted. Did he resent the baby enough to do this? But where could Joshua be? No one had disappeared like you would expect if they had kidnapped the baby.

Sharee rested her head in her hands. So many people acted in the program, all with opportunity. And she had felt so pleased and encouraged about how many were taking part! If she'd only substituted a doll for Joshua's part...substituted...

Her mind whirled and held the thought. But that was too crazy. Think real, Sharee. That's too improbable. Or was it?

Sharee bowed her head and prayed.

Ten minutes later, the CR-V's engine came to life. She knew how out of place one thing appeared. If she took that one thing and put the other information around it, then things made sense. She could be wrong. Other evidence that she did not have could prove her wrong, but she could be right, too.

Go.

She hesitated, her hand on the gear shift. John would think what she planned foolish and dangerous. She shouldn't worry. She knew, and he must, too, that their relationship wouldn't work. He didn't want to be pushed, and she wanted someone with whom she could serve God. She'd push for sure, and she'd make him miserable. Her heart jerked at the thought. Pain enveloped it.

Her hands tightened on the steering wheel. He got angry too fast, anyway, and was way too protective. She understood about his wife and Alexis, but she could foresee the problems. Again that erratic jerk of her heart. It didn't matter, anyway. Joshua topped all priority lists.

Go now.

She dug her phone from her purse and texted a reply to his last message. How long ago? Two nights ago? It seemed like forever. At least, she had used her head, her common sense, and texted for back-up. That should make him happy.

She stepped on the gas and headed back to church. All around her, the air seemed to vibrate.

Hurry.

Her foot pressed harder on the accelerator.

Chapter 32

She drove through the parking lot at the church, praying under her breath. The air still vibrated with urgency. She passed the office, the work buildings, the parking lot full of cars, and pulled onto the back road where she and John had jogged. The Honda slowed to a crawl. She wasn't exactly sure which house, but she would recognize it.

The Dodge van stood in the driveway. A straight line could be drawn from the house through the cypress trees across the field to the fellowship hall. The lawn needed mowing even in winter. It spoke of neglect.

Sharee parked in the street, climbed from the CR-V and glanced around. John should have seen her text by now. Perhaps she should wait. She wrapped her arms around herself. *Not so brave now, are you?* Her gaze went back down the road toward the church. He'll be here. Unless he put his phone down. She rubbed her fingers across her forehead. He did that sometimes—took it off the belt clip and laid it down somewhere. She tugged her jacket tighter, feeling the sense of urgency still. *I can't wait forever.*

She started for the front door then slowed, eyeing the van. An older model. Good. Perhaps...

She walked to the driver's side and saw the car seat in the back. With a quick movement, she snatched open the driver's door. Her breathing sounded loud in her ears. Could she do this? A quick prayer went to heaven, and then she leaned forward and yanked on the hood latch. Two minutes later, she eased the hood down and headed for the front door.

A dog hit the fence on her left, snarling and barking. She jumped back. Shock leaped through her, and her hand rose to her chest. She should have remembered. The dog leaped at the fence again. The barking grew louder. A vicious display of teeth joined the noise. She sprinted for the front door.

Her knuckles made quick, loud knocks on the door. No answer. She knocked again, the sound mingled with the pit bull's growl and the whine from the fence as he jumped against it. Minutes passed. Sharee pounded, thumped, banged.

As she lifted her sore knuckles once more, the door flew open.

"What do you want?" Roseanne glared at her then whirled toward the dog. "Shut-up, Bull! Quiet!" The dog subsided, but a continual snarl rolled their way. "What do you want? I'm busy."

Sharee stared. The red hair was now brown, and the bright clothes with matching earrings had changed, too. The woman was dressed in all black and had one slender necklace circling her throat. Behind her, the room was bare except for a sofa, coffee table, and lamp. Nothing else, and nothing on the walls or tables.

She brought her attention back to the woman. "I want Joshua."

Roseanne blocked her way. "I don't know what you're talking about. I'm busy." She tried to close the door.

Sharee stuck her foot out and grabbed the door.

The other woman tried to yank it free. "What are you doing? Let go!"

"No. Let me in."

The dog's barking increased. Roseanne turned and shouted at him. Sharee, feeling the urgency, stepped past her into the room. Suitcases were stacked next to the door.

"Hey! What are you doing?" The woman tried to step in front of her.

"I told you. I want Joshua."

"I don't know what you're talking about."

"Oh, don't you?" Sharee leaned over and lifted a diaper bag from among the luggage. If she'd had needed something to confirm her hunch, the diaper bag did it.

"Leave that alone!" Roseanne yanked it from her hand and dropped it to the floor.

"Besides Bruce and Pedro, you were the only one who didn't search for Joshua last night. Pedro left way before the program ended. And Bruce, well let's just say Bruce has God for an alibi. Do you have an alibi, Roseanne? You came back and talked to the police, but then you disappeared again."

"I came home to check on my dog. All the lights and sirens last night upset him."

"Like he is now, you mean? Is he the one who found that first doll and carried it off to the field and left it? Where had you put it? Wherever it was, your dog found it, didn't he? We all know he gets out of that fence once in a while. You recognized it that night, didn't you? That's why you were so horrified."

"I told you, already. I don't know what you're talking about." She looked past Sharee and shouted at the dog once more. Her eyes shifted. She glanced over her shoulder.

Sharee's gaze followed hers down the hall, and she took a step forward. Roseanne shifted her position and blocked her.

"You need to get out of here."

"Not without the baby."

Roseanne's hand shot out, grabbing her arm, shoving her back toward the open door. "Get out!"

Sharee struggled with her, yanking free. "Tell me why you have a car seat in your van. You couldn't have bought one just to carry Joshua around when Marci needed help. She has one for him. No, you got it because even before he was born, you planned to kidnap him, didn't you?"

"You're crazy!" Roseanne grabbed the door and tried to force Sharee back so she could close it. In the background, the dog's snarl continued, and the woman's eye flicked its way.

Where was John? Hadn't he got her text? If he didn't come soon, how would she get Joshua away from this woman?

"I told you I'm busy," Roseanne said. She glanced at her watch. "I want you to leave. If not, I'll call the police."

"Yeah. Do that. In fact, I might."

Roseanne's eyes narrowed, her face drew tight, and then her look changed. She hesitated a moment. "Okay. You want to see the baby? Okay. Come on. I'll show you." And when Sharee hesitated, she smirked. "You do want to see him, don't you?"

A horrible feeling went up Sharee's spine. *Dear God*, she prayed, *please let him be okay. Please.* "Yes," she managed. "Yes, I do."

Roseanne made a motion with her hand, waving Sharee inside; and when Sharee stepped forward, Roseanne closed the door.

❧

John stood at the office window when Sharee drove past. He frowned. She hadn't slept long, if at all. Well, he hadn't either. He craned his neck to see where she parked. Behind the buildings like Ted? An alarm went off inside, but he relaxed. He'd seen Ted go out with another search party just a short time ago.

Behind him, the pastor moved around the office, picking up things, putting them down, stacking books that lay on the receptionist's desk.

John turned to him, "What's wrong with you, Alan? You're turning into a fidgety old man."

The pastor looked up, distracted. "I don't know." He thought for a moment, shrugged, and began to pace. Under his breath, he began to pray.

John watched him and shook his head. "Look, I'm going to go find out which area we need to search next."

"Yeah. Do that." Alan reached for his chair and turned it so the seat faced him. He knelt down. He motioned to John. "No, John, wait. *Pray.*" He put his elbows on the seat of the chair, leaned over, and began to pray.

John watched for a minute. His gaze ricocheted between the door and his cousin. He started to sit down in the other chair, but stopped, took the cell phone from his pocket and placed it on the desk. The clip had broken during the night's search. He sat in the nearest chair and bowed his head.

❧

Sharee stood looking down at Joshua in the portable crib. The small room cocooned him. Besides the crib, a chest of drawers, a changing table, and a rocking chair crowded the space. Roseanne had planned well. The hair on the back of Sharee's neck rose, but she leaned over the baby. His sound sleep and easy breathing soothed her worry.

God, she prayed, *you have to stop this woman—for her own sake and for the baby's.*

Her eyes rose to meet Roseanne's hard gaze. It's strange, Sharee realized, but I'm not afraid right now.

"Roseanne, this baby has done nothing to you. He's only two months old. Let me take him home."

The woman's eyes darkened. "He hasn't done anything, but his mother has. She killed my son. Killed him. She took mine; now I'm taking hers."

"How did she kill your son?" But she knew already. It's why she'd come here. And the woman had already confirmed what she'd thought, what God had showed her. A substitution—'She took mine; now I'm taking hers.'

"In a car accident. Oh, she and the police tried to blame me. They said I ran the red light, but she was speeding!" Her voice grew louder. "Look at Bruce. Look what she did to him. He goes around all the time acting like it's okay. Being so sweet and kind to her like they were still friends, but I know how he feels."

"I was on vacation when the accident happened. I only heard a little about it. Marci doesn't talk about it much."

"Of course not. Sweep it all under the rug, you Christians. She only called me once and didn't even come to the funeral." Her face stilled. "She killed my son, and he was all I had."

"Roseanne, I'm so sorry. I had no idea." Two years. She's waited two years to get revenge. Had the pain built until she could stand it no longer? Sharee noticed her dead eyes. "But the other woman's name, wasn't it Sheraton? Something like that?"

"Yes, Midge Sheraton, that's me. You didn't think I'd come here and give my real name, did you? I watched for weeks in the mall, waiting until I saw a woman who looked something like me and then followed her until I could steal her purse."

"But the detectives they…"

"Think I am Roseanne Sawyer as they're supposed too. I told them last night I had my purse stolen and then moved down here, so my new ID has my old address. If the other woman filed a report, that's all they'll see. A stolen purse. They'll figure it out, but not before I'm gone." Her eyes narrowed.

"But the deputies canvassed the area last night."

"I was in and back out of here before they started. Dropped off the baby with a little cold medicine that put him to sleep, and I went back to the church." Her mouth stretched into a sneer. "And answered all their questions. I gave them everything they wanted on everyone else. They think I'm a gossip, but it got them looking at others, not me."

"But...how did you away without any of us seeing you? And the dogs. They weren't able to track you."

"You think I'm stupid because I dressed like that? I made up that persona. You all laughed behind my back, I'm sure, but that's what I wanted. And when I volunteered for your little Christmas program, I knew it would give me the chance I wanted, and I was right."

"But..."

"I suggested the manger in the back to Marci. It went like clockwork. When everyone was singing—so nice of you to have us all sing at the end—I just slipped away, slipped through that little door, grabbed Joshua and walked into the night."

"But the dogs. They should have tracked you."

"Ha. Dogs aren't miracle workers. A few feet from the road, I grabbed the scarf I had for the costume." She stopped and grinned. "Now you know why I was so upset when I couldn't find it? It was just the size to cover him completely and stiff enough not to smother him when I put him into the bag."

"Into the bag?" Her voice elevated.

"Yeah, it was actually one of those insulated diaper bags. I fixed it so no one would know. I wrapped him in the scarf and put him in the bag and zipped it up."

Sharee felt her eyes widening. The woman sounded crazy. Was she really going to try to fly out of here with Joshua? Suddenly, a cold chill crept up her spine. Where was John? She needed help.

Midge Sheraton laughed. "Yes, I did have it figured out. I carried him home in the diaper bag—all wrapped up so no skin cells got out. Insulated bag. Tracking dogs have their noses to the ground, but they weren't tracking me, and I had used that route so many times, it wouldn't have made a difference, anyway. Even if they tracked me to the house. I've walked home that way every night during practice."

"But why didn't you leave last night?"

"And let them know for sure who to look for? This way, they have plenty of suspects. Bruce, Ted, even Marci. Those girls. That homeless man that's been hanging around. I even implied that you knew more than you were telling." The satisfaction in her voice slithered over Sharee's nerves. "They'll take another day or two checking everyone's information, and I'll be gone before that. No one but Marci will miss me for days, and Marci has too much on her mind to consider what it might mean."

Sharee's heart stuttered. No one would miss her for days unless Sharee sent up the alarm. *Dear Lord, I need help.* "You can't do this, you know. It's wrong, and you'll never get away with it."

"You think I care about what's right or wrong?"

"Yes, I think you do. If you want revenge, then you know there's a right and wrong." She studied the woman. "You couldn't have known about Marci's pregnancy when you came. Had you planned something else?"

Roseanne's mouth thinned. "I wasn't sure. I dyed my hair and wore those outrageous clothes. I knew she'd never recognize me. She'd only seen me once. I could do whatever I wanted after I got here. When I heard she was pregnant, then I knew. But I didn't want her to be happy about it. I wanted her miserable. So, I got the dolls. But you know about that, don't you? You kept interfering. That's why I left one on your door." She spun around, grabbed a purse from the rocking chair, and yanked something from it. When she swung back, a gun pointed at Sharee's chest.

Everything stopped. She could only stare at the gun. *Either I'm going to die, or I'm going to walk out of here with Joshua. Which one, Lord?*

"Get in the closet." Midge Sheraton ordered.

"You can't do this." Sharee kept her voice soft.

"You don't know what I can do. I came to get revenge, and it doesn't matter how I do it. But Joshua…Joshua will replace Kenny. God is smiling on me."

Kenny, Sharee repeated the name to herself. Sharee felt compassion wash over her.

"Roseanne…I mean Mrs. Sheraton, God isn't smiling on you. Satan is tempting you. You're not a kidnapper. You're a mother who has lost a son. You're hurting."

"Don't give me your platitudes. What would you know about it?" The words erupted with emotional debris.

Sharee leaned back, took a long breath. "I don't, but other people do. John lost his wife. Ryann lost her baby. Look at God, His Son died, too."

"That means nothing to me."

"But it should. God's Son died for you because He loves you."

The woman's look hardened. The gun rose higher. "I don't need his love. Get in the closet, or I'll pull the trigger."

Sharee didn't move, but her glance slid toward Joshua. *Lord....* "Let me take the baby home, Mrs....Sheraton. He's innocent. Just like your son was."

"Don't talk about my son!"

"Tell me about him."

"I don't want to talk about him!" She waved the gun. Pain rolled across her face. "He was only ten. Only ten. He was all I had."

Sharee remained silent, praying, asking for the right words, the right tone, asking the Lord to heal this woman whose pain had led her to such devastating actions.

The woman focused on Sharee again. Her face straightened. The gun focused. A cold shiver ran up Sharee's spine.

"Mrs. Sheraton," Sharee kept her words soft, "your son wouldn't want you to do this."

"Don't tell me what my son would want."

"Your son was a child. Children don't like to hurt things. He wouldn't want you to do this."

"Stop saying that!" She put both hands to her ears, but still clutched the gun in her right one.

Sharee started to move, then halted. In the movies, the heroine would jump the other woman, grab the gun and get free. Should she? The distance between them, getting around the crib, looked impossible. What if they struggled? What if the gun went off and the bullet hit Joshua? She stopped. *I'm not the heroic type, Lord. And I can't risk Joshua. Help.*

Sharee cleared her throat. "What would Kenny want you to do?"

The woman lowered her hands and pointed the gun at Sharee's chest.

Chapter 33

The late afternoon sun slanted across the field. John paced back and forth in front of the bleachers, his mind jumping from one thought to another.

Three years had passed since he'd done any substantial praying. When he'd let himself out of the office a few minutes ago, Alan still knelt, still prayed. *How long can you pray without knowing what you're praying for?* His own prayers had centered on Sharee and Joshua and their safety. He hadn't understood why he'd included prayer for Sharee's safety. She should be here somewhere. He needed to find her.

He started to pass the bleachers but stopped. A memory had intruded— of teenagers holding hands, deep in prayer. At seventeen, he'd stood with them, seeking God with all his heart. The reality and the emotions of that time swept over him, along with the passion God's love had created in him.

His heart jerked; his head lifted. *What do you want from me?*

Will you serve me?

Pain rolled back and forth like the thrust and withdrawal of the tides. If he never understood about Janice, he still needed to make a decision about God. Was God good? Was He righteous? Was He worth serving as John once thought?

Life wasn't what you wanted. It wasn't heaven, and maybe that's what created the problem. His desire for heaven on earth. Like Abraham, he'd looked for a city whose builder and maker was God, a place of no sorrow and no more tears. But those words talked about heaven, not earth.

Will you serve me?

John raised his head again. *I promised that if you saved Joshua, I would serve you.* Silence encompassed him. *That's not what you want, is it? You want me without the strings, without conditions, like Sharee said.*

Swallowing, he sat on the bleachers, his soul challenged. He pictured Jesus on the cross, and he bowed his head. Anguish and repentance washed over him. *Forgive me, Lord, my hard-heartedness, my anger. You have loved me even when I wanted nothing to do with you. Forgive me. Yes, I'll serve you.* God's presence seemed to envelope him as it had the night before, the residue of anger and pain washed from him.

Rising, he began to pace again, praying in repentance and submission, and mumbling, "Whatever you want, Lord. Whatever you want."

᷎

The gun looked enormous. Around it, everything wavered. The chill chased up Sharee's spine again. She raised her eyes to the woman before her. Midge Sheraton's blank expression seared Sharee's heart.

"You don't want to do this, Mrs. Sheraton. Let me take Joshua home."

"Get in the closet."

"Please. You cannot—"

"Get in the closet!"

Sharee hesitated.

The woman's hand moved, the gun pointed at Joshua. "It doesn't matter to me. Either way, I get revenge."

"No! *No.* Stop. I...I'll get in the closet."

The gun arced back her way. It indicated the closet's direction. Sharee slid her foot back.

"All the way."

Sharee glanced around and took another step back. "You can drive away or catch a plane. Whatever. Just leave the baby."

"Shut up." The woman leaped forward, and Sharee flinched backward and hit the door. "Open it. Get in."

Sharee turned and fumbled with the knob. When she opened the door, a hand hit her back and she lurched into the closet. The door slammed. Darkness swallowed her. She stood immobile, transfixed, fighting waves of nausea. A loud scraping sound came from the room. Something slid across the floor, followed by a rocking echo and thud. A hard and heavy object landed against the door. Pitch-blackness amplified the sound.

Sharee felt for the door and put her hands against it. "Mrs. Sheraton, please. Leave Joshua. He's done nothing to you."

No reply.

Then she heard something else slide across the floor, a bang, and an additional thump on the door. Sharee fought the cold, sticky feeling that swept over. *I will not faint. I will not faint.*

"Mrs. Sheraton!"

Nothing. Quiet.

She waited, listening.

Nothing.

She called again. The silence answered.

Leaning forward, she slid her hand over the door, feeling for the knob. When she found it, she grasped and twisted it, pushing outward. Nothing happened. She tried again, throwing her weight against it. A slight movement? Her heart jolted with hope, but the next instant, she froze.

A scrabbling, clawing sound reached her ears. The sound seemed to come from the hall, growing louder each second, and then it filled the room. She stepped back from the door.

"There!" Mrs. Sheraton's voice rose in triumph. "That will keep you!"

Sharee's hand clutched her chest. "Mrs. Sheraton! Please, leave Joshua…"

Ferocious barking cut off her words and filled the air.

Chapter 34

The outside door slammed shut. Sharee's heartbeat accelerated, and her hand rose to her throat. She heard the beast sniffing and stepped backward. A second later, the dog hit the door, clawing at the opening near the floor. Her breath caught and her heart hammered. Whatever the woman had propped against it hadn't kept him away.

She began to shake. *No, please, Lord, no.*

Trembling started in her legs, and she threw her hands out in the darkness. Nothing. She'd seen a shelf above her, filled with objects, and she grabbed for it. Her hands closed on something hard, but it shifted and fell. The metallic crash caused an explosion of barking. She jumped back and grabbed for the overhead shelf again. This time, her hands closed on something soft. In another instant, it toppled over and dropped on top of her. She tried to drag it from her head, stumbled into the wall and crashed to the floor.

The dog's barking reached a new level. He tore at the door, scratching and snarling. Sharee pushed herself backward, her prayers loud and fervent, her voice merging with the dog's.

The slice of light from under the door leaped at her. Shadows jumped across it as the pit bull clawed harder. Sharee's breath came in shallow gasps.

Think, Sharee, think. God's with you. You can do this. She forced herself to her feet. What had she heard?

Midge Sheraton had dragged something over and tilted it against the closure, then added a second one. But they hadn't kept the dog away. They must have legs. The chest of drawers and the changing table. That had to be it. What else was there except the crib? Sharee took a deep breath, trying to ignore the dog's growling. If she pushed hard enough, maybe she could rock them upright.

But she'd have to deal with the dog to get out. Cold cloaked her for a moment then she shook herself. *No. He can't get in, Sharee. Even if the door opens a couple of inches, he won't be able to get in.*

She moved the soft object to the right, climbed to her feet, and repeated all the scripture she could remember. When she grasped the door handle, she took a long breath. A moment later, she turned it and threw herself against the door. Immediately, the dog's howl filled the air.

She dropped back, pain slicing through her side.

Had she imagined the slight give?

With the animal's constant noise, it was hard to think.

She stepped back, turned the handle again, and flung her whole body against the door. Pain shot through her shoulder. She collapsed backward, but two inches of yellow light brought highlights to her prison.

The dog's nose pushed against the gap, snarl rising. Sharee's hand rose to her mouth. She stepped back, swallowing hard. The dog's teeth gnashed against the door like jagged rocks. Her stomach clenched.

If it opened more, the dog would attack. She scooted to a back corner of the closet and collapsed, sobbing.

❧

It took a few minutes, over her own fear, before she realized the dog had quieted. She glanced at the door. His nose was pushed against it, but he'd stopped gnawing, stopped growling. She swallowed and wiped her face.

Lord, I've always wanted to do things myself, but I can't now. Where's John? Where is he?

She shifted her position, and the dog snarled. She froze.

I have to do something. I have to. I can't stay here. Lord, you're with me. I want John, but you're here, and you're enough. She shoved herself to her feet. Through the crack at the door, she saw the dog rise, too.

A weapon. She needed a weapon. Her gaze dropped to the floor. The ribbon of light lay across the comforter. Not exactly what she what she wanted, but it did offer protection. She yanked it from the floor. For one second, the dog's eyes were level with hers, teeth bared, deep guttural snarl emitting from its throat.

She started to step back but stopped. "Hush," she commanded. "Be quiet!"

The words set him off. His barking rose to a deafening din. She shuddered, but shook herself and caught the comforter under her chin. Gripping it with both fists, she pulled it to cover her legs and feet then edged toward the door.

Perhaps, with luck—no, with God—she could stop him. She stood for a moment, blocking out the dog's noise and prayed.

Swallowing, she grasped the knob and fumbled with the comforter in her hand. The dog shoved against the door, barking wildly. She tried the doorknob again. When it turned, she took a deep breath and leaped forward. A thump and a crash, and the door jolted wide. The dog leaped for her.

Her arms shot up and out for protection even as she screamed. The pit bull hit her and sent her spiraling back into the closet. The comforter was wrenched from her hands, and the dog yelped, the tone different from anything she'd heard.

She scrambled to her feet and stood paralyzed for a moment as he spun under the weight and blackness of the spread. The bedding twisted around him.

She raced for the door. Yanking it open, she jumped through and slammed it behind her. Her head dropped for a moment. Yes. Yes. Yes! She tore down the hall and skidded into the living room.

The front door stood open, and the suitcases had disappeared. Only one thing was left. Joshua sat gurgling and bubbling in his car seat. Sharee stared in amazement. She ran to the front window in time to see Mrs. Sheraton bang the van's hood down and start back toward the house.

Sharee backed up next to Joshua. In another moment, the woman stepped through the door. Her eyes widened.

"How did you get out?"

"It doesn't matter." Sharee tried to steady her breathing. "I'm taking Joshua home."

The other woman's face drew into a sneer. "You won't get past me."

They surveyed each other. The door still stood open. Freedom beckoned. Sharee's breathing slowed, and she realized the woman held no gun. Her gaze swept the room. No purse anywhere. No gun. In the car?

"I'm taking the baby." Sharee's own voice surprised her. Its depth and determination came from someone or somewhere else.

"No."

"Do you think your son would want you to do this?"

"I don't care! He's not here. Not…alive…any longer."

"Think about him. Would he want you to steal another person's child?" And when the woman did not answer, she asked, "Would he want you in prison?"

The woman's mouth worked. Pain crossed her face. Sharee let the silence speak, allowed God to work. Tears formed in the woman's eyes.

Sharee licked her lips. "Let us go. Both of us."

The woman didn't move. Sharee leaned forward and started to pick up the car seat.

"No!" The threat in the woman's voice rang clear.

Sharee froze as the Mrs. Sheraton moved, blocking the doorway.

"You have to let us go," Sharee spoke with authority. "Your van won't start, and if you were flying someplace, you've missed your plane by now or you will. All your plans have fallen apart."

&

Pastor Alan paused in the middle of rising to his feet. He knelt back down, bowing his head again, his heart reaching to God.

&

"It's not going to work," Sharee said. "All your planning. Nothing will bring your son back, and you'll ruin his memory."

The tears flowed in silent streams down the woman's face, but her eyes never left Sharee.

"Jesus can help you, though, with the pain."

This time, the woman's eyes closed. A moment later, her face crumbled. She bent her head and began to sob.

Sharee hesitated. Compassion filled her. Joshua gurgled. She leaned, unbuckled Joshua from the car seat, and gathered him into her arms. The car seat would be too heavy to carry and take too much time to strap in. She could go faster by foot. She had only to cross the road and then she'd be at the backside of the pond with the field and the church just beyond.

Midge Sheraton's sobs rent her heart.

Go.

She edged around the woman, cold insides waiting for her to make a move. But she made none. Sharee slipped out the door, and Joshua began to squirm in her arms. Nerves drew like taut fingers throughout her back; her arms shook. Behind her, the sobbing stopped. Sharee's step quickened. Her back felt like a huge target. If Midge Sheraton got the gun...

She started to pass the van and stopped. Shifting Joshua to her left arm, she tugged open the van door with her right hand. The purse sat in the middle of the seat. She leaned over and grabbed the purse. Its heaviness confirmed her suspicions, and she slipped it over her arm.

Sharee turned and rushed past her SUV. On the other side of the street, she stumbled down into the dry ditch and up the other side. To her left, the cypress trees rose tall and thin, close together like a wall. Pencil straight sentinels. The pond was on her left now, and relief began to pump through her body. She concentrated on not falling and began to cross the field. A glance behind showed no one following. She stumbled and caught herself, squeezing Joshua to her chest. The baby gave a small cry.

"Sharee?" John's voice, thrown across the field, brought her head up.

She saw him standing in front of the bleachers, staring her way.

"*I've got him, John!*" Her voice rose, emotion spilling forth. "I've got Joshua!"

Chapter 35

John stared. She'd found him! He shot a glance over his shoulder. Some people stood talking by the fellowship hall. He saw Deputy Richards. "She's found him!" He shouted and began to run across the field.

Seconds later, he reached her and skidded to a stop. Wide-eyed joy filled her eyes. "Where? How did you—"

"Roseanne. Roseanne had him."

"What? But—"

"You found him?" Deputy Richards jerked to a stop beside them. His hand moved from the holster on his hip to touch the baby's cheek. "This is Joshua? You're sure?" When Sharee nodded, he reached out. "Let me have him for a moment."

Sharee's brows rose. She glanced at John, and he lifted a brow, too. After a pause, she leaned toward the deputy and let him take the child from her arms. He cradled him against his chest, talking to him, soothing him, acting like a new father. John stared, knowing his mouth hung open.

The deputy raised his head. "Got one at home the same age. Sure didn't want anything to happen to this one."

Other people began arriving. Before long, a crowd made a tight knot around them, craning their heads to see Joshua. Voices grew louder each moment.

"Let's get back to the fellowship hall." The deputy nodded toward Sharee. "We'll need a statement."

"The baby's parents are here!" Someone yelled.

The mass of people parted, and Marci and Stephen pushed forward. John slipped his arm around Sharee and watched Marci grab Joshua from Richards' arms. Stephen enfolded them both in his.

Cameras appeared over the crowd's heads, and reporters pushed through the crowd, shouting questions. John heard Sharee's name mentioned and saw the swarm of reporters break and half slide in their direction. He pulled her closer.

The Deputy stepped in front of them just as the detectives arrived. In a few minutes, the detectives led them away, and Richards kept the media at bay. They made their way back to the fellowship hall.

"I've got a gun," Sharee said in an abrupt tone.

Michael O'Shay straightened, and the other detective's hand slipped under his coat.

"It's Roseanne's...Midge Sheraton's. That's her real name. It's in this purse. She kidnapped Joshua." Sharee slipped the purse from her arm.

The detective took it, opened it, and checked the gun.

Detective O'Shay frowned. "We need a statement. How did you..."

A chill radiated through John. Roseanne had a gun? How did Sharee get the gun and the baby?

The men spewed questions at her. At the end of her brief story, both detectives threw him wide-eyed looks. She'd gone alone to confront Roseanne, and Roseanne had threatened her with the gun, locked her in a closet, and put the dog to guard her. Another chill went through him.

The detectives scrambled for their cars, and they watched them whirl out of the parking lot. Other law enforcement followed them, and the reporters raced for theirs. Deputy Richards walked their way.

So many emotions rocketed through John that he didn't know which one to go with. Relief, disbelief, thankfulness, anger.

Anger won. "What in the world were you thinking? Why didn't you come for one of the detectives? Or me? Anyone?"

Sharee didn't answer but turned to watch Marci, Stephen, and Joshua.

"You went over there alone." He stared at her averted head, wanting to pull her back around, wanting to shake her and hold her all at the same time "Why? Why didn't you wait? Didn't you think—"

Sharee raised her head a moment but turned back toward the others again.

His anger deflated like a flattened football. "She locked you in the room with the dog?"

Sharee shuddered, and he reached for her, pulling her into his arms.

"Yes." Her voice was low. "I don't know how she knew."

"I'm sure she didn't, but she could bet that dog would scare anyone."

"I knew I had to get Joshua. I couldn't let the dog stop me."

"If you had called..."

"I did. I mean, I texted; but I knew God would help me."

He stared over her head, willing himself to calm down, to keep his mouth shut. She'd never cared for her own safety. Never took precautions. The girl needed someone to take care of her. She needed protection—from herself.

"John? They won't hurt her, will they?"

"Hurt her?" He paused. "Roseanne? Not if she doesn't resist."

"I feel for her, John."

"You feel for her?" She'd surprised him before, but not quite this way.

"She lost her son."

"But was taking someone else's."

"I know, and I know it's wrong, but she has no one else. He was all she had. I can't help feeling sorry for her."

"Okay."

The compassion that came from her shouldn't surprise him, but it did. Given so quickly, so easily. They both stared as the crowd a few yards away began to break up. People headed for the parking lot, for home. The reporters that didn't follow the detectives still surrounded Marci and Stephen, but even they were beginning to leave.

Sharee pulled away. "I want to see Marci."

John kept hold of her arm. "We can see Marci, but we also need to talk. Before the police get back with a hundred other questions."

Deputy Richards cleared his throat. "The police—make that the Sheriff's office—is already here. Waiting. And I do have some questions. Not quite a hundred."

"You didn't go with the others?"

His face showed the wisp of a smile. "One woman, one dog. A dozen law enforcement officers." He shrugged. "I don't think I'll be missed."

"She'll be okay?"

He nodded. "Should be. The dog on the other hand… But we have a dog lover on the force. He's there. Should be okay, too."

Sharee breathed a sigh of relief. "Good."

The deputy's face showed surprise. "You're worried about them both?"

"Mrs. Sheraton, really. She lost her son, and I have a hunch she cares for the dog."

John's hand tightened on Sharee's arm. "You never know what she would have done."

The deputy vaulted a look between them. "That's right. You never know what people are capable of—good or bad." He paused. "What made you think Roseanne Sawyer was the kidnapper?"

"Well, I remembered she had a car seat. John and I saw it one evening when she brought Marci back from the store. She had Joshua in a car seat. And Matthew took him out of it and put him in his own. I didn't think about it until later. She always complained about being short of money, so why buy a car seat for Joshua when Marci had one? And I remembered what John said about the dog bites on the first doll. He didn't think Cooper did it, so what dog did? Who had a dog? That kind of narrowed it down. Also, she dropped Marci and the girls off at the church the evening Marci found the doll in her car seat. It would have been easy for her to circle around, jump out of the van, leave it, and then drive home. And she had a key to the nursery."

"Anything else?"

"I eliminated Bruce. He wouldn't kidnap Joshua to get back at Marci. I mean, what would he do with him? Kill him? No way. And Marci would never hurt her own child. Neither would Ted. He's obnoxious sometimes, but he wouldn't do anything to hurt Marci. So, that left them out. I could see Abbey "murdering" the dolls for spite, but not actually kidnapping Joshua. Again, what would she do with him? I started thinking about substitution and thought of Ryann, but that had the same problem. Whoever took Joshua would have to disappear with him. I didn't think Ryann would leave her family and just disappear. And then I remembered about the boy who died in the accident. What about his mother? And how would she kidnap him? The easiest way? Join the church. Then when the time presented itself, that person could snatch the baby and go. So, I asked myself who was new that might fill the requirements, and the only one I could come up with was Roseanne. It all fell together."

"Why didn't you tell the detectives all this? Why go over there by yourself?"

"I don't know. I...you probably won't believe me."

"Try me."

"I felt God leading me."

He inclined his head but only said, "That was risky."

"It didn't matter. Joshua mattered."

John muttered something, but the deputy said nothing.

"I told you it wasn't John."

John shot her a glance. "What?"

The deputy's mouth lifted. "I didn't think it was."

"But you..."

"I was trying to shake you enough to find out what you weren't telling me."

"But I wasn't..." Sharee halted; her face grew hot.

"She took my lead, I think," John said.

"I thought so. You covered well for her."

John shrugged.

"For what reason?"

"I didn't want to say anything about the note. Or Abbey."

"Abbey?"

"Yes. At the time, we both thought the note was from Abbey. I couldn't bring you," John smiled an apology, *"the Law,"* down on her without more evidence."

The deputy said nothing for a moment then shook his head. "You know, you should trust us next time. We're the good guys."

Chapter 36

At midnight, John stretched his legs under the table and cupped his hand around the hot coffee Lynn had fixed for them. Pastor Alan and Daneen drew their chairs up to the table in the fellowship hall and set their mugs on it. Lynn and Sharee sat across from him.

Finally, law enforcement, the media, and the others had gone. The relief sliding from his shoulders was like a turtle sliding from its log perch into the dark pond water.

"It's hard to believe Mrs. Sheraton just waited until the police got there," Sharee said. She warmed her hands on her cup, also. "Just sitting there, rocking."

"You took her gun," Pastor Alan said. "Maybe at God's leading."

"She might have killed herself, you mean? Her life has been so hard these last few years."

Lynn shook her head. "I don't know. Yes, she lost her son, but she kidnapped Joshua. Not to mention what she did to you."

"I know, but, well, I can forgive her."

Lynn shook her head.

Pastor Alan nodded. "God's all about forgiveness. And speaking of that, Bruce said you would have to forgive him, Sharee. He just couldn't believe that after all God had done, you showed up at Anderson Park to tell him the police were looking for him."

John straightened. "What are you talking about?"

"When Pedro told me he knew where Bruce might be, I wanted to find him before the police did."

"You what? Wait. What has Pedro to do with Bruce?"

"When you sent me to get some sleep. I spotted Pedro on the road, and he mentioned that Bruce often went to Anderson Park—"

"You picked up Pedro *and* went looking for Bruce?" He tried to keep his voice level. What else didn't he know? His shoulders began to tighten again.

Pastor Alan cleared his throat. "John, you were telling me about Matthew earlier."

John's glance raked him. He rose from the table and began to pace up and down. His eyes went to Sharee, lingered a moment, then skipped back to the pastor. "Yes, we were wrong about Abbey. Matthew wrote that note."

"Matt?" Sharee's voice left no doubt of her surprise.

"Yes. Ryann came to tell me about an hour ago. I guess Deputy Richards mentioned that I found it."

Daneen shifted in her chair. "Does this have to do with the adoption?"

Everyone's heads swung her way.

"What adoption?" Pastor Alan asked.

Daneen threw a look at her husband. "Marci and I went to lunch a while ago, and she told me that Matt's girlfriend became pregnant. She placed the baby for adoption. She asked me not to say anything to anyone." She threw another look at her husband. "Sorry."

He shrugged and shook his head.

"When Joshua was kidnapped, Matt told Marci he knew how devastated she was because not only did he love Joshua, but he loved his own baby, too. He also still wonders about him. Fathers have no say. He really thought when the girlfriend didn't want the baby, that his parents would take him. But it was so soon after the accident, and Marci was overwhelmed with guilt. She couldn't do it. She just told him to place the baby for adoption like his girlfriend wanted. Now she feels terrible."

"I can't believe this. I had no idea." Sharee's eyes were wide. "I never knew, and Marci is one of my closest friends."

Daneen put her hand out. "It has nothing to do with that. She felt she had to protect Matt. That if anything was said, it should come from him. I just caught her on a terrible day. She felt nothing was going right and wondering where God was."

Lynn sat forward. "And Matt's all right with everyone knowing now?"

Daneen shrugged. "The investigation brought out a lot."

Sharee set her cup on the table. "Maybe that's why he helps at the Pregnancy Center. It seemed odd when John and I saw him at the park."

Lynn pulled the band from her long hair and ran her fingers through it. "I didn't think guys cared for babies that much."

"Have you ever watched Matt with his siblings?" Daneen asked. "He's more like a father than Stephen, but then Stephen works long hours to bring in money just to feed that family."

Sharee propped her elbows on the table. "You know who I feel bad for? Abbey. I really judged her. Her clothes. Her attitude. And yet I never took the time to know her. Not like Ryann did. Ryann just reached out when Abbey joined the church."

"But why did Ryann keep the note?"

Sharee nodded at John. "Did she say?"

"She said she had it in her Bible to remind her to pray for Matt. Anyway, after Ryann told the detectives who wrote the note, they asked him to come and talk with them."

"Okay. But let's come back to Roseanne or Midge Sheraton or whoever." Lynn settled in her chair and took another sip of coffee. "You mean she came here with the idea of revenge?"

Sharee nodded. "Yeah, she did."

John stopped pacing and caught Sharee's look. "She might have killed you."

"I don't think so. The strangest thing is I wasn't scared. Well, until she brought in the dog."

"Huh!" Lynn said. "I guess so."

Sharee grinned. "Petrified of the dog, but even then God was there."

"She might have killed you," John said again as if they had not interrupted. He couldn't stop the emotion this time. His voice was rough with it. She'd endangered herself so many times.

Sharee stood and put her hand out to him. "John, I wanted you there."

"Did you even think about what you were doing?"

Her hand dropped. "Of course, I did. I told you already. I texted you. Not that it did any good."

"Texted?" He picked up his phone from the table. "I never got a text."

"You must have." Sharee grabbed his phone, looking down at it, her fingers gliding over its face. "I replied to your text from Friday."

"Friday?" His brow wrinkled. He reached over and plucked the phone from her hand. "I didn't text you Friday. I was too busy with all the last-minute stuff you wanted. We talked two or three times, that's all. And Saturday, we didn't talk." He stopped at that. They both knew why. "I picked up Pedro Saturday, took him to lunch, and brought him here that evening."

"*You* picked up Pedro—off the side of the road? A hitchhiker?"

"It's different."

"It is? Why? Because you're a man?"

"Yes. Face it. It's just the way it is."

Her jaw clenched. "That's ridiculous. And what if I see Pedro on the road? Do I just wave and keep going?"

"All right. There might be times…"

"Ha! There are times."

He gritted his teeth. "This has nothing to do with Roseanne or what we were talking about."

"I think it does."

"Sharee." Pastor Alan's voice rose. "I texted you the other day. I haven't looked at my phone today. Too much was happening. In fact, I left it in the back office. You were late the other night and things were getting rowdy, so I texted you. Didn't you see my number?"

"No. I just glanced at the message. I was running out the door and assumed John sent it." She had wondered briefly why his picture hadn't appeared. Too much going on that night. Right.

John shoved his phone into his pocket and put his hand out to her. Their arguing only clouded the issues and got them nowhere. "Come on," he said.

"Where to?"

"Outside. We need to talk."

"Talk?" Her voice dropped, and something changed in her face. "No, let's do that later."

"Later? You said that before. We have some things to discuss. Come outside."

"No."

He raised an eyebrow and studied her. What was the problem now? Joshua was back with his family, and he'd wanted to talk with her for two days. He frowned at her, and she lifted her chin. The woman was more aggravating than the flashing cameras and nosy reporters. He stepped forward, grabbed her, and lifted her into his arms.

"Hey! What are you doing?" Sharee squirmed against his chest. "Put me down!"

"No. We're going to talk." His grip tightened, and he indicated the door with a nod. "Alan, do you mind?"

Pastor Alan grinned, stood, and moved past the two other women, before shoving the door open.

"Hey!" Sharee struggled to get free.

The door slammed behind them. Okay, door stops. All over. He stood a minute in the darkness, getting his bearings.

"Put me down." Sharee's voice sounded hoarse. "John—"

"I told you we need to talk. I've got something to tell you." He walked toward the bleachers, into the moonlight, holding tight while she pushed against him.

"You can't just pick me up like a sack of potatoes!"

He shook her. "Only if you make me. Stop struggling."

"John, I..." her voice broke this time.

He halted, moved his head out of the moon's light and tried to read her expression. When she shoved against his chest once more, he dropped her to her feet.

"What is your problem?" Impatience filled his voice. Great. How could he tell her what God had done in his life when he couldn't keep his voice level?

"I don't want to talk. It's been a long day. I... Can't we just concentrate on the good things?"

Then remembrance hit, and he swallowed his irritation. Friday night seemed a lifetime away, but they'd left their relationship in the air. Was she afraid of that?

He tugged her to him. "Please. Just hear me out."

She didn't respond.

"Sharee?"

She shook her head, keeping it against his chest. "I've given you to God once. I don't know if I can do it again."

His hand went to her hair. "You gave me to God? Gave me up, you mean?"

She nodded.

"When was this?"

"Friday night."

Just what he thought. He leaned down, lifted her into his arms again, and walked toward the bleachers. "Well, I guess you don't have much to say about anything then. You need to hear me out."

He stopped at the bleachers and set her down on the first step, clasped her hand in his and led her to the highest row. Silence enveloped them. The moonlight highlighted everything, painting the program scenes the color of warm butter. Stars shimmered against the night sky. Across the field, from the houses on the next street, multi-colored Christmas lights flickered here and there through the cypress trees.

Her head stayed averted. He stared past the program site, past the yellow crime scene tape, and wondered how to begin.

"Look, you're going to have to get used to having me around." He waited until she looked up. Moonlight lit her face, and he couldn't control his wide smile. "You've got what you wanted, you know. I've committed—no, recommitted—my life to God."

She straightened. "You what?"

"I recommitted my life. God did move during the Christmas program and afterward, even during all this...horror... that we've been through. Between you, and God, and Joshua, and the program, even talking to Abbey...well, you've got what you wanted."

She met his look with a frown as if she didn't believe him. "You recommitted your life to God?"

"Yes."

"But when? When did this happen?"

"During the program, and again today." He felt lightness inside but wasn't sure how to explain that to her. Instead, he caught her hand and squeezed it.

"You're serious?"

He almost laughed at her tone. "Yes. You should never have given me to God if you weren't prepared for him to do something."

She threw her arms around his neck. He slipped his around her waist and drew her close. She leaned into him, and he kissed her hair, tilted her face up and kissed her mouth.

In a moment, she traced his jawline with her finger. "When Joshua disappeared, I kept wondering where God was and how he could let this happen."

"That's natural."

"To you, maybe, but…"

"But you aren't used to that?"

"No, I…" Her voice stilled. "I guess it's easy to be full of faith when you have nothing that challenges your faith."

"You've had challenges."

"But not like yours. Or Abbey's. Or Ryann's."

"Are you disappointed with yourself, or do you think you disappointed God?"

"Both. I've been pretty prideful about my faith." She took a long breath. "And about taking care of myself. I…I wanted you so much when I was at Roseanne's."

Surprise went through him. She'd wanted him? Needed him? "Sharee, it's okay to need help others sometimes. No one can handle everything."

He heard her ragged breath. "I know. It's just…"

"What?"

"It was so hard for mom and dad to let go. I was just determined to make it on my own when I got out."

"But you're close to your family."

"I know. It doesn't mean we don't have issues."

He laughed. "It's good to hear you're not perfect."

She slugged him on the arm. "I love you."

"I love you, too." His thumb rubbed her mouth. He bent his head toward hers, but the thing he'd never told her filled his mind. He lifted his head. "Sharee, there is still something I need to tell you. I—"

"Wait," she interrupted him. "Wait. Say that again."

"There is something…"

"No, the other."

He stopped, reflecting. "That I love you?"

"You've never said it."

"Haven't I?" He smiled. "I love you." And he kissed her again, his mouth moving, searching, drawing her response. When he drew back, his uneven breathing fogged the air between them. Better say it now, or he'd get side-tracked for sure.

"I need to tell you something." His voice sounded rough to his own ears. "Okay." She put a hand on his chest and pushed away. "Okay. Tell me."

"It's about Janice and me." She didn't move, but something of her vulnerability, of her immediate uneasiness, came through to him. He pressed her close.

"I told you that when I met Janice, she'd just become a Christian. Her enthusiasm for God drew me to her. After we married, we planned to go overseas as missionaries."

"As missionaries?"

He nodded. "My father's a pilot, and I've been flying since I turned fifteen. After I received the Lord, I heard about Nate Saint and that whole story of their work with the Wuaorani Indians. By the time I met Janice, I already knew God had called me overseas—to be a missionary pilot."

He paused before continuing. "Satan tripped us up, though. We were still in church. I studied all I could about small one- and two-engine planes, how to fly them, how to fix them; but something happened. I don't know what, exactly. We began to drift away from God." He paused, feeling the regret.

"John, it's okay. You don't have to explain."

"Yes, I do. I told you the truth when I said before that we were enjoying all that the world had to offer. We chased after the world." Another pause. "When Janice died, I couldn't deal with the guilt or the pain. Anger at myself and at God took over. But I have to give up my right to know why, to be god; and to admit that He's sovereign, whether I like what happens or not." A long pause. "I know we live in a fallen world. I know this is not heaven, but that's what I wanted. Heaven on earth. I wanted everything to work out right. All the time."

He stopped, eyeing her, feeling the vulnerability within himself now. Things could still happen that he might not like, that could cut deep. But if so, he would hold onto the One who had created him, who had saved him.

Sharee huddled against him, shivering. He rubbed her arms.

Seconds later, she reared back, sitting bolt upright. "Wait. You *knew* God called you to be a missionary?"

"Yes."

"But…you mean, through everything that's happened, you knew you were called to be a missionary?" She jumped to her feet. "Why didn't you tell me?"

He stood, also. "I knew if I told you, you wouldn't leave me alone. As it is…" He remembered his words just before she appeared with Joshua. "God has me where He wants me, anyway."

He watched the moonlight and the breeze play with her hair. After a minute, he said, "You're right about the omission, though. I seem to have done a lot of that since Janice died. Forgive me?"

"Hmph," she said. "Too easy."

He laughed and kissed her. She snuggled close, the resistance gone. He could feel the warmth of her body leaning into him. He dropped his arms about her waist.

"John?"

"Hmm?"

"This is the best Christmas gift I could have."

"Is it?" He looked down at her and pulled on a stray curl. "Well, you have another gift coming."

"I do?" She curled her body against his. He drew the sides of his jacket around her, wrapping them both inside.

"Uh huh." He wanted to kiss her mouth again, her chin, her neck... He could generate some heat for her. Aloud, he asked, "Sharee?"

"Yes?"

"Are you going to be as stubborn about that purity thing as you are about everything else?"

She raised her head. "Yes."

He groaned and said nothing. Not, as he'd said before, that he'd expected any other answer from her. Not that he would take advantage. He'd just have to marry the girl. He slipped off his jacket and put it around her. Something between them would help right now. "I'm buying you a coat or jacket for Christmas."

"I can get my own jacket. I—"

"You can come with me, or I'll pick something out myself. I refuse to let you freeze all winter. Especially in Florida." And before she could protest further, he said, "Look, about Bruce and Pedro. What did you think you were—"

"What do you want for Christmas?"

He dipped his head, studied her and lifted a brow. "Okay. You're off the hook for now." He thought a moment but nothing came to mind. "I don't know. We don't do gifts much in my family."

"There has to be something you want."

He slipped his arms back around her, squeezed her. "I think I have it."

She rested her head against his chest, and he stared out over the field. The moonlight and the Christmas lights filled his vision. Hope and joy filled his heart.

"John." She pulled back and raised her face.

"Yes?"

"The gifts and callings of God are without repentance—without change.

You said you knew what God had called you to. Well, he's still calling you."

He looked deep into her eyes for a minute and nodded. "I know that, girl. I know that."

"For unto you is born this day in the city of David a Savior,
which is Christ the Lord.
And this shall be a sign unto you;
Ye shall find the babe wrapped in swaddling clothes,
lying in a manger.

And suddenly there was with the angel
A multitude of the heavenly host
Praising God, and saying,
Glory to God in the highest,
And on earth peace,
Goodwill toward men."*

*Luke 2:11-14, KJV

I hope you enjoyed reading *Amber Alert*.
Authors need and appreciate book reviews.
Could you please take a few minutes
to put a review on Amazon?

Amber Alert is Book 1
in the *Dangerous Series*.
As Long As You Both Shall Live is Book 2.
Splashdown, Book 3, will be out this summer.

Looking for Justice, a later installment, follows John's sister to Tennessee.

Be sure to join Linda's email list
at www.lindarodante.com
to get the latest news on Linda's upcoming release
Splashdown.

All of Linda's works are available
on Amazon in both print and eBook.
The next few pages will give you a peek
at *As Long As You Both Shall Live.*

As Long As You Both Shall Live
Prologue

She was always on time.

He could see the church parking lot from the edge of the woods. Glancing at his watch, he shifted position and made sure the trees concealed him. Cars exited the main road, bumped down the drive, and pulled in for the evening service. A steady stream of people parked and entered the building.

The woman who called earlier had not given her name—only a message. "Sharee's getting engaged. She's going to get married. Just thought you'd want to know." And although he'd fought the urge to come, he had surrendered to the rising anger before the afternoon ended.

His fists clenched. Just like anyone else, he had the right to be here. He could even walk into the church. They couldn't do anything about it. She couldn't. Not like before. He contemplated doing that, going in, finding a seat near her, and listening to the sermon.

No.

He didn't want to play games.

His head rose in time to see her Honda CR-V turn into the long drive. Parking next to the side door, she jumped out and hurried inside. She hadn't changed. Same petite body, same untamed hair and, he was sure, the same puritanical attitudes.

No, he didn't want to play games. What he wanted was not nearly so innocent.

Chapter 1

John Jergenson's head bounced against the window when the airplane's wheels hit the runway in Tampa. He tried stretching his six-foot-two body in the cramped seat as he'd done numerous times over the last twenty-seven hours. The long flight had taken a toll.

As buildings and cement roared past outside, he shoved the tiredness away. For four weeks he'd flown into the jungles of Indonesia and hiked through muddy terrain to reach villages lost to time. Tired and dirty, his group had emerged from the wild to be met as if they were kings or royalty. Being put on such a pedestal had humbled him, and that taste of humility had not left him yet. He wouldn't ruin it by complaining.

"Home." His eyes focused on familiar objects. "And home safely."

In the seat next to him, Bob Ferguson chuckled. "Did you doubt it?"

John sent Bob a sardonic smile. "Only a half dozen times."

"One time being that crocodile, and another that logging mess we got caught in. Dugout canoes aren't the safest transportation in a river full of logs."

"I wish they'd warned us."

"And taken the chance that we'd back out?"

John's mouth lifted. They'd have made that downriver trip no matter what. The month he'd spent under Bob Ferguson's tutelage had brought appreciation for the man's wit, intelligence, and spirituality. At times, though, he'd questioned his mentor's sanity.

His smile widened. "With you, they had no fear of that."

"God was with us."

"That He was."

John grabbed the backpack from under the seat in front of him. He'd come through situations he'd never faced before, and each one had sent him to his knees in thanksgiving and praise.

He shifted his gaze to the airplane window. Sharee should have been there. At night, after a long day of work and ministry, he'd lie on the dirt floor in a crowded hut and think about her. He wanted her beside him. Her love of helping others would fit perfectly with the work that needed to be done. Next time... Next time, she would be with him.

Something stilled inside him. Had the ring he bought in Jakarta arrived? Had Bruce picked it up as he'd asked?

Around him now, people began to stand and edge into the aisles. The phone conversations swirled and rose and then grew silent as the passengers dragged baggage from the overhead bins.

Bob rose. "Sharee picking you up?"

"Yes." John met his friend's grin with his own, squeezed into the aisle and joined the assembly line inching forward.

They passed through the gangway and caught the tram. When the doors opened again, he stepped out and let his gaze slip from person to person until he saw the mass of auburn curls. She wore a blue dress of some shiny material and the gold necklace he'd given her before he left. Heels lifted her five-foot-two-inch frame to average height. A frown creased her forehead, but even with the serious expression, she looked beautiful. His heart kicked up a notch.

As their eyes met, relief flooded her countenance. He side-stepped Bob's family reunion and continued forward to stop in front of her. Her head tilted back, eyes looking deep into his. She'd worried about him. He saw it in the way she searched his face, and he dropped his bag and pulled her into his arms.

&

They turned in at Howard Park; and drove past the oaks, pines, and palms that surrounded the picnic shelters; and headed across the causeway to the small island beach. On either side, sunbathers stretched out on beach towels, catching the last rays of the sun. In the water, windsurfers flaunted their aerial stunts and flipped their boards over in quick, broad arcs. The spray from their acrobatics swept like long fish tails behind them.

Sharee sighed—content and relaxed as she hadn't been for weeks. Maybe since he was home, her concern about their relationship would cease. Her heart stumbled as she thought about Dean. She'd made a mistake by rushing it. She wouldn't do that again. But John was not Dean, and she needed to remember that.

And she'd tell him about the phone calls. He'd know what to do.

John glanced her way, smiled. He parked the truck facing the Gulf. The white sand glistened in the late afternoon light, and the roughened waters stretched to the horizon. Light sparkled off the wave tops—a million tiny reflectors, shifting, winking, moving.

They kicked off their shoes, climbed out of the truck and walked along the beach. When they stopped, John drew her around to face him.

The wind caught her hair, twirling it in front of her eyes. She moved it behind her ear and studied his coffee-colored hair, the deep-set eyes, and tall, wiry build. "Four weeks was a long time."

"Was it?" A light appeared in his dark eyes. "For me, too, although it was an amazing trip."

"Tell me about it."

He ran his hands up and down her arms. "I wish you'd been there."

"I think I would have liked that." After the last couple of weeks, she had to agree. Instead of spending time in a jungle of emotions here, the idea of spending time in a real jungle sounded intriguing.

He took her hand and turned to walk the beach again, his voice deep but passionate as he talked about traveling through the jungles, staying in the villages and helping with needed building projects. "Then each evening, we took turns preaching. We'd begin after dark and only had the lanterns, but when we lifted them high during the meeting, we could see that the entire village had gathered in the dark." He stopped and turned to face her. "Sharee, mission trips change people. We both know that. The anointing and the presence of God seem so strong. You know I've felt called to overseas missions. I believe this trip confirmed it."

She smiled. "I can hear it in your voice."

"I need extra flight training, especially landing on those short airstrips. I'm sure we didn't see the shortest ones." He chuckled. "And it takes an extra dose of faith to fly some of the planes. I studied maintenance and repair before, but I need a refresher."

He stopped. Sharee felt his hesitation. She lifted her head, keeping her hair in place with one hand, and searching his face.

"I'd like to go back in six months."

"What?" Something dropped into her stomach. The smell of the sea spray reached them. "But you just got home."

"I know."

She had wanted him home, wanted his confidence in fighting the sudden uneasiness in her life. He couldn't be leaving again. Not this soon. "What about the schooling you just mentioned? Won't it take a while?"

"I'll start immediately. I was studying aviation mechanics when the crash happened." He paused a moment. "Doing a refresher won't take long."

"And you don't want it to."

Her voice must have risen because he moved his head to inspect her. "No."

The sun's last cusp slipped beneath the horizon, and the gold lights disappeared. "I don't know how you can do all that you want in six months. You're being unrealistic."

His brows rose, and he pulled her close. "We need to talk about it. I'd planned to tell you all that happened on this trip. About the dangers we could face in the jungles, but God is so real there, so present. Not that He isn't everywhere, but you've been on mission trips. You understand. I want to go back, and I want you to go, too."

She put a hand against his chest. "John, I'm not sure about a mission trip. I just...I..." What? How could she say she wasn't sure about anything right now?

"Not just a mission trip." His voice had deepened. His lopsided grin and his next words made his meaning clear. "Marry me."

"What?"

His arms tightened around her. "I love you. You know that. God is calling us both. Don't you feel it?"

She didn't know what she felt these days. She had just wanted him home, wanted the anxiety gone, wanted things the way they were before he left.

"Marry me. We'll go back together."

She dropped her head. *I'm not ready for this, Lord. Please.*

"Sharee?"

His puzzlement was clear, but she couldn't look at him. His question was a formality only. In fact, it wasn't even a question, and he expected her to say "yes" with the same enthusiasm he exhibited.

"John, I can't. I..." How could she explain her recent feelings? The uneasiness about their relationship, how she'd messed up before, and then the phone calls... A sudden wave of emotion swamped her.

He put a finger under her chin, lifted it, and pushed the hair from her eyes. His smile disappeared. He studied her face a moment longer and dropped his hand.

&

What is wrong, Lord? Why do I feel as if I'm on a tilt-a-whirl?

Sharee blew out a ragged breath. John had returned from a life-changing experience feeling certain she'd say yes to marriage, and yes to serving the Lord with him. And before he left, her heart had said the same. How could she explain the feelings that swirled inside now, that had grown over his month-long absence? She couldn't. Instead, she'd asked him to give her time, a week or two at least, before she gave her answer.

On the ride back, she sensed his pain. She wanted to say something, anything to make it better but couldn't.

Her eyes slid to the clock. Just three hours ago. She grabbed another tissue, swiped at her eyes then blew her nose. Why this indecision? Why?

The phone shrilled, and her muscles tensed across her shoulders. She didn't want to talk to anyone. The music came again, and she leaned forward to check the screen. Pastor Alan. No. No way. He'd know something was wrong immediately. But why was he calling? It shrilled again. Was there a problem? Someone homeless with whom he needed her help?

She snatched the phone from the end table. "Hello?"

"Sharee?"

"Yes."

"It's Pastor Alan. We're at the hospital, but don't worry. They're just doing some tests. I'm sure he'll be all right."

"Who will be all right? What are you talking about?"

"John."

"John?" Her voice rose. "What about him?"

"There's been an accident."

Author Biography

Linda was born and raised in Florida. She is married with two grown sons, a daughter-in-law, and three grandchildren. At twenty-six, she discovered the miraculous love of Jesus. God blessed her with a passion for the written word—especially mysteries and romantic suspense novels, from Nancy Drew to Agatha Christie, from Dee Henderson to Kristen Heitzman.

She speaks about and works against human trafficking. She blogs on this subject and on commitment to Christ at www.lindarodante.wordpress.com (Writing for God, Fighting Human Trafficking).

To learn more about her books, this series, and the author, please visit www.lindarodante.com.

Made in the USA
San Bernardino, CA
16 July 2016